RAOUL &
HANNAH

Dear Gills. This is Bea's
new book

Thought you might
like a copy.

Muriel.

Raoul and Hannah

Published by The Conrad Press in the United Kingdom 2019

Tel: +44(0)1227 472 874
www.theconradpress.com
info@theconradpress.com

ISBN 978-1-911546-47-4

Typesetting and Cover Design by:
Charlotte Mouncey, www.bookstyle.co.uk

The Conrad Press logo was designed by Maria Priestley.

Printed and bound in Great Britain
by Clays Ltd, Elcograf S.p.A.

RAOUL & HANNAH

BEA GREEN

For Esther Morales and my parents
Leycester and Piedad Coltman

1

Hannah Anderson has been my guiding star.

She has been the one who inspired me to believe that I could do amazing things with my life. Her faith and belief in me meant I never doubted myself. She gave me the confidence to believe that as a Mexican from a poor district in Mexico City I could have success in a career I loved. Hannah meant everything to me. I have special memories of her branded in my mind; the way she smiled and laughed, her intrinsic kindness and the multitude of little mannerisms that made her unique. Every girl I've met in my life since has always been compared to her and they've all fallen short of Hannah's beauty and magic.

I'm Raoul Morales. I'm twenty-eight years old, a Mexican citizen. I'm not a writer by trade, (you'll probably notice that as you read on) but an interior designer. I try my best to make people's houses look wonderful inside. The way I see it, the world can be pretty terrible, so home is what matters most. I like to think I make my customers' lives better, and I hope I do.

By nature I tend to be someone who's normally content to trundle along at a placid pace, but today I'm uncharacteristically shaken and anxious. It all started with a phone call I got at around nine-thirty yesterday evening. Right now it's three twenty-six in the morning, on the fifteenth of January, a Monday.

Earlier, at around two in the morning I think it was, I was tired and unable to sleep so I threw the pillows out of my bed in anger and frustration. I decided to get out of bed.

Right now, I'm sitting at the desk in my sitting-room, trying to write out my thoughts because at this time of the night there's no one I can speak to.

I've accepted I'm unlikely to get any sleep tonight so I've decided to release some of my emotion into this notebook. Tell me, have you ever reached the point where your inner turmoil is so great you've had to put pen to paper to release some of the tension?

Maybe you haven't been there, in which case I can only say you're lucky.

I feel exhausted, so you'll have to forgive me if my writing degenerates into incomprehensibility.

As a matter of fact looking at it now, my writing does look a complete mess.

I think it's partly the fault of my hand, not my pen. My hand's shaking slightly and it's leaving an ungainly thin black scrawl (there's really no other word for it) across the page when I write. Not that my writing was ever neat in the first place but I'm struggling to read it now, which isn't helpful. No doubt I'll end up repeating myself.

Hopefully, if I can calm myself down a little, my hand will steady itself and I'll be able to write legibly again.

Right. If you'll kindly excuse me, I'm going to take a few deep breaths before I continue...

The problem is I've had a bit of a shock tonight and it's come in the guise of that unforeseen and startling phone call.

I'm sitting here at my desk, in my flat in Bosques de las Lomas which is situated to the west of Mexico City, and I'm wondering how many people around the world just now are receiving distressing phone calls that catch them unaware. Blindsided. That's the word that describes perfectly how I feel tonight.

2

I can remember vividly what I was doing when the phone rang. I was midway through an episode of a television drama and I really wasn't in the state of mind to receive unexpected news. I was chilling out after a busy day at work like millions of others on this planet.

Truth is I haven't been able to sleep at all since I received that phone call. I can still feel the adrenaline flowing through my veins, and tightness in my chest, with the shock of it. It was an old school friend of mine, Austin Mitchell, who made the call.

He didn't take long to tell me the unexpected news; he told me he's currently in the middle of divorce proceedings with his wife.

The real issue here is that Austin's wife happens to be my childhood sweetheart, Hannah Anderson.

I fell in love with her during my teenage years and I've never really fallen out of love with her.

Hannah Anderson.

My goodness, I had blocked her out of my mind. Now I can't stop thinking about her.

It's complicated. My feelings are complicated.

I've always wondered whether Hannah and I would've married each other had we been living in the same country. There's always been a very deep connection between us, a sense of belonging almost. The only real obstacle there's been between us is that I now live and work in Mexico City, whereas she lives and works in Edinburgh.

Three years ago I flew out of Mexico to attend her wedding in Edinburgh. It was a big affair, full of smart hats, kilts, an expensive bridal gown and several bridesmaids.

I have to admit I left the wedding celebrations early and I cried copiously in my hotel room that night. I cried my heart out despite the fact I haven't been in a proper relationship with Hannah since we both started college and university.

It's embarrassing to acknowledge my tears now, but you see Hannah's always been incredibly special to me. We grew up together and she's the keystone of my childhood.

She's been married three years and I thought I had reached closure. For a very long time I've carried an imaginary picture of Austin and Hannah, and their 2.5 children, in my head.

Now tonight my mind is spinning in every direction. All the assumptions I've made about Hannah's life are starting to fragment into little pieces.

I'm going to nip to the fridge and drink some wine before I continue. There's nothing like wine to loosen the tight coils in one's mind. I'm strongly tempted to drink myself into oblivion but I have to be at the studio early this morning, and I'm not going to let this one phone call disrupt my design work.

I really am struggling to comprehend why Austin's news has rattled me so much. I mean, it's not something I wished for and yet right now I feel both excited and guilty. Guilty? Why would I feel guilty?

I mean, I feel bad for Austin; he's a decent man.

Come to think of it, he hasn't mentioned why he's divorcing

her, which is a little strange. I mean he knows Hannah and I were very close, so maybe he just felt uncomfortable telling me why he's divorcing her. After all a divorce is never amicable, is it?

I think I'll call him tomorrow and try to find out more details. Or maybe I should call Hannah.

No, no, that's never going to work. Austin was the one to call me so I should really be speaking to him. If Hannah had wanted to speak me, she'd have done so by now.

Why hasn't she called me? She hasn't completely forgotten about me. After all I still receive regular emails from her and a yearly Christmas card.

I'd like to speak to her.

3

All this nostalgia from the past is reaching into my heart and gripping it tight. I feel a lump building in my throat. This is crazy. I need to snap out of this. I reckon the tiredness must be hitting me. I can't even see the page I'm writing on clearly, and I'm continually rubbing my eyes.

I'm sure the wine isn't helping my lethargy either but I don't regret drinking it. This wine's so good. It has a crisp, almost bitter, tang to it but you can taste the mellow, tropical notes in the after flavour, or the finish as a connoisseur would say. It's an elegant Chardonnay wine, from Casa Madero in the Valle de Parras region here in Mexico.

Tonight the wine's served its purpose, because it's both refreshing and soothing. There was a time when I only drank beer. My taste has been refined since then, probably as a result of my job. My clients like good wines.

I'm digressing now, which is probably a good sign. It means some of my raw emotion has eased off a bit. And I'm getting tired. Writing this has definitely helped me unwind a little, so thank you for your patience.

Tomorrow I'll share my news with Christina, my wise friend and business partner. No doubt she'll have some helpful advice to give to me. Christina has experienced it all as far as relationships go.

My life here in Mexico City is a good one. I need to move past this. Austin's call has yanked me back into the past and I really wish he'd never called me. I know the news that Hannah's getting a divorce is never going to leave my memory now. It's difficult for me to believe that I can carry on as normal, knowing that Hannah will be single and available soon.

But Hannah and Austin belong to my past and I should be looking to the future.

Enough! I've got a long day's work ahead of me tomorrow.

I'm going to sign off and crash onto my bed. I need to get at least an hour's sleep or when she arrives at work tomorrow, Christina will find me fast asleep on my keyboard.

4

In a brief moment of abstraction I look up from my computer and reach out for my mobile phone, which has been buzzing incessantly with texts since this morning.

As I lean across my eye catches sight of the bright Christmas card on the shelf in front of me and I automatically reach out to pick the card up, as I have done many times since it arrived a couple of weeks ago.

The slightly fatuous snowman on the front of it is a little incongruous as today in Mexico City, midway through January, it is pleasantly mild and the window of the studio I work in is open. Outside, the collection of cacti assembled by my business partner Christina and me are a splash of colour on the patio in their bold coloured plant pots.

Inside the Christmas card, my childhood friend and sweetheart Hannah, has written in her clear, almost childish, handwriting; *Dear Raoul, Hope you have a lovely Christmas and a Happy New Year! Love to your family. Come and visit us soon! Lots of love as always, Hannah.*

I wonder again why Hannah omitted to tell me she was divorcing Austin. Maybe it really is time to give Hannah a call and see how things are in Edinburgh. However before I call her I want to think meticulously about what I'm going to say to her.

I carefully put the card back on the shelf.

With a sigh I look at the pile of unfinished projects on my desk and realise it will be a long time before I'll be able to take time off to go and visit Scotland again. The downside of being self-employed is that you're never fully able to switch off from your work.

The amount of work we're getting now is giving me sleepless nights and I envy my partner's laidback attitude to life. Christina never worries about the business. If too much work comes in she says it's time to raise our prices but even this doesn't seem to slow down the workload piling up on our desks.

We're lucky. People here in Mexico City are willing to pay astronomical prices for our services. I suspect some of our well-heeled clients actually prefer to pay more, in a snobby kind of way it makes them feel they are getting a better quality of interior designer.

Christina, who will be fifty-eight years old this year, has been doing this for much longer than I have. She built up a good reputation for the firm long before I joined her six years ago, after graduating from my interior design college in Santa Catarina.

Looking briefly at my mobile phone, I reflect for a moment on how far I have come from my inauspicious start to life and think again of my mother, who did all she could to give me a decent education.

5

My mother fell pregnant with me at the age of fifteen and my grandparents were poor fruit farmers who lived in a small two-bed apartment in the district of Iztupalapa, in the east of Mexico City. My mother lived with her parents until I was six months old, at which point she secured a job in a diplomatic residence on the other side of the city. My mother told me a long time ago how one of the most painful moments of her life was when she had to tell her parents she was pregnant with me, at the age of fifteen and after a one night stand. What made this episode worse for my mother was the fact that my grandparents are devout Catholics and had to live with the shame of having a teenage daughter pregnant out of wedlock.

I have never known and will never know who my father was. My mother knew his first name (John) and that was basically it, but she did say he was an American.

Despite having a father who is an American, I will always identify myself as Mexican. The only other nationality I could feel a kinship to would be British, possibly because of the many years I spent growing up with the Anderson family in Mexico, and then in Scotland. But don't get me wrong my heart will always be locked up in this beautiful, vibrant and dangerous country of ours. I think as an interior designer I would fail to be a success somewhere like Britain as my palette would be too forceful for the subtle neutral taste of the majority of the people there.

The door to the studio slams open and startles me out of my reverie.

Tall and graceful, Christina walks in carrying as usual several fabric books and a briefcase. She dumps these in an untidy heap by her desk. Apart from the small area around my desk the studio as a whole looks like a cyclone has hit it.

My fastidious temperament hates the mess but I have learnt the hard way that this is how Christina works. Move a paint pot out of the way and she will complain for days how she had to spend hours trying to find it. She applies a strange logic and order to the mess that surrounds her. I have had to learn to live with it.

'Well, how did it go?'

Christina grimaces. She has just been to visit a notoriously awkward client who is married to a prosperous business-man. They both own several well-known furniture shops in Mexico City.

'She and Mussolini would have made the perfect couple. I really don't know why she needs us. She's very obviously decided what she wants and you can't convince her otherwise.' Christina restlessly looks through her client's file, flicking through the pages with impatience. 'I'm strongly tempted to call her up and say we can't take her on.'

Christina closes the file abruptly and pushes it away from her in disgust. She swivels round on her chair to face me.

'For a start it'll damage our reputation if she gets her way, as I've never met anyone with less taste. She thinks because her husband owns some successful furniture shops she knows everything there is to know about interior design.'

'I'm up for dropping her from our books. We've more work than we can cope with as it is.'

'Could you call her and tell her that please?' Christina looks at me pleadingly.

I can't resist her puppy dog look. I nod and make a note on my phone to call the client tomorrow. Christina and I are good at supporting each other. Christina has stepped in many times to save me from the mistakes of my inexperience and no client who knows her is ever late with their payment. The Mexican government should really hire her to solve the spiralling debt crisis in this country.

We work silently at our desks for the next three hours with only the background roar of road traffic disturbing us. By about five fifteen in the afternoon Christina stretches and gets up.

The turquoise and silver bangles she wears tinkle softly. Long silver earrings hang from her earlobes and a necklace made of silver and turquoise fish hangs down the front of her dark blue suit. Christina's work is flamboyant and innovative but her taste in clothes is conservative. It's only in her taste in jewellery and shoes that she betrays the artistry in her nature. Today, despite her height, she's wearing a pair of stylish silver Prada wedges.

'Espresso, Raoul?'

'That would be great, thank you. Oh and I've finished the room plan for Amaya Perez. I'm meeting her on Friday.'

'Great! That was fast. Let me know what she thinks of it.' Christina disappears into the kitchen.

Both of us know we'll be here until late tonight. We order take outs to the studio so often the staff at our local Italian take-away, Bella E Buona, now recognise my voice when I call them to place our dinner order.

Christina plonks an espresso and a couple of biscochitos (Mexican sweet biscuits) by my computer. I finish amending a detail on AutoCad and turn to take a sip of my espresso, at which point I notice Christina watching me as she nibbles on her biscochito. I lift an enquiring eyebrow at her.

'Have you called her?'

'Who?' I answer defensively, stalling for time.

'Idiot! Hannah of course.'

'No, I haven't.'

'Why not? And don't tell me you haven't had time to do it because I don't buy that excuse.'

'I'll get round to it. There's no hurry.'

Christina shrugs.

'I don't understand you. If Hannah was such an important part of your childhood, why don't you just call her? I've seen you looking at that ridiculous Christmas card so many times now. Call her.' As if to emphasize her point Christina reaches over and pats my arm. 'Courage, my friend, courage.'

I laugh but say nothing. I'm not sure yet when I'll contact Hannah, or even then what I'll say to her.

Christina raises her eyes up to the ceiling in mock exasperation and then gets back to work. I can be very stubborn sometimes and she knows there's no point in trying to change my mind.

6

When I was younger my mother would frequently say I was so obstinate I should join the GAFE (Mexican Special Forces). She used to say even if my enemies tried to torture me, they wouldn't be able to get me to do what they wanted.

Personally I believe you can't go against the tide of your genetic inheritance, and thankfully my friends and family have accepted my occasional inflexibility.

Later that night, when I'm back at my spacious apartment in Bosques de las Lomas, I dig out some of my old photo albums from the walnut sideboard and take all four of them to the glass coffee table. I'm over tired and I know I won't be getting any sleep any time soon.

I flop down on my only armchair.

I've had this armchair for five years and I love it. The chair's a lovely cerulean blue. The chair's broad arms are covered in loose threads where Gordo, my pale brown Burmese cat, has attacked the thick fabric and the seat has sunk with use, but it's so comfortable I often fall asleep sitting in it.

The walls of my large sitting-room are coloured the palest lemon yellow and hanging on them is my treasured collection of Mexican graffiti art, in plain white frames.

In the privacy and comfort of my own home I can indulge in political art. One of my paintings depicts a Mexican with the caption '*ningún ser humano es ilegal*' (no human being is illegal). There is a spray paint picture of Frida Kahlo wearing diamond jewellery, a direct contradiction of her socialist views, and lastly a skeleton in a suit addressing the Mexican parliament against the backdrop of the Mexican flag.

I flick through the pages of my old photo albums, looking at the faded photographs of Hannah and her family.

In one photo my mother, in her maid's uniform, has her arms around Hannah and they're both facing the camera laughing. My mother is small and, even at the young age of eleven, Hannah is slightly taller than her.

I find it hard even now, all these years later, to see my mother in a maid's uniform.

I understand how many people in my country would see my mother's employment as a maid, in a diplomatic residence, as a lucrative job. I can only say that as a young boy, growing up with the Anderson family, I was always painfully aware of my mother's low social status in comparison to theirs. All the kindness and generosity the Anderson family showed us never changed that for me.

7

So there we have it. My mother worked as a maid and I met Hannah Anderson because my mother happened to be employed as a maid by Hannah's parents, who were British diplomats. Otherwise our paths would have never crossed.

In my view, any maid who works in a diplomatic residence is essentially making a valuable contribution to their country's interests. After all, how would diplomats manage without the invaluable help of faithful servants to ensure the smooth running of all the dinners and functions in their homes?

How would diplomats manage without trustworthy servants to take care of their children, enabling them to immerse themselves in necessary diplomatic work and social networking?

Servants to diplomats have to learn to be discreet and silent witnesses around the house, for they'll have unprecedented access into the private lives of their diplomatic employers. In certain countries it's readily assumed servants working in diplomatic residences might also be spies, paid by the host state to spy on their employers.

My mother was sixteen when she started working as a maid and this wasn't exactly what she had hoped or planned for her life but what could she do when she had a baby and no means of support except her parents? My grandfather, after searching desperately within the close-knit Mexican network of our friends and relations, managed to secure her an interview with the Swedish consul, newly appointed to Mexico City and looking to recruit a maid.

My mother, with her waist-length ink-black hair tied back and dressed in her smart new suit, made a good impression during the interview and despite her complete lack of experience, she was hired.

My mother hadn't trained to be a maid when she went for her first job interview. So before she started her new job her Swedish employer had to arrange for her to go to a colleague's house, for a couple of weeks, to be instructed in the rudiments of working for a diplomat.

As a result of her new job my mother had to leave our home in Iztupalapa, on the east side of Mexico City, and move into the diplomatic residence in Polanco. Polanco is about an hour's drive from Iztupalapa and it is an exclusive area of Mexico City, situated west of the city centre, with many high-end shops, restaurants and museums.

I think my mother did well given her circumstances.

8

Let's face it, there's high unemployment in Mexico and, add to that the nepotism that exists at all levels of society, it isn't easy to get work at the age of sixteen with minimal qualifications.

Nobody I know here takes work for granted. Even my mother's interview with the Swedish consul only took place because of a little nepotism (my mother had a second cousin working as a secretary at the Swedish embassy and she put in a good word for her).

Four years after working for the Swedish diplomat, my mother's hard work and dedication to the job meant she was recommended to his successor at the residence and this thankfully meant the new Swedish diplomat who took over the residence also decided to keep my mother on as his maid.

Although her position at the diplomatic residence was considered a good one among my family's acquaintances, my mother was always looking out for any new opportunities for advancement. She was very aware of how temporal and uncertain her contracts with her diplomatic employers were.

Her work certainly intrigued her.

She'd come home at weekends talking about the high profile Mexican politicians who'd come to dine at the residence where she worked, or the Swedish writers, artists as well as the businessmen and women who'd come to stay for short periods of time.

This was a world that enticed her.

The contrast between the various nationalities wining and dining at the residence on a frequent basis, and their cultural differences, fascinated my mother.

One weekend I remember she had brought home from the residence a collection of brightly coloured wooden horses and soldiers, hand painted in Sweden.

As I lined them up on a bookshelf I couldn't help admiring their red and white artistry. 'Who gave these to you, mum?'

My mother was sitting on her bed, watching with pleasure as I examined the toys.

'Jan often gets given gifts from visitors that he can't use. He tends to give them away and he thought you might appreciate these.'

I nodded. My grandmother had gasped with delight at the beautiful red and white embroidered table linen my mother had brought home a few months ago. Another cast off from the Swedish residence.

'I like the way they've painted these. Each one is slightly different. This one must be the colonel because his outfit is more complicated than the others', I said, lifting up the soldier to show her.

'Who gave Jan these?'

'These were given to Jan by the Swedish military attaché who was paying him a visit from his usual post in Colombia. Jan has so many interesting things in the house.' My mother shook her shoes off and curled her feet up on the bed.

'Mexican artists have given Jan lovely pictures, and he has

many other gifts from different nations. People in the embassy are not allowed to receive or give gifts above a certain amount but it's lovely to leave a country with a lot of mementos to your time there. To be given something original and inscribed to you is very special I think.'

My mother picked out the trumpeter in my collection and looked at it curiously.

'These are so pretty. I don't think our *alebrije* carvers could produce something like this.'

'Yes, they could', I contradict her, feeling defensive about our local talent. 'They're more creative. They make things the Swedish would never dream of making.'

My mother nodded in silent agreement, momentarily lost in thought.

Here in Iztupalapa there are many shops selling alebrijes, although the truly skilled carvers sell their wares to the United States and to the up market tourist shops in Mexico.

Some of them sell for thousands of dollars. Our skilled carvers and artists have depicted nearly every creature you can think of, as well as local peasants in various traditionally Mexican scenes.

I glanced briefly at my mother looking for her affirmation. She didn't take long to respond.

'Yes, that's true, Raoul. I think the *alebrijes* made by our carvers are unique in the world and their use of colour is very special.' My mother yawned, lying back lazily on her pillows. 'Creativity's in our blood I think. Look at the silverware, the glassware, the ceramics and the *alebrijes* that are so popular now in the States.'

9

My mother's proud of being Mexican. I think working in a diplomatic residence fostered this. As a young boy I didn't really appreciate how my mother's work opened her up to a cosmopolitan world she never would have had access to otherwise.

She liked her employer and she enjoyed learning a little about different cultures. She'd even learnt a few words of Swedish. I could tell she felt proud of the opportunities Mexico had to offer these very different countries.

Of course while my mother worked in Polanco I was left to my grandmother's care.

My grandparents' home was situated in a quiet street in Iztupalapa. Their street was called Calle Amistad. I've always thought Friendship Street is a lovely name for a street.

The buildings on our street were an eclectic mix of sandy stone, red brick and soft grey concrete. Black electrical cables hung in a criss-cross across the road. My grandparent's little house only had two bedrooms so on the weekends, when my mother could make it back home; she shared a room with me.

This made the days when my beautiful mother wasn't there very painful for me. I can only describe what felt like a big black hole welling up in me whenever I looked at her empty bed during the week. It left me with an acute sense of abandonment and, even today, it can come back to haunt me from time to time.

I don't even know if my mother was ever aware of how hard I found her long absences from home. We've never talked about it. She must've been aware of my sadness to some degree, but regardless of this, she did go on to make a great success of her job.

My mother's always been defined by her persistent desire to be independent; even now when I'm in a position to help her financially she wants nothing from me. Maybe I get my ingrained obstinacy from her.

10

I have to confess my memories of growing up in Iztupalapa with my grandparents are somewhat coloured by the acute boredom I suffered during that time. I do remember my grandfather occasionally taking me up to his small fruit farm in Tecamachalco.

Getting out of Mexico City certainly livened things up a bit for me, and I remember searching for the burrows of large hairy spiders in the grass while my grandfather took care of the fruit trees.

Tecamachalco was approximately a three and a half hour drive south from our home. When my grandfather had first inherited this plot of land it was practically worthless, but Tecamachalco was becoming increasingly urbanised and my grandfather planned to sell this little plot of land as a nest egg for his retirement. For now he was holding off until the prices for land in Tecamachalco went up as high as they possibly could.

Unfortunately for me, even tending to the fruit trees in Tecamachalco with my grandfather soon lost its appeal for me.

Nowadays I credit the enforced boredom I suffered during my early years for the start of my creative career.

Getting under my grandmother's feet continually, because I had little else to do, finally spurred my grandmother on to find something to occupy me. She found some old typewritten pages in her cupboard, and a pen, and sat me down at the kitchen table to draw on the reverse side of the pages.

From there I gradually progressed to owning a decent set of pencils, charcoal and chalk, as well as a sketchbook.

I've recently read articles written by psychologists on creative thinking. They warn the technology we use today is inhibiting creative thinking in our young children. I disagree with this.

I think creativity can be expressed through technology as well as more conventional means. I do however think a certain amount of boredom is an excellent conduit for creative thinking.

11

My grandparents, to be fair to them, did their best to provide me with a happy childhood.

Let's face it, other children have to grow up with parents who are dysfunctional and find themselves in dire situations. My main problem was boredom and loneliness, which ironically enough is usually the burden of the elderly.

I'd never go so far as to say it affected my mental health, but I do remember how painfully alone I felt the years I lived with my grandparents in Iztupalapa.

The only real friend I had was an elderly gentleman called Manolo, who lived across the road from us.

Manolo was an eccentric and familiar presence on our street, as he'd been living there for at least the last fifty years. You could spot him from a distance because he always wore a wine coloured fedora hat on his head and he also tended to drag his feet in a shuffling walk.

He blamed his walking style on having broken his toe when he was younger, apparently he injured himself running away from a bull at the bullring in Tijuana, but not everyone believes this story.

He always wore baggy trousers held up by a belt and a carefully ironed shirt. Manolo would announce his presence to us, if we weren't outside, by knocking loudly on our front door and shouting out '*¿Café hoy, Carmela?*'

My grandmother often invited Manolo in for coffee during the day, recognising he was lonely and in need of company.

When she heard a few bitchy neighbours were gossiping about her coffee mornings with Manolo she decided, to my horror, to confront those rotund middle-aged ladies after mass one Sunday. I had the misfortune to be by her side at the time and I can still remember cringing in embarrassment as she spoke to them. My grandmother's always been a feisty woman.

'I've heard you've been talking about me having coffee with Manolo. I hope you don't have a problem with this?'

Three of the women in front of her shook their heads vigorously in denial, but one unfortunately made the mistake of smirking knowingly. My grandmother then snorted contemptuously in response.

'You should be ashamed of yourselves. As God is my witness' at this point my grandmother, like a diva, histrionically made the sign of the cross, 'Manolo's wife was, as you all know, one of my closest friends. Before she died I promised her we would make sure Manolo was OK. Tell me, what exactly is the big deal about that?' My grandmother put her hands on her hips, bristling with hostility.

'Manolo's a sad and lonely old man and he enjoys having coffee and churros at our house. May God forgive you if you thought otherwise, you sex obsessed *putas*.'

My grandmother then squeezed my hand tightly and swept out of the church at a furious pace, dragging me along behind her.

Manolo, like me, was very isolated and I think because of this we became kindred spirits despite the big age gap between us.

Manolo's two children had left home and rarely visited, even though they both lived relatively near by in an affluent district of Mexico City. Manolo did eventually, thanks to me, find permanent companionship in the form of a mongrel dog called Campanita.

Campanita was a very beautiful mongrel and she'd been ruthlessly abandoned as a newborn puppy. I'll always be proud to remember she was discovered by me. She was a tiny puppy and my first philanthropic act, as far as I can recall, was saving her from the trash where she'd been thrown.

I found her when she was just a tiny scrap of fur, lying help-lessly in the filthy garbage container where she'd been dumped.

Hearing her plaintive whines one afternoon, I climbed into the smelly garbage container and pulled her out from among the heavy plastic bags. I gagged at both the smell of garbage and the sight of the other dead puppies. She was the only puppy out of the litter still alive among the mounds of stinking garbage bags.

However when I'd finally scrambled out of the container, holding tightly on to the puppy, I not only realised I'd soiled my clothes completely (which would anger my grandmother terribly) but I also knew my grandmother wasn't going to be at all pleased to have another responsibility foisted on her.

She definitely would not want the puppy.

It's at this point I decided to go up the stairs to Manolo's apartment and ask for his advice.

I rang his doorbell and waited impatiently for him to open the door. I could hear Manolo's familiar shuffling tread down the corridor before he opened the door.

'¿*Hijo, qué pasa?* What've you done with your clothes?'

I held up the now quiet puppy to Manolo. I could feel the tears trickling down my face but I didn't care.

'I found it in the garbage, Manolo. It's the only puppy left alive but I don't know what to do. *Abuela* will not want to have to look after it when she already has me to take care of. But I can't let it die. It didn't ask to be born and have some idiot dump her in the trash.'

Manolo patted me gently on the shoulder.

'Son, calm down. First you're going to have to get yourself cleaned up before Carmela sees you like that. Go to the kitchen, get a cloth and some soap and scrub those stains off your clothes. Give me the puppy, she's going to need a clean and some milk too.'

By late afternoon Campanita was fast asleep on a towel in a cardboard box on Manolo's kitchen floor, her fine white whiskers twitching in her sleep.

From then on I was allowed to visit Manolo and play with Campanita without worrying about what my grandparents would say.

I exercised Campanita whenever I could, because Manolo was getting too old to throw balls and chase after a young energetic dog. Compared to the occasional stray dogs wandering along the street with their ribs painfully showing through their fur, Campanita grew into a healthy striking white dog with a black patch over her eye.

Manolo sensibly made sure Campanita was spayed so she wasn't able to contribute to the growing number of unwanted dogs in the city. So many dogs in our neighbourhood were feral, slinking around the dusty streets with mangy tufted hair and with their eyes turning in hunger and fear.

Until I started school in the autumn of 1992, I only had old Manolo, and Campanita, as friends. That's it, an old man and his dog. Not exactly what I would call ideal preparation for life, or for school, as I was soon to discover.

In fact, I think in this respect my mother and grandparents sadly neglected me, but don't we all say such things when we look back to our childhoods? My life was to change for the better in the autumn of 1996 when, thanks to my mother, I'd be home schooled with the Anderson children.

However, at this point in time, I still had four years of school in Iztupalapa to get through first.

12

In the autumn of 1992 I started primary school in Iztupalapa and I quickly became the target of bullies in the school.

Looking back now, of course, I'm not surprised. I mean I'd spent all my formative years with adults only and I'd no siblings or friends my age. This in itself was always going to be a big handicap. But at the time I couldn't figure out why I was a target. I often wondered if it was because I was new to the class, or maybe because I was taller than most of the kids my age.

In the end I decided the bullying was happening because I was so pale skinned; the neighbourhood called me '*el blanquito*' (the white one) whereas at school I'd always be called '*el gringo*'. I have to confess I did curse my American father many times for the colour of his pale skin every time the kids called out '*gringo*' in the playground.

They used to wait for me when I walked out of the school gates to go home. There was always at least three of them waiting for me, for although I was quiet, I was tall and broad for my age.

Sometimes they used belts on me as the other kids slunk away, trying to pretend they couldn't see what was going on. Sometimes they had more inventive tools to hand, pocket-knives, or pieces of broken glass. The cowards were always careful to hold the sharp pieces of glass in a thick piece of canvas cloth.

In the beginning there was rarely a day when I didn't return home with some interesting cuts and my clothes ripped or torn. My grandmother would shake her head and purse her lips as she incessantly mended my clothes.

The bullying only stopped when a boy called Miguel Cortes decided to get involved, and told the bullies to back off or he'd ask his dad to sort them out.

Strangely, from that moment on, the three boys who'd picked on me left me alone and I began slowly to build friendships with my classmates. I'll never forget what Miguel did for me then. I've lost touch with him now, but like everyone else who has ever been bullied, I still retain vivid memories of those hideous days and the relentless way the bullying ground down my self worth.

Although Miguel was in the year above me, I always made sure to greet him when I saw him, and Miguel often stopped to chat to me in recess, when most of the other boys were kicking a football around the dusty playground (a game that interested neither one of us).

How do I describe Miguel? He was quite nondescript really, a rather small, dark, slim boy with intelligent eyes.

What made him stand out was the quality of his clothing. He came to school with a Tab watch, authentic Nike shoes, Levis jeans and Lacoste shirts; this in a school where had there been a school uniform many of the parents would've struggled to pay for it.

It took me some time to understand Miguel's background, as I was excessively naive for my age to be honest.

Everyone else in the school knew that Miguel Cortes's father was a prominent local drug lord. He subsidised the school as well as the local hospital, ensuring that the teachers had their salaries paid and weren't tempted to look for more lucrative jobs in other parts of Mexico City. Even the school building, it was rumoured, was built with some of his money.

When I eventually found out about Miguel's family background, I suddenly understood how such a small boy had been able to wield so much power over those bullies. From that moment on I would always associate wealth with power.

My grandmother unfortunately learnt about my friendship with Miguel too.

A friendly neighbour called Fabio also had a grandchild at the school. When I came home from school that day my grandmother told me Fabio had dropped by at lunchtime to have a word with her, and being no fool she knew straight away something was worrying him about me.

Manolo was there too at the time, sitting in my grandmother's kitchen slowly devouring some sugared churros, bits of which disappeared under the table where Campanita was eagerly awaiting her share.

My grandmother, who by the way was called Carmela, stood up anxiously as soon as Fabio entered.

'Fabio is everything all right?'

'Yes, yes Carmela. Everything's fine. I just came to have a quick chat. Do you have any more of that coffee available?'

'Yes, of course.' My grandmother turned round to lift the cafetièrre pot off the hob, poured coffee into a small espresso cup and placed it in front of Fabio.

'There you go. Have you had lunch?'

'Yes, thank you. Though one of your *churros* would be greatly appreciated.'

My grandmother gave him a plate and moved the basket of churros towards him. After that she sat down in her chair, folded her hands, and waited patiently for Fabio to speak.

Fabio took his time to drink his coffee and eat a churro. Manolo looked silently at my grandmother, his thick white eyebrows raised, but she refused to turn her eyes away from Fabio.

Finally, after chewing and meditating for a few moments, Fabio decided to speak.

'It's nothing very important but I thought you might want to know. My son's told me that Raoul's formed a new friendship at school with a boy called Miguel Cortes. Apparently Miguel stopped those idiots at the school pushing Raoul around and now Raoul's become a devoted follower. Has he told you any of this?'

'Yes, he said that he'd made friends with a boy in the year above him. I didn't know his name was Miguel Cortes, he's never mentioned his name. But if he helped Raoul we're grateful to him.'

'You might not realise that Miguel Cortes is the son of Sancho Cortes.'

'Ahh,' Manolo exhaled loudly and nodded his head up and down as my grandmother froze.

'And Sancho Cortes, as you know, is *el Lobo*.'

'*Dios mio*. I can't believe it. Raoul's a friend of *el Lobo*'s son? How on earth did that happen? *Madre de Dios*, what are we going to do now?'

My grandmother's eyes watered with unshed tears as she looked across at Manolo.

Manolo shrugged his shoulders fatalistically and shook his head.

Fabio patted my grandmother's shoulder reassuringly as if what he had just said was of no great importance.

'There's nothing you can do, Carmela. Don't make a big drama of it. They're too young to get into trouble but I thought you should know. Miguel's a nice kid, well brought up, and probably has no idea of what really goes on in his father's line of business.' Fabio looked intensely at my grandmother, trying unsuccessfully to convince her. 'Nothing's going to happen while they're at school. It could end up being a problem possibly later on when they become teenagers.'

Fabio picked up a churro and slowly munched on it. However seeing my grandmother's anxious face he continued to speak with his mouth full.

'Personally, from what I've heard, I don't think Miguel's cut out to join '*el Lobo*'s' activities and from what I understand from his teacher Miguel's a good scholar. His father's keen for him to go to university and not get involved in his business.'

My grandmother was horrified and shook her head in disagreement.

'I don't like it. It isn't good for Raoul and it won't be good for us.' She looked helplessly at Fabio. 'I know we can't say anything or do anything but I'll have to tell his mother when she's back home again. She really won't be happy about this friendship, she's working hard to provide Raoul with a future one day.' My grandmother sniffed loudly. 'This is not part of her plans for him. But there's no point saying anything to Raoul. Raoul's stubborn and very loyal.'

Fabio shrugged his shoulders.

According to Manolo, who was following the conversation with interest, it was clear Fabio thought things would work themselves out eventually and he thought it doubtful that I'd ever be a part of *el Lobo*'s plans for his pampered son.

'Carmela, let it run for a bit. They're just children. Things will work themselves out. Trust in God.'

My grandmother nodded and made the sign of the cross. Still looking worried she proceeded to be hospitable and asked Fabio how his family was.

Her fears and concerns about my friendship with Miguel were passed on to my grandfather that night, to my great annoyance, and to my mother at the weekend.

I was sitting in my bedroom, drawing in my sketchbook, and I could hear their raised voices through the thin plasterboard wall, as well as the concerned tone in which they spoke of my friendship with Miguel.

As a result of Miguel's unsavoury connections my grandparents were reluctant to have Miguel come and play at our house after school.

I was thoroughly infuriated by this but finally, when they saw I'd no intentions of letting my new friendship with Miguel dissolve, I was given permission to have Miguel come round to visit after school.

This happened mid-way through the autumn term in my second year at school, which only goes to show how bloody persistent I can be when I put my mind to it.

13

I saw my grandmother's anxiety visibly diminish when she met the polite, well-mannered boy who accompanied me back home.

I sat with Miguel on the plastic chairs in our dusty back yard, drinking a glass of Coca Cola, chickens pecking at the ground around us. At this stage I didn't feel in any way inferior to Miguel, although I was aware his home life would be very different to mine.

I remember bluntly asking Miguel why my grandparents would be so worried about having him round to their house.

Miguel turned to look at me with intelligent dark eyes and grimaced.

'Most people are funny about my dad, he has a bad reputation and he scares people.'

'So is he scary?'

Miguel smiled.

'No! If they'd let you come to my place you might meet him and see for yourself...'

'Not that he is home that much,' he added sadly.

I smiled at the thought of being invited out to Miguel's home.

At the end of each school day a blacked out Land Rover would pick Miguel up from the school gates and take him home. I had often wondered who sat behind those blacked out windows and I'd feel incredibly proud because my friend was so very wealthy.

Miguel, kind and polite, never gave the impression he thought me impoverished or that he found my home drab.

He was enthusiastic about my primitive sketches of Manolo and Carmela, and liked my drawings of the buildings and cars in our street. He admired some of my drawings so much I ripped them out of my sketchbook and gave them to him.

He appeared to enjoy feeding the hens in our back yard, and most of all eating my grandmother's homemade pastries.

It wasn't long before the invitation came for me to visit Miguel's home and my grandparents went to tremendous effort to smarten me up.

I was thoroughly annoyed when they literally forced me to wear my church clothes and shoes. I protested vigorously at putting on a tie. Nothing would budge me from this stance; they had to be content with getting me to wear a shirt.

I was very thankful I was visiting Miguel's house on a Saturday so no one from school would see me dressed up like this.

The blacked out car came to pick me up at ten in the morning with Miguel smiling and sitting in the back seat. My grandparents stood at the door and waved us off anxiously.

They were not the only ones watching the car's slow progress up the street. Many windows along the street had faces peering out, watching my first visit to *el Lobo's* house.

A gated community and some scraggy wasteland several miles away, bordered Miguel's house. The house itself sat up on a slope that gave a clear view of the surrounding city. I wondered if the house was high enough to rise above the smog that sometimes engulfed our city.

The road up to the house was pretty isolated, and all I could see were a few cattle grazing on each side of the road and some well-fed horses twitching their ears towards our car as it came towards them.

The wall surrounding the house was high and there was a plump sentry by the front gate.

As soon as he spotted our car he allowed the electric gates to open and our car drove up to a large house built in the style of a Spanish villa with white walls, black metal ironwork on the windows and a red tiled roof.

Miguel rang the doorbell and a short, round lady in a maid's uniform opened the door with a big smile.

'Hola Miguel. Here's your friend Raoul! How smart you are Raoul! And handsome too!'

She chuckled as she saw my discomfort and patted me on the back.

'Come to the kitchen and have some food. Miguel, your mother's out just now but she'll be back in an hour.'

'That's fine Nuria. We'll have something to eat and then I'll show Raoul around.'

Nuria waddled in her flat ballerina shoes towards the kitchen and opened the swing door to let us in. On the sparkling clean breakfast bar, ready prepared, were two plates with tortillas and two large glasses of fresh orange juice. It didn't take us long to eat the food and begin a tour of the house.

I'd seen many houses like this one on television but the reality of being in such a house was quite overwhelming for me. Artwork in bright primary colours hung on the walls. I remember standing in front of one particular painting in the living room.

My eye zoned in on this painting because of the brightly coloured geometric figures dancing in it. Miguel seemed amused by my interest.

'Do you like the paintings?' Miguel asked me. 'My mother loves his work. The painter is a guy called Carlos Merida. My mother says it reminds her a little of Picasso's work. You know Picasso, right?'

I nodded my head sagely even though I'd absolutely no idea who Picasso was. I mean if you think about it, how many young primary school kids know about Picasso?

That was Miguel for you. Like me, he clearly spent too much of his time with adults but unlike me, he was learning something useful along the way.

'She also likes pictures by another artist called Gunther Gerzso. She likes the way he puts colours together. Those are the ones in the dining room,' Miguel added.

Miguel opened the double doors to the dining room, where a glass and marble dining table stretched across the room surrounded by fourteen high backed dining chairs.

On either side of the room hung the strong geometric paintings by Gunther Gerzso, the artist born of German Hungarian parents but who's now considered a Mexican national treasure. Even now I find it hard to believe I saw his original paintings hanging on the walls in Miguel's house.

'My mum says he's also compared to Picasso. I think my mum's a little crazy about Picasso.'

Miguel walked nonchalantly back again, past the leather sofas, marbled floors and glass coffee tables and started to make his way up the stairs to the upper floor.

I reluctantly left the paintings and followed him up.

From Miguel's bedroom window I could see out to the back of the house. At the back of the house there was a large garden with a swimming pool that looked as though it was never used. Miguel's bedroom was large enough to accommodate a pool table and a large sofa and television.

Everything was spotlessly clean and tidy.

I became intrigued by the pictures on the wall of different buildings in New York.

The bookcases in Miguel's room were stacked with books but also contained some cleverly built buildings made of matchsticks. Some had internal stairs curving round to the upper floors; others had lifts built in or attic rooms.

'Did you make these?' I asked Miguel in surprise.

'Yeah, because we live so far away from everyone I spend a lot of time on my own and I get bored. I started making some small Indian huts and then went on to make more complicated houses out of matchsticks. Making these buildings distracts me and I enjoy it. I prefer it to Lego to be honest. I also design them on the computer. I can show you on the computer if you like.'

'I'd love to see them.'

Miguel switched on the computer and went into his files to show me some of his 3D buildings and 2D room plans.

Looking back now, I'm sure the room plans Miguel had designed were very basic, but of course to my young and impressionable eyes they were stunning.

I had no access to a computer at home and only occasionally at school. I suddenly felt ashamed of my hand drawn sketches, which had none of the accuracy these computer based drawings had.

'When my father saw how interested I was in buildings, he got one of the architects who works with him in the business to come and show me how it to use it. This is a program that most architects and interior designers use to draw. It's so much easier than doing it by hand. Very few people can draw well by hand.'

Miguel, having shown off his plans to me, looked at me and seemed to perceive the negative thoughts running through my head.

'I can't draw like you can. None of us at school can. You shouldn't compare your drawings to these. My father's architect said if you want to start studying and designing buildings you need to be good at art.' Miguel exited the program as he spoke.

'It's not enough to be able to design on the computer. You've got to be able to see the space, and be able to sketch out your ideas. But anyway,' he said, shutting down the computer. 'This isn't much fun. Why don't we have a go on the go-carts in the garden?'

I followed Miguel out of the room and walked outside, where we spent the rest of the afternoon racing go-carts around a small racing track at the bottom of the garden.

Visiting Miguel's house was a pivotal moment in my life. I'd never forget my visits to Miguel's palatial home (at least so it seemed to my young eyes) and later on as I grew up, my memory of those clever computer drawings and Miguel's beautiful home spurred me on to relive something similar in my own life.

I certainly developed an aesthetic appreciation of art and home interiors after seeing Miguel's house.

When I left Iztupalapa to live with my mother I gradually lost contact with Miguel.

Initially Miguel and I'd send each other sporadic emails, but eventually I lost touch completely with him as most people do with friends they once knew in early childhood.

A few years later, acquaintances in Iztupalapa told me Miguel and his family were forced to leave Mexico after a brutal and destructive turf war between rival drug gangs. Miguel's dad lost control of his business interests in Iztupalapa and as a result the family ended up fleeing to San Paolo in Brazil.

I often think nostalgically of Miguel now I'm older, and hope that where ever he is now he'll be living a relatively normal and fulfilling life.

After all, Miguel was the one who convinced me to leave Iztupalapa, and to go and live with my mother in Chapultepec.

If it hadn't been for his encouragement I'd have never agreed to leave my grandparent's home and I'd have never met Hannah Anderson and her family.

14

I've never claimed I made life easy for my mother when I was a young boy. I resisted, like most children, any change in my circumstances. My life was comfortable enough and I felt secure in my friendships both at school and at home.

It had never occurred to me I'd ever have choices to make, or whether the unspoken cost of taking my studies forward would mean choosing to leave behind the friends and family I knew in Iztupalapa.

However I underestimated my mother, who'd always have higher expectations for me, just as my grandmother had once had for her.

My mother had been working for the last year as a maid for a British diplomatic family, the Andersons, who were based in Chapultepec.

In 1996 I was to meet the Anderson family for the first time and move into their home in Chapultepec. Or to be more accurate, I moved into the maid's flat next to their house.

I was nearly ten years old at the time.

Mr and Mrs Anderson lived with their three children in a large two-storey house in Avenida de Aconcagua in Chapultepec. Chapultepec is a well to do area in Mexico City, popular with many diplomats because it is full of museums and art galleries, as well as bohemian cafes.

The Andersons lived approximately half an hour by car from Iztupalapa, although it would take my mother and I almost an hour to get there by bus.

However close the physical distance was between our homes in Mexico City, there was a huge gulf in terms of culture and language.

I didn't know it at the time of course, but living with the Anderson family was to change my life for the better. I can guarantee you I wouldn't be working as an interior designer today, if it hadn't been for their support and encouragement.

It took a while to persuade me to move to the Anderson's home. To this day my mother still goes on about how stubborn I was.

Personally I don't know why she complains so much because, until I moved in with her, I'd spent ten years living with my grandparents and my grandmother never complained about me in this respect.

Maybe my grandmother could see herself in me, I don't know. But I accept I did stress my mother out when I staunchly refused to entertain the idea of moving with her to Chapultepec.

'Mum, if you make me go and live with you in Chapultepec I'll run away and come home again. I'm not going there with you.'

I remember my mother looking at me with quiet exasperation. She then tucked a stray strand of black hair behind her ear and leaned back on her chair.

'Raoul, you'd be an idiot to let this pass you by. Think about it. Don't you envy the kind of life Miguel has? I know you do. All the times you see his house and all the times he gives you presents and you can't afford to give him something as expensive back. With the right education you can make a better life for yourself, without all the danger and trouble Miguel's family will one day have.'

My mother paused dramatically and looked at me. 'Sometimes, you just get one chance in your life to make a difference, to go and do something you really enjoy.'

I said nothing.

My mother clasped her hands together so tightly I remember her knuckles stood out.

I wasn't oblivious to the fact she desperately wanted me to join her in Chapultepec, and was keen for me to be educated alongside the Anderson children.

Mrs Anderson knew my mother had a young son living in Iztupalapa and had generously offered for me to come and share the maid's flat with my mother. She also offered to home school me with her three children. Apparently Mrs Anderson had told my mother she felt learning English would be of enormous benefit to me, but equally my Spanish could also benefit her children.

Mrs Anderson, or Marion as I later came to call her, had taken a tour of Greengates, the large international school in Mexico, and decided against putting her children there. It was a huge school and she felt her children would lose their individuality.

So they were all going to be home schooled by a semi-retired primary school teacher called Mrs Cumber.

Many of the diplomatic wives, if they didn't have roles within the embassy itself, were keen to support and work with local charities during the term of their diplomatic posts. Mrs Anderson, however, was a strong believer in charity starting at home and had early on taken an interest in my mother.

15

My mother at twenty-five years of age was a beautiful and intelligent woman but also extremely competent in her work at the residence. Mrs Anderson, having managed lazy and incompetent staff in her previous postings, now thoroughly appreciated how well run the diplomatic functions were in her household and how little she had to interfere in the day to day running of the house.

Meanwhile, back in Iztupalapa, my mother would plead with me to accept the invitation made by Mrs Anderson.

'Please don't blow it. I'll tell Mrs Anderson we need a little more time but don't take too long, Raoul, or you'll lose this opportunity. I promise you, you'll live to regret it later on.'

Like you sometimes must regret having had me, I remember thinking to myself at the time.

'Are you sure this isn't all about my friendship with Miguel? I know you don't like me to be friends with his family. This is all very useful for you now isn't it? You know I'm happy here, I like my friends and I like my school. You've no idea what it'll do to me to leave everyone here, and go and live somewhere else.'

'Raoul, we're worried about your involvement with Miguel's family. But this is not about that.' My mother waved her outstretched hands to emphasize her point, as she always tended to do when agitated. 'Mrs Anderson's given me a really generous offer and it could give you a chance to do something special with your life. You haven't even met her or her children. She's offered for you to come up and meet them any weekend that suits us. You can have a look around and decide then.'

'Mum, I get what you're saying, and what you're wanting me to do, but like all the other diplomats they'll leave after four years and what'll happen to us then? What's the point?'

'*Madre de Dios*, Raoul!' my mother said impatiently, 'The Anderson family are well connected and very generous. They want to try and improve our lives and to be involved with us. It's just the way they are.'

'You haven't answered my question, mum. What do we do when they leave?'

'I trust them to work something out for us when the time comes for them to move on. After four years your English could be fluent for a start and it would be an amazing skill to have.' My mother stood up, tired of repeating herself and anxious to get on with things. 'Raoul, don't throw it all away. Have a think about it and we can get abuelo to drop us off one Saturday to meet them.'

It took a long time to convince me of the merits of going to study in Chapultepec with my mother.

Thankfully though, the summer holidays were coming up and there was no immediate pressure for me to leave Iztupalapa, as the Andersons would soon be away in the United Kingdom on holiday. My mother was desperately hoping that I'd start living with her and the Andersons in the autumn.

Like most of the children in my class I wasn't thinking at the time of my adult future. Not many children do at the age of ten. My preoccupations were of a trivial nature.

Back then I'd have to confess to thinking about what food or drink I'd be having for lunch, and whether I'd get a chance to make a good swap of baseball cards at recess. The more pressure I got from my mother to change my life the more I grumbled and resisted.

My determined mother started to look sorrowful and made it clear I'd break her heart if I didn't accept Mrs Anderson's invitation to stay in their household.

Finding even Manolo determined to encourage me to go I began to feel hurt and unwanted. My only sympathetic friend appeared to be Campanita, probably because she was a dog and couldn't talk back to me.

One hot afternoon, as we sat in the cool shade of his small terrace, old Manolo looked at me as I stroked Campanita and clearly noticed how depressed I was about the whole situation.

'You don't need to worry about her when you go, Raoul. Pedro says he's happy to walk her. He's just as fond of her as you are.'

'I haven't said I'm going to go and live in Chapultepec and I'm not worried about Campanita.'

'Then why are you walking around like a bear that's lost its pot of honey, Raoul?'

'I'm upset because everyone's trying to force me to go to Mrs Anderson's house in Chapultepec and I don't want to go. But if I don't go they'll blame me for it, for not making something of my life and for not helping out my family.'

Manolo smiled.

'If you go and you don't like it you can always come back. You haven't even given it a go. Your mother's not going to force you to stay if you don't like it. What's the harm in trying?'

'I don't want to be in a house where my mum will be working as a servant and I'll just be allowed to be in their home when they want me. I don't want to have to be friends with some rich, stuck up British kids who won't know anything about us or about Mexico.'

'You haven't even met them. No one's going to respect you when you haven't even tried to meet the family or seen their house. Everyone will understand if it doesn't work out and you come back.'

'Exactly. I'm getting forced into this because everyone's behaving like I'm throwing away a lifetime's worth of *pesos* if I don't go. Even you are saying no one will respect me if I stay. Everyone's just pushing me into this and I don't want to go.'

'Raoul, we'll still be here for you and love you if you stay. But you're foolish if you ignore what the people who love you the most think is best for you.'

'I don't care. I don't care if I'm foolish. You're not the ones having to go away and live somewhere else. You'll get to stay here. None of you have a right to tell me what to do because you're not having to do it yourselves.'

'OK, Raoul. Let's not talk about it anymore. It's not worth a fight.'

In the end it was Miguel who convinced me to go.

Both of us were stretched out on hammocks in the large terrace at Miguel's house one Sunday afternoon, with glasses full of ice and lemon Fanta. For once I was uncharacteristically silent. Miguel looked across to me and decided to join the fray.

'I understand why you don't want to go, Raoul, and I'll miss you of course, but you shouldn't think things will always stay the same here. In a few years half the class will be out working as *alebrijes* carvers or working in a factory as glass artists. Some of them will be working in the supermarket.'

I looked away from Miguel, not wanting to engage with him on this subject, but he seemed undeterred because he carried on regardless.

'Things change. My family have no idea if they'll be here for the long term. In a sense we've no more stability or security than those diplomats your mum wants you to stay with. Everything changes. This could be an opportunity for you to do something different and if it doesn't work out you can just come back here.'

I sighed impatiently.

'Would you go if your mother asked you to leave here?'

'I wouldn't have a choice. Until I am old enough to get a job and be independent I have to stay with my family and do what they decide is best. It doesn't mean I like it, being dependent on them, but most families just want what's best for you.'

'I can still stay with my grandparents. I'll always have a home here.'

'Your situation is different to mine because you can choose between staying with your grandparents here or going away with your mother. But your grandparents aren't going to be around forever and they're getting old. Manolo's getting old.'

I reflected on this for a moment. I didn't like the thought of my grandparents and Manolo aging.

'Yes, Manolo's getting old. My grandmother lives in dread of him tripping and falling down the stairs of his apartment. His legs are really weak. At least he has a walking stick now.'

'Anyway if you did go,' Miguel, unusually persistent, wasn't letting the subject drop, 'we could keep in touch through email.

I'm sure you'll be allowed to use a computer to email us.'

'I just don't understand why everyone thinks me going away to Chapultepec is such a great thing. I'm happy where I am and I don't need anything else.'

Miguel sat up and looked at me in surprise.

Miguel, from my childish point of view, had bad moments when he was just like an adult in the way he looked at life. He often managed to make me feel like a silly toddler.

'Are you sure you're happy here? In a school where the teachers have no expectations for most of the pupils? I'm probably going to be moving to a private school in a year or two.'

I shrugged dismissively, as if to say what's that got to do with me?

'My parents want me to go to college but don't think the teaching at our school is going to get me there and I'm already getting extra tutoring at home. Your mother's only trying to do for you what my parents are doing for me.'

I thought about Miguel's dad, who I'd met only a couple of times. Miguel's dad was a boisterous, cheerful man who'd welcomed me like I was a member of the family.

A question that had been niggling me for some time resurfaced in my mind and I decided now was the time to ask Miguel.

'Doesn't your dad want you to join him in his business?'

Miguel suddenly looked away from me as though the question made him uncomfortable.

'You know what my dad does right?'

'I've an idea. I'd have thought he'd want you to get involved.'

'Just because he's making his money through crime doesn't mean it's what he wants for his son. He knows I couldn't cope with it.'

Miguel lay back into his hammock, letting it envelop him, so all I could see was the outline of his body dipping in a V shape, with his trainers sticking out at the top. Was it shame or horror that made him withdraw? I didn't know.

His disembodied voice carried on talking, sounding eerily like a distant radio.

'He's lost all sense of reality and he's done some really brutal things. I only know of a few things he's been involved in but they're bad enough. It's hard to explain... It's like you have a kind father who loves you and enjoys the time he spends with you, showers you and your mother with gifts and money....' Miguel paused for a moment to take a drink and I could hear the ice cubes clinking in his glass.

'Then you remember the kidnapped boy, whose ransom his parents weren't able to pay. They found him dead a week later on the side of the motorway and he was my father's victim. This boy happened to be the son of a businessman who'd refused to pay my father protection money. My mother and I have tried to talk to him about it and to find a way to pull him back but it's too late, he's used to this way of life and it doesn't affect him anymore.'

Thinking about this, I swung myself a few times on the hammock, pushing on the whitewashed wall with one hand. I wasn't surprised at what Miguel had shared with me. The whole school knew what '*El Lobo*'s' activities were about.

'So what you're saying is we can both get better teachers and one day, who knows, maybe we can meet up and start a business together.'

Miguel's head suddenly popped out of the hammock. He smiled at me.

'Exactly! We both have a chance to do better for ourselves and it doesn't really matter how we get there.'

When I went home that day I waited until my mother had left for work, and then told my grandmother I would go to Chapultepec to live with the Andersons. I was too proud and immature, of course, to admit to my mother I'd changed my mind about living with the Andersons.

My grandmother was delighted and relieved, mostly to be fair to her, on her daughter's behalf.

16

On a Saturday, in the middle of August 1996, I went with my mother to visit number 32 Avenida de Aconcagua for the first time.

My first impression was of a huge brown metal gate and a high ivy covered wall surrounding the building inside.

As we stood outside the gate waiting for someone to let us in, I looked at the completely empty tree lined road and immediately missed the sight of a mangy flea bitten dog, the noise of trucks and cars coming in and out of the garage in my neighbourhood, the women walking down the street to go to the market and the old men sitting outside playing chequers.

This road was eerily quiet.

Once we were buzzed in, we walked up a paved stone pathway with white Cala lily flowers on either side. Peach trees heavy with fruit stood at regular intervals on our left hand side, the large two-storey brick house was on our right hand side.

My mother squeezed my elbow in an effort to reassure me as we walked up to the large house.

A tall lady, with loose fair hair in a frizzy halo around her head, popped out of a side door with a friendly smile and came towards us.

She was informally dressed in jeans and a pale blue shirt, and I instantly felt very overdressed and aware of my black and shiny polished shoes.

However I also remember feeling an almost immediate liking for this lady, who seemed to be so relaxed and welcoming.

Which wasn't what I'd expected to be honest.

'Hello Esther and Raoul, how lovely to see you! Hannah's been bursting with impatience to meet you. Patrick's in his usual spot, busy in the kitchen making himself a snack.'

'My name's Marion,' Marion said, holding out her hand for me to shake.

I noticed she spoke Spanish well although with a very pronounced accent. Not used to shaking hands I shook her hand clumsily and then followed my mother into the house.

The front door opened into an enormous square hallway with a high ceiling stretching upwards.

The stairs went up in three stages to the upper floor. I noticed ugly plywood squares attached to the banisters all the way up to the top floor.

Marion noticed me staring at the plywood panels.

'Those were put there to stop my youngest boy, Stephen, who's a terror isn't he Esther? from falling through the metal railings. We'd only just moved in when Hannah found Stephen hanging completely silently by his hands, on the edge of the stairs up there. We managed to quickly pull him up before he fell to the ground.'

Marion turned away from the stairs as if the memory pained her.

'Bless him he burst into tears because he'd had as big a fright as we did, but he's not to be trusted and after that incident we decided he'd have to go to nursery in the mornings or goodness knows what else he'll get up to when we're not watching him.'

A tall slim girl, with her long fair hair tied back, appeared out of what I was to discover later was the kitchen.

'Ah, here's my second child, Hannah.'

Hannah was almost as tall as me but I thought she looked to be a good deal younger. My mother had told me she was the same age as me. Hannah had a small nose and her cheeks were covered in freckles but what struck me the most were her large, very pale blue eyes because I'd never before seen blue eyes in the flesh, only on television.

I tried very hard not to stare into them. Something I found difficult to do as she was clearly equally as interested in inspecting me.

Hannah decided she approved of me because within the space of a minute she smiled, and held out her hand.

'Hello Raoul!'

I returned the handshake with a tentative smile.

'Right. Now we only have to find where my oldest son is, and my husband, and all the introductions will be finished! Esther, I think if you take Raoul into the kitchen you'll find Patrick there and you can fix yourselves up a drink or something to eat, while I go and see if I can find David. I think he was in the study watching the news.'

Marion disappeared off up the stairs as my mother and I went into the kitchen, with Hannah following close behind us.

Patrick was sitting at the kitchen table with a loaf of bread in front of him and a sea of crumbs around it. He was busy making a cheese sandwich and only stopped for a moment to gruffly greet us.

He was a broad shouldered boy, somewhat heavily built, with a shock of blond hair hanging over his eyes.

'Paaatrick! What a mess!'

Patrick looked uncomprehendingly at my mother until she gestured at the crumbs. He immediately looked apologetic and went over to the sink to fetch a cloth to wipe up the mess.

As he mopped up the crumbs my mother went over to the moka pot and filled it with water and coffee, and then went to one of the cupboards and brought out a tray in which she laid out three small espresso coffee cups and a plate with some biscuits.

'Raoul love, what would you like to drink? You can have some milk or some Coca Cola?'

'Just water, Mum,' I said, feeling suddenly more confident as I watched Patrick obey my mother and clean up the crumbs.

Hannah was talking to Patrick in English but as she wasn't whispering to her brother, I didn't feel uncomfortable about not understanding what they were saying. Patrick just nodded from time to time and carried on chewing his sandwich with bovine intent.

'Raoul, follow me out into the sitting-room. Can you carry the coffee jug please?'

I obediently walked behind my mother as we walked out of the kitchen and into an open plan room on the left hand side of the square hallway. Potted plants stood at intervals between numerous cream sofas and glass and bamboo side tables. Brightly coloured paintings were on the walls in complementary shades of purples and pinks.

A large bright pink rug occupied the space in front of what looked like an unused fireplace.

Photo frames with various pictures of the Andersons stood on different side tables. Hardback books from the National

Museam of Art and the National Museam of Anthropology lay on the enormous coffee table in the middle of the room.

Marion appeared soon afterwards, walking down the stairs followed by a gangly man wearing a pair of round tortoiseshell framed glasses. He was tall like the rest of the family, making my mother and I look small by comparison. He had on a pair of smart trousers and shirt because, as it was quickly explained, he was off out to a formal drinks reception at the Indian residence.

He greeted me in very fluent Spanish and laughed at my evident surprise.

'Did you see Marion? Raoul must've had a very bad impression of your Spanish ability to be so surprised when I speak to him. Raoul, you'll definitely be a great help to my family if you decide to stay here with us.'

I looked blankly at David Anderson, confused and not comprehending how I could be of help to them.

'Just take a look at Hannah and Patrick, Raoul. So far they've learnt to say hello in Spanish and I don't think they know how to say much more. I'm sure within a few days you could teach them an awful lot about your language and they could help you learn English. So it would be a win/win situation, don't you think?'

I nodded numbly, a little bit overawed by this pale man who spoke Spanish so well.

David turned to Marion and my mother.

'How soon do you feel Raoul would be able to come and stay with you here, Esther?'

'Hopefully he'll be ready to move in in a couple of weeks time. He'll want to say a proper goodbye to his friends and family in Iztupalapa before he comes,' my mother said quickly.

65

I could see she was desperately hoping I'd not contradict her in a fit of rebellion, so I kept quiet. In any case I felt quite intimidated by this house and its family. It was a struggle to imagine living here at all.

'That sounds perfect, Esther. If you need anything else for the garden flat just let us know obviously.'

'Thank you very much, Mr Anderson. I'll take Raoul to see the garden flat before we leave. I don't think we really need anything else.'

David smiled and emptied his espresso cup, before standing up and making his apologies as he headed out of the house.

Once David had left I immediately felt more relaxed, and leant back on the comfortable sofa as my mother and Marion discussed their plans for schooling once September started.

I wondered what Hannah and Patrick were up to in the kitchen but I waited patiently for my mother to get up and show me round the rest of the house.

17

The back garden was large, not as large as Miguel's garden back in Iztupalapa, but large enough to hold a Jacaranda tree with an enormous swing tied to it, a stone fountain with strangely no water in it, a big playroom and up some winding metal stairs behind the playroom, a small flat.

My mother's flat was quite basic with a shower room, toilet and two bedrooms.

My mother had made the flat nice and homely with some of my grandmother's bright crochet cushions, a colourful bedspread and rug, as well as some eye-catching framed posters with Aztec illustrations.

I was glad to see there was a television in the flat and I appreciated getting a chance to see where my mother lived, and how the room had been made cheerful by her small homely touches.

By the time we were on our way back home to Iztupalapa on the Sistema de Movilidad bus I was starting to feel very tired.

As I looked out of the window at the traffic congestion, snarled up in typically Mexican fashion, I felt relieved and also strangely drained. It had been a stressful time leading up to the visit, and now the visit was finally over I felt deflated.

'What did you think, Raoul?' my mother asked calmly.

'It was OK,' I said shrugging my shoulders casually.

This seemed to satisfy my mother who put her head back on the seat and shut her eyes.

'Their children are good kids, you know. I'm very fond of them,' she said before she started to doze.

I did feel more positive about the move, especially now I'd actually seen where I was to stay, and to my surprise I felt I'd like to get to know Patrick and Hannah better. In those days I didn't possess the confidence to believe I had anything to offer.

Realizing I might be able to teach Patrick and Hannah my own language made me feel valued in a new way.

18

'Raoul, wake up now please. *Raoul!*'

I let my face emerge from the sheets and I stretched both of my arms out over my head, but my eyes remained shut.

I finally tried opening my eyes.

'Is it time?'

'Of course it is, Raoul. Come on! You have to get a move on, I've got to go in five minutes.'

'OK, OK. You go ahead. I'll get ready.'

I threw back the bed sheets and my mother, satisfied that I was really going to get out of bed, left the room to get ready.

Eventually, when I was ready to leave the garden flat I stood for a moment at the top of the spiral staircase and breathed in the cool autumn air.

Down below the blue flowers of morning glory climbed up the side of the playroom, it was so early the petals on its flowers were still folded shut. I shook my shoulders back, ran down the remaining stairs and let myself into the back of the house, which my mother had left open for me.

The smell of coffee assailed me, as did the sight of fresh pastries laid out on a basket ready to be taken through to the dining room.

I sat at the kitchen table and pinched a French Palmier pastry from the basket.

'Raoul, not from there!' my mother said, playfully swiping at my hand but it was too late. I'd taken a big bite out of it.

She carefully replaced the Palmier I'd taken with one from the cupboard.

She fetched a tray and laid out five glasses of fresh orange juice alongside the coffee jug.

'I'll be back in a minute,' she said as she walked through the swing door to the dining room.

I went to the cupboard and picked out a plate and a glass, pouring myself a glass of milk from the jug in the fridge. The milk in this household was carefully boiled up before it was available to drink, mainly because of the Anderson's fear of catching amoebas.

My mother came back and carried through the basket of pastries to the dining room.

When she returned she picked up her mug of coffee and sat at the table with me.

In an hour's time the household cook, Aida, would arrive and take over the kitchen but this early in the morning the kitchen belonged to my mother and I so it was very peaceful.

'So what lessons do you have today Raoul?'

'We're getting maths and history, I think. Although Mrs Cumber said she's going to do some English writing. I'll just do what she asks in Spanish. She said once my English is good enough I can try to write in English but the main thing is to be able to write creative stories at the moment, and it doesn't matter what language it's in.'

'Very good. Antonio, the driver, said he'll pick you up at four to take you to football.'

'Cool. Aren't you going to eat anything, mum?'

My mother smiled.

'I've already had a piece of toast and as you know once Aida gets started there'll be lots of leftovers she'll be trying to get us all to finish.'

'I know. I'll be looking in at break to see what's available.'

The door swung open and the youngest member of the Anderson family walked in.

'Good morning Raoul,' said Stephen, walking up to me and giving me a hug.

Stephen had a rather confrontational relationship with his older brother and soon after meeting me seemed to have decided I was the kind of older brother he would've preferred having. I guess from his point of view I was never too bored or busy to play football or cricket in the back garden with him, unlike Patrick who preferred to spend his time talking to his friends, or on his laptop.

'Stephen, your breakfast's on the dining table, my love,' said my mother.

'I know.'

Stephen smiled, turned and went through the door to the dining room.

A short time later the bell rang, letting my mother know the table was ready to be cleared.

Under the dining table, hidden under the carpet, there was a bell for the master or mistress of the house to summon the maid from the kitchen.

A hilarious and embarrassing situation had arisen at one formal dinner when David, who was sitting next to a French diplomat, was trying to find the floor button to summon my mother to the dining room to clear the table for the next course in the meal.

He had to quickly explain to the nervous diplomat next to him that he was not trying to rub against her ankle; he was actually just trying to find the service button under the carpet.

My mother went through to the dining room with her tray and I heard her talking to Marion Anderson.

Marion was going to be out for lunch today with some other diplomatic wives, but before she went out she'd get a list of the necessary food shopping needed for the reception at the end of the week from Aida, our cook.

Shortly afterwards my mother came back through with a tray full of dirty crockery and cutlery, at which point I got up and went through to the dining room to help clear the table.

I found it very hard to see my mother waiting on others but I did understand how in a country with huge unemployment this job was considered a lucrative and privileged one.

I also knew the Andersons were considerate employers and were sensitive to how I might feel watching my mother waiting on them. They never gave orders and were always polite with their requests.

Often Hannah would give my mother a hand if her mother allowed her to. Marion was keen for Hannah to help out because it worried her that her children would grow accustomed to this lifestyle, and would struggle to adapt to reality once they were older and on their own back in Britain.

19

However kind the Andersons were the indefinable barrier between employer and employee always stood between them and us.

At the weekends we'd return to Iztupalapa whereas the Andersons often went on extended trips to Acapulco or to Yucatan. They also visited the Teotihuacan pyramids and the well-known Popocatepetl volcano. On other occasions they went horse riding in the mountains, away from the bloated and polluted capital city.

I was in some inexplicable way ashamed when I came to the realization the Andersons had seen more of Mexico than I had.

Hannah, who told me all about their trips away, was at first hurt and then annoyed by my gruff responses, but I think she soon realised I felt isolated by my circumstances because she stopped telling me about their weekends.

One day she asked her mother if I could join them on one of their weekend trips. Unknown to Hannah and Marion, Stephen was also listening and told me about the ensuing conversation afterwards.

'Well Hannah, he has to see his family back at home too and it's good for us to have a bit of time together as a family don't you think?'

'Yes, but I feel it's so unfair Raoul's never seen the places we go to and all these places are a part of his country. Mrs Cumber is teaching us about Aztec history and he's never even seen the pyramids made by them.'

'I'll speak to Esther about it. Maybe next time we go to the pyramids at Teotihuacan he can come with us. Try not to worry about it too much Hannah. Raoul knows he has a different family and background to us. He also likes going to see his grandparents and his friends in Iztupalapa at the weekend. In fact Esther's invited us to visit her home in Iztupalapa one weekend so we'll have to organise a trip there too soon.'

I was horrified when Stephen told me this. I couldn't imagine anything worse than showing the Anderson family around my grandparent's small two-bedroom home.

However when the trip to my grandparent's home did take place, it didn't actually go as badly as I had feared.

20

One November weekend, two months after I'd moved to Chapultepec, the Andersons' came to Iztupalapa to meet my grandparents. The Andersons driver, Antonio, drove Marion, Hannah and Stephen to our home in Iztupalapa on the Saturday morning.

I was so relieved neither Patrick nor David were taking part in the visit, that I consequently felt pretty relaxed showing Hannah and Stephen around my back yard and neighbourhood. Meanwhile Marion had coffee with my grandparents, Manolo and my mother.

Stephen with his dark eyes and dark hair was nicknamed affectionately 'el Mexicano' by all who saw him and Hannah was called 'guapa' (pretty) or 'rubia' (blonde) by everyone who greeted us, which didn't bother her in the slightest once I'd explained what they meant.

Stephen and Hannah didn't suffer from shyness so they weren't afraid to use the little they'd learnt of Spanish on our acquaintances.

Waving goodbye to the Andersons later on in the afternoon I felt a sense of contentment descend on me. To have shared some of my background and my home with the Andersons seemed to build a bridge between our lives and to blur the perimeters in which we all lived.

21

Mrs Cumber looked up from her desk and caught me looking out of the window again, fiddling with a rubber on my desk.

Our eyes met briefly before I quickly put my head down to the textbook in front of me.

I heard her sigh quietly. She by no means despaired of my ability to learn but I have to confess I had a very low attention span when it came to learning things like grammar and algebra.

Mrs Cumber was a retired teacher and she was acutely aware her teaching was very much 'old school'. She knew her teaching was good enough to get the Anderson children to pass entrance exams at schools back in England.

However she often said to me she felt her teaching didn't connect with me, and she felt she'd let me down.

Initially she'd punished me with written homework for my moments of abstraction but despite my mother pleading with me to pay more attention in class, it had no noticeable effect. Nowadays she just seemed to wonder desperately what to do to get me motivated and interested.

'Raoul, *¿que pasa?*' she asked me in Spanish that spring afternoon, early in 1997.

'*Nada, profe,*' I replied with a smile.

'*Nada,* Mrs Cumber,' my teacher corrected.

'*Nada,* Mrs Cumber,' I repeated obediently. '*Estoy flojo.*'

'Raoul, laziness isn't an asset in the classroom.'

'Asset?'

'Asset means *ventaja.*'

'I know, Mrs Cumber. I'm sorry. I know it's hard work to teach me. I'm trying but I can't find this kind of maths interesting.'

'I'm aware you struggle with algebra, Raoul. But you can't just learn "new maths". You have to know the basics.'

'I know but I can't help feeling there must be a fun way of learning this.'

'What do you think Hannah and Patrick?'

'Well I think Raoul has a point,' said Hannah, kicking Patrick as he smirked at her.

'I think we should be using the computer more; there's loads of fun maths games you can download and play. There're also loads of Utube videos that can explain tricky maths. We could set the computer up on the television screen in the playroom,' said Patrick eagerly.

'OK, Patrick,' said Mrs Cumber decisively, pushing back her tinted blond fringe from her eyes. 'Do you think you could set it up for me in the playroom tomorrow? I'll have a look tonight at some teaching clips and some maths games. It's a good idea. Raoul, do you and Esther own an a laptop or computer?'

'No. We don't have one,' I said rather defiantly.

There was an awkward pause.

'Well I'll have to see if we can loan you one because it would help you catch up if you could practise your English and your Maths on it. I'm not very technical but if we should run into any problems I'm pretty sure we could rely on Patrick to sort us out. Patrick can be our head of IT. What do you think Patrick?'

Patrick briefly nodded his agreement but his flushed face revealed how pleased he was to be chosen to help our small class.

Mrs Cumber paused for a moment, clearly wondering if she could come up with something that could keep us all attentive in the meantime.

'Right. let's give algebra a miss just now. Stephen, you can work on your times tables exercises. As for the rest of you, I suggest we work on some measurements. I want you all to imagine what your future home might be like. I want the three of you to draw up a sitting-room with all the furniture in it and measure out each piece with the ruler as we did last week. I want to see the width and length of all the pieces of furniture in the room.' Mrs Cumber held up a piece of A4 paper. 'The sitting-room should be the size of this A4 piece of paper and it should be done accurately, to the usual proportions of 1:10.'

I saw Mrs Cumber watching us as we all bent our heads to the task. Her pale blue eyes turned to me and looked thoughtfully at me. There was no doubt in my mind she had decided I would relish the task and would produce the neatest drawing out of the group.

I was also pretty sure she sometimes wondered if Mrs Anderson was doing me a disservice by getting me involved in this small class.

I had on two occasions overheard Mrs Cumber question my mother about my future.

'What's going to happen to Raoul when the Andersons leave Mexico in a few years time? Having learnt and seen as much as he has, how can Raoul be satisfied with returning to life in Iztupalapa?'

I know my mother had to fight the urge to tell Mrs Cumber to get on with her job and to stop worrying about us. But it didn't do to get on the wrong side of a teacher, so my mother didn't reply in the way she clearly wanted to. She'd just parry Mrs Cumber's questions with practised ease. My mother would have made a good diplomat.

Looking back now, I can understand Mrs Cumber's concerns about me. Marion seemed to look on life with a constant determined optimism, but Mrs Cumber had spent many years in Mexico working in the ex pat community and wasn't sure there'd be much of an opening somewhere for a boy like me to finish my studies.

Still, despite her worries, she did her best for me and certainly my mastery over the English language was impressive. Children at the age of ten are like sponges when they learn languages.

Instead of spending hours learning grammatical rules, I learnt to speak English first and this is definitely (in my view) the best way to learn a language.

I'd also made a credible effort to teach the others Spanish. Both Hannah and Stephen were making progress in the language, Patrick not so much as he didn't like to look a fool and often refused to repeat tricky words or phrases.

I looked over to Hannah, who as usual had her frizzy hair escaping in all directions from her ponytail, and had her freckled face bent over her page. A silver chain with a little silver mother of pearl fish hovered over the page she was working on.

Hannah was very competitive and would no doubt be trying to draw up a diagram that would be better than mine.

I was subconsciously aware Mrs Cumber disapproved of how attached to my mother and I Hannah was. Maybe the inevitable separation Mrs Cumber saw looming between us worried her.

Mrs Cumber was a plump widow who lived with two black poodles in a house a few streets away from us. It probably wasn't healthy for her to become so enmeshed in our lives but as she didn't seem to have much of a life outside of the classroom, it was probably inevitable. She certainly could have done with doing some yoga or mindfulness classes to help her chill out a bit more.

Later on, back in the kitchen of the main house, I had my afternoon snack while Marion sat on a stool going over the lunch and dinner menu with Aida, the cook.

In the background the kitchen radio crooned a Mexican love song *'La Culpa ha Sido Mía.'*

Tonight there was going to be an important reception for several Mexican government ministers and their wives. Marion liked to provide a typically British menu, as this was always a novelty, and provided a ready topic of conversation for her guests.

Marion generally always relied on her cooks because, to be frank, her cooking skills were pretty poor. Since arriving in Mexico she'd gone to cookery classes twice a week and now owned a large collection of recipes she liked to make use of.

However Aida, who was a gifted cook, was never terribly keen to make use of Marion's recipes or ideas.

'Aida, I bought two legs of lamb at the meat market yesterday and I would like to us to do another roast lamb dinner with the mint sauce, as we did in March remember?'

Aida, who was rolling out pastry to make small hors d'oeuvres, grunted in assent.

'And what do you think we should do for the soup?'

'¿*Caldo de queso*?'

'Cheese soup?' Marion wrinkled her nose. 'What about that recipe for London Particular soup?'

'I don't like it. It's too tasteless. These people who are coming are Mexicans and we're used to flavour, spices.'

Marion sighed.

'All right then. You decide the soup.'

'And the *postre*?'

'For dessert we'll just use the *crème de menthe* cake you made yesterday. That'll be perfect.'

'Very good, *señora*.'

Marion left Aida in the kitchen, her sturdy arms working away at the pastry mixture, and went to see if the dining room was set out appropriately. She knew my mother would've taken good care of laying the table, with their smart crockery and table linen, but Marion always wanted to check anyway.

22

Later on I had a look at the white finely embroidered linen, the silver cutlery and the crystal glasses. So much work was involved in these meals, not only in preparing the food but the crockery, the glasses and the cutlery, all had to be washed by hand afterwards as they were too fragile to cope with the dishwasher. I've never understood why people pay so much for tableware that needs so much extra care.

No doubt tonight, while David and Marion entertained their guests, Stephen and Hannah would be hanging over the banisters to catch a glimpse of the well-dressed guests.

My mother would remember to send them up some desert once the guests were finished with the meal.

According to Hannah, a few years ago when they were living in Brazil, Patrick had spotted a cake carefully prepared for a function hosted in their house and had stuck his fingers into it to scrape off some of the icing. Their cook had been absolutely furious and apoplectic with rage. By now the children knew to stay out of the kitchen or Aida would shout at them, but my mother was always willing to steal away while the guests had coffee and take them up some treats.

Marion came back into the kitchen to grab a cup of coffee and announced she was heading upstairs to check on her outfit before heading out to a spinning class.

Marion was a keen cyclist and told me she was determined to keep up her cycling so that when she returned to the UK again she could get back to her road cycling. She said traffic in London was bad enough to cycle in, but there was absolutely no hope of being able to cycle safely alongside the crazy and dangerous drivers of Mexico City. If you weren't mugged, kidnapped or worse, you'd soon be run over with impunity.

The levels of physical activity varied within our household.

I went along with Patrick to football sessions once a week but I also relished, once I had my new trainers, running several circles around the Anderson's garden in the afternoons. I remember having to get rid of a lot of excess energy.

Hannah went to ballet lessons but she was starting to lose interest in them. So I would say Stephen and Marion were the most active members of the Anderson family in those days. Apart from the odd game of golf, David and Patrick were generally content with playing a few rounds of cricket in the garden before heading indoors again.

The Andersons only had one car and a driver for the family so we were limited in how many outings we could make. Marion often arranged, with other ex-pat parents, parties where the ex-pat children could disappear and mingle separately.

If at any point we wanted to walk somewhere, we had to be accompanied by my mother or Aida.

Nowadays, unfortunately, Mexico is even more lawless than it was back then so I don't know these days what diplomatic families do to keep their children safe in Mexico City.

23

Outside the little garden flat the rain belted down onto its flat roof. Flashes of lightning were followed by loud bursts of thunder. It was late August 1997 and an especially harsh storm had broken that evening.

My mother was in the main house and I was lying on my bed, in the maid's flat, reading The House on Mango Street by Sandra Cisneros.

Mrs Cumber had given me the book to study. Hannah, who's an avid reader, also offered her book collection to me and had recommended an English translation of a book by Raquel Jaramillo.

Suddenly the lights in the flat went out and I scrambled to my bedside table drawer to find my torch.

Approximately twice a year the storms were bad enough to cut off the electricity in the house.

I didn't like to be left alone in the dark but my mother had a number of candles laid out in our rooms in case the lights went out.

I found the torch and switched it on. I then went through to my mother's room to fetch the matches and one by one I lit all eight of the candles in my room.

I knew this was very wasteful but the bright light from the candles was very comforting.

I'd just settled back down on the bed to read my book when suddenly there was a loud knock on the front door of the flat.

Surprised, I went and opened the door only to see in front of me the two bedraggled shapes of Hannah and Stephen, who had streams of water descending down the hoods of their yellow raincoats.

Stephen had a torch in his hand too.

'What are you two doing coming out on a night like this?' I demanded, letting them both come in.

Before answering Hannah and Stephen took their shoes and sodden raincoats off, hanging the coats on the pegs behind the door.

'We asked your mother and she said it's fine for us to come across. She has to stay at the house because they're clearing up the dinner and the guests still haven't left... '

Hannah grimaced.

'They're probably all dressed up and you wouldn't want to go out in this weather in your best clothes.'

'Is the house without electricity too?' I asked.

'It was. We had a blackout but the generator's kicked in now so they're OK. I kind of wish they'd been left in darkness because then they might've decided to go home. By the way, this place looks cool with all the candles lit. It's really cosy.'

Hannah looked curiously about her, taking everything in.

Stephen meanwhile was busy emptying his raincoat pockets. Inside each pocket there were some rather squashed looking chocolate truffles. He laid them all out on a side table.

'There we go. That should keep us going.'

I was suddenly filled with affection for the pair of them, grateful they'd thought about me while the storm lingered.

The unfortunate side of inhabiting a city high up on a plateau, surrounded by mountains, was that inevitably the clouds liked to gather in the valley and the storms could be very terrifying.

I've memories as a young child of sitting in the bath in Iztupalapa and the lights suddenly going off during a bad storm. I felt sheer panic until my eyes grew accustomed to the dark, and I managed to find my way out of the bathroom. Meanwhile my grandparents were clattering ineptly about the kitchen trying to find matches and candles.

'What's Patrick up to?'

'What do you think?' said Hannah wrinkling up her nose and suddenly looking disapproving.

'Playstation?'

'Yes, Minecraft as always.'

'Don't you get bored here, Raoul?' asked Stephen, uninterested in anything his brother was doing.

'Not really. I used to live with my two grandparents, more or less as an only child, so I'm used to my own company.'

'So you just read when you're here?' asked Stephen, looking rather surprised.

'No, not exactly. I also work on my art.'

'Can we see your artwork?' the two of them asked simultaneously.

The two of them looked expectantly at me.

I hesitated for a moment. Although I liked and trusted Hannah and Stephen, I was very protective of my artwork.

My artwork's always felt like an extension of myself.

In those days I didn't have the confidence to pursue my hobby in the face of criticism, and I knew I was sensitive enough to be affected by their comments on it.

I reached behind my cupboard and dragged out a bulky art portfolio, bought for me by my mother.

Stephen and Hannah quickly knelt down on either side of me and started looking through my collection of drawings.

I'd drawn pictures of buildings around Mexico, Palacio de Bellas Artes, the Metropolitan Cathedral, Palacio de los Deportes and the Torre Mayor, the tallest building in Mexico. I'd also drawn sketches of the Eiffel Tower, Grand Central Station in New York. Many other pictures were squeezed into the portfolio. Needless to say I didn't take them all out.

'These are amazing, Raoul. You're really talented,' said Hannah and Stephen nodded his agreement.

I was pleased with their wholehearted praise.

'You can see where I've gone wrong in some of them. Here the lines aren't quite straight,' I said critically, pointing to the picture I'd drawn of Grand Central Station. 'And in this one I've had to shade the contour because it wasn't in the right place.'

I pointed to a picture of the Albert Hall.

'Stop! Raoul, just stop! It upsets me when you talk like that. These are beautiful. I can't believe you've drawn them and never showed us. Where did you copy them from?'

'I've mostly used the computer in the playroom to do them as the clips I've found on Utube explain how to do the perspective... I hope nobody minds me using it,' I added anxiously.

'Of course, nobody's going to mind. Mum's already told you to use it any time you want to. She wanted to make sure you could keep in touch with people back home.'

I smiled to myself reminiscently at the thought of Miguel's erratic email correspondence and Manolo's tentative weekly efforts to master email at the local Internet cafe.

Manolo's emails usually followed the same format:

Hola Raoul

How are you doing? Campanita and me are doing very well as are your grandparents. Hope you are behaving yourself and making us all proud of you.

Hugs,

Manolo.

'Have you done any of Teotihuacan or Palenque?' asked Hannah, bringing me back to the present.

'No.'

'I'm going to see if we can arrange a trip with you to one of them. You have to sketch them, they're so beautiful.'

'Too many stairs,' said Stephen, disagreeing. 'There're too many stairs to climb on all the buildings there. The Aztecs must've liked climbing up stairs a lot. As if Mexico doesn't have enough high places to climb.'

'It's all part of their religion, Stephen, and their sacrifices. They're trying to get as close as possible to the heavens,' Hannah explained patiently.

'It all seems pretty weird to me, cutting people's hearts out and then giving their hearts to the Gods. What's all that about? It's a good thing the Spanish came along and stopped it all.'

'The Spanish were worse, as you well know, because Mrs Cumber taught us about it last year. They killed and took everything they could from the Mexican people to fund their wars.'

'I still think they're better than the Aztecs,' said Stephen stubbornly.

I diplomatically didn't intervene in the discussion and started putting my drawings back in the portfolio.

Stephen wandered around my room, looking with interest at the photos on my bedroom wall.

The main light suddenly came back on again, momentarily blinding us all with its brightness.

The power cut was over.

'Who are these people, Raoul? Are those your grandparents?' Stephen asked, pointing to a photo with a dark haired couple. In it their eyes were wrinkled and screwed up with the sunshine. The woman was wearing an embroidered apron and the man had a straw hat on.

I went across to look.

'Yes, those are my *abuelos*.'

'Oh, I didn't recognise them. They look so much younger in that photo. And who's this?' asked Stephen, pointing to a photo of Manolo sitting in a doorway and hugging a large white dog whose friendly face looked earnestly into the camera.

'That's Manolo. You met him remember?'

'Oh yes. I remember. That dog's Campanita, isn't it?'

'Stephen, trust you to only remember the dog. How rude can you be? You shouldn't be looking at Raoul's photos. These are his private and personal things.'

'Hannah, it's fine. Really. I don't mind,' I said, giving Stephen a reassuring pat on the shoulder.

'Is that your dad, Raoul?' asked Stephen, emboldened to ask more questions and pointing at another photo.

'No, that's my friend Miguel and his dad. You never got to

meet him but he's a good friend of mine.'

'Oh right. So where's your dad then?' asked Stephen, turning to look at me.

Hannah looked anguished but said nothing.

I took a deep breath. How did you explain not having a dad to a conventional family like theirs?

'I've no idea,' I said quietly.

'Don't you want to know?'

'Not really, no.'

'Do you even know who he is?'

'No, I don't.'

'I don't understand, haven't you asked your mother about him?'

Stephen, deliberately ignoring the sharp pinch Hannah had given him, continued to wait patiently for an answer.

'If my mum had wanted me to know about him, she would've told me. Either way I don't think my father would have any interest in me. I came along by mistake and both my parents were too young to deal with it. My grandfather's like a father to me because he's the one who's always taken care of me and my mother.'

Stephen went and sat on my bed.

'Fathers are a pain if you ask me'.

This puzzled me.

'What do you mean?'

'I mean I could be quite happy without a father sometimes.'

There was an awkward pause in the conversation.

Eventually Hannah sighed.

'He doesn't really mean that Raoul. It's just not always easy in our house.'

'I'm sorry but I don't understand what you mean. Is there a

problem with Mr Anderson?'

Hannah and Stephen looked at each other and shrugged.

'It's just hard at times in our home,' explained Hannah. 'Our parents argue a lot. It's one of the reasons we so like having your mum in the house. They keep the lid on it when there's other people around.'

Stephen nodded in agreement.

Hannah looked across at my photos again.

'Holidays can be the worst. Once when we were little, after a nasty argument, they left us in the hotel room while they went out in the car to try to sort it out. It was stressful because we'd no idea when they'd be back, and we were far away from home in a hotel, in a strange city. I think they thought they were better trying to sort the argument out in the car, instead of in front of us.'

'I see. I hadn't realized.'

Hannah smiled sadly at me.

It was at this point I recognised her vulnerability for the first time, and in that moment I began to realise how much Hannah meant to me.

'No doubt you thought we were the perfect family! I don't think they exist. Dad fell in love with another woman when we were based in Belgium, at least that's what mum says.' Hannah rubbed her eyes angrily, refusing to allow herself to cry in front of me. 'She's never really forgiven him for it and she's struggled to trust him again. Dad's always out at different dinners and mum finds it hard, as she doesn't know exactly what he's up to. When he gets home she gives him a hard time and he's quite often tired or stressed. They both have explosive tempers so you can imagine.'

I shook my head.

'Actually, I really can't imagine. Mrs Anderson's always so nice.'

'Mum's nice,' chipped in Stephen.

'They both are,' said Hannah firmly. 'It's hard for dad because he has to work all these long hours, and he gets quite stressed with things we know nothing about. Mum gets bored, which is why she does all these cookery and leather binding classes. It's a bit of a let down for her because when we were in Belgium she had a good job working for the European Union as a secretary.'

Hannah looked at her watch.

'Anyway, we'd better get back now, Stephen, or they'll come looking for us.'

I watched the pair of them disappear into the night, down the curving metal staircase. I then wiped up the wet puddles where their raincoats had dripped water onto the floor.

After talking to Hannah and Stephen I felt more grateful than ever before for my grandparents, and the strong bonds of affection they had in their marriage.

Would my mother ever have that, I wondered. I knew my mother was better off on her own, instead of being with an unreliable man, but it would be good to think some day she'd find someone nice to take care of her.

24

One Friday, at the end of September 1998, I woke up with a sense of deep anticipation.

Hannah had wrought her magic and persuaded Mrs Cumber to take us on an educational school trip to Palenque. It was really just an excuse for all of us to have a vacation together.

Hannah's suggestion it would be good for me to see ancient Aztec or Mayan buildings was met with approval from all the members of the family and Mrs Cumber was put in charge of the arrangements.

An easy option would've been to drive to Teotihuacan, which was situated only 40km northeast of Mexico City, but Mrs Cumber preferred the Mayan ruins at Palenque.

Despite the quantity of tourists visiting this jungle site, the intricate and detailed engravings at Palenque as well as the buildings, were in her view more impressive than those found at Teotihuacan. She assured Marion the whole distance southwards to Palenque and Cancún was heavily policed and safe to drive.

The embassy loaned out their minibus for the trip and Marion paid Antonio, our driver, overtime to take us to Palenque over the weekend. We would stop over two nights at Palenque, the next night at Mérida in Yucatán and finally the last two nights at Cancún with friends of Marion's who owned a hotel resort by the coast.

We'd be flying back on the Wednesday to Mexico City; Antonio after dropping us off at Cancún was going to make his own way back to Mexico City.

I was slightly apprehensive, as I'd never flown in an aeroplane before. As I hadn't mentioned this to anyone, it was clear it hadn't occurred to anyone else going on the trip. When I mentioned my fears of flying to my mother she squeezed my hand in silent sympathy (she'd never flown before either).

The drive from Mexico City to Palenque was going to take nine hours.

It became quickly apparent that the three Anderson children were in the habit of quarrelling acrimoniously over who got to sit next to the window in the car.

I could only imagine how fraught the long three-hour drives to Acapulco, or other places the Andersons were in the habit of travelling to at the weekends, must have been when in their car.

Thankfully the minibus allowed plenty of space for everyone to sit by the window (if they so wished) and in any case Stephen decided he wanted to sit next to me so wasn't fussed, for once, at having an aisle seat. Hannah insisted I had to have the window seat on the mini bus because this was my first trip away with them.

We left for Palenque early on the Friday morning, when the dew was still hanging on the garden's grass and the morning chill was enough to make us put on a jumper. Antonio had greeted us brusquely and had quickly loaded our small bags onto the minibus.

Despite the early start it took some time for us to reach the outskirts of the city.

Carretera Federal 95 (Highway 95) led us up to the sombre pine forests of the encircling mountain range, leaving behind us the grimy clouds of city pollution, before descending again.

'OK everyone,' said Mrs Cumber, twisting round to address the sleepy faces behind her. 'Do you remember me telling you about Emiliano Zapata? Please tell me you haven't forgotten!'

'Yes, I remember. He's from a place called Morelos, isn't he?' said Hannah.

'Yes, Hannah, he was. The state we're passing through now is the State of Morelos and Emiliano Zapata was born in a town called Anenecuilco. If you visited Amenecuilco you would see many statues of Zapata and paintings as well. Does anyone remember what he was famous for?'

There was an embarrassing silence at the back of the minibus.

'Come on guys. Patrick do you remember?'

Patrick looked slightly startled, like a rabbit transfixed by a car's headlights.

I gleefully noted how his blank expression annoyed Mrs Cumber, as she'd clearly been so certain he knew the answer to her question. Patrick had written his history essay last month on Emiliano Zapata.

If things carry on like this on the trip, I thought to myself, Marion's going to sack her for being a useless teacher.

'Come on, Patrick. Tell us what you know about Zapata.'

'He's the Mexican national hero', said Patrick cautiously.

'What did he do to deserve that?'

I caught Hannah's eye and tried not to laugh. This was so excruciatingly painful. Why didn't Mrs Cumber just give up on the history lecture?

'He fought to overthrow the elite who had control over most

of the land in Mexico and he fought against the dictatorship running Mexico at the time.'

'Well done Patrick.'

We all collectively heaved a sigh of relief.

Mrs Cumber turned back to the front again and the rest of us exchanged quick grimaces behind her back.

I looked out of the window and watched the flat green plains pass by, with large mountains breaking up the horizon in the far distance. Mostly the landscape tones were subdued shades of moss and crocodile green. The green plains were broken up at regular points by bushes and trees. Occasionally, near water, a beautiful willow tree would appear, its long branches trailing the ground. Often orange-brown cinnamon coloured cattle appeared standing in close groups, their ribs sticking out as they chewed away at the sparse grass.

Wisps of white cloud hung around the mountains in the distance, but otherwise the sky was a bright clear blue.

I felt Stephen's head roll onto my shoulder (Stephen was clearly feeling the early start that morning) so I rested my head on the headrest behind me and started to doze too.

After a few hours the minibus came to a halt at a roadside stop and I looked out of the window.

A couple of plump women dressed in brightly embroidered shirts and long red skirts had set up a roadside stall selling watermelon and various other antojitos, which means 'little cravings'.

Antonio had gone off to smoke a cigarillo and Marion and Mrs Cumber went up to the stall to buy a large plate of water-melon slices.

I nudged the dead weight on my shoulder.

'Stephen, wake up. It's time to take a break and get a snack.'

The word 'snack' seemed to energise Stephen and he sat bolt upright in his seat. He groggily followed my pointed finger to the plate of watermelon.

Patrick and Hannah were already exiting the minibus, relieved to stretch their legs.

Stephen jumped off his seat and raced out of the minibus.

'Mum, can we buy some *gorditas*, please?'

Marion turned back to the stall with Stephen in tow.

'All right but we're not buying any *gorditas* with meat in them, we'll stick to cheese instead,' said Marion firmly, ever suspicious of the food quality.

She bought a few quesadillas and gorditas from the ladies who exclaimed with delight when they saw Stephen. Stephen, accustomed to getting attention from friendly Mexicans, ignored them and waited patiently while the ladies carefully placed the food onto a large plastic plate and handed it over.

Patrick and Hannah were sitting on a wooden bench with Mrs Cumber, eating the watermelon and spitting out the black pips into their paper napkins.

I thought about the bright colourful Diego Rivera paintings Mrs Cumber had shown me. How cleverly the obese artist had captured the richness of the agricultural market and the peasant women selling their produce.

Sitting by the dusty roadside, looking out into the dry green pasture, I thought food had never tasted so good.

'We're having a picnic later on,' Stephen informed me.

'A picnic?'

'He means a lunch outdoors,' Hannah explained. 'Dad's not very keen on picnics because he's a bit of a foodie, which really just means he's snobby towards the ready made food you have on a picnic. Dad would always try to find a restaurant to stop at on our road trips.'

I could well believe that once you were used to Aida's cooking anything else would be a bit of a let down.

'That watermelon's delicious,' said Patrick, looking at the now empty plate. 'I could eat three of them.'

'Well, we'll buy one more plate and take it with us for lunch time,' said Marion. 'Here you are Patrick,' handing him some pesos, 'go and buy another plate for us.'

Patrick wandered off to the food stall and waited in the queue that was rapidly building as more cars stopped to buy some snacks.

A few people gave us curious looks, clearly intrigued to see the blonde Andersons sitting alongside Antonio, Stephen and myself, as they ate their quesadillas.

Before long we were back on the minibus and heading south again.

25

The next morning I opened my eyes and found Stephen wide-awake and staring at me with a big grin on his face. I sat up and saw that Patrick too was awake.

'What's the time?'

'It's nine o'clock and we need to have breakfast before ten so you need to hurry up and get dressed.'

Stephen and Patrick were both dressed and looked to have been awake for some time.

I shook my head trying to wake up. It had taken me a while to fall asleep in the strange hotel room, and Patrick's snoring last night had been both loud and irregular.

I felt exhausted but hopefully a cup of strong Mexican coffee would keep me going the rest of the day.

The hotel was a pleasant building; its white painted front was covered in cascades of bright pink bougainvillea flowers. The front garden consisted of neatly tended bright orange bird of paradise flowers contrasting with bright yellow Mexican poppies and bright orange sunflowers.

The inside of the hotel didn't feel very Mexican.

The owners had gone for a rustic Texan decor and I personally found it too neutral in tone. Brown leather, a lot of dark brown wood in the wood beams and furniture and neutral tones on the walls all felt a bit too bland to me.

Already at this age I liked and related to the bright primary colours you could find in any Mexican food market, in any ceremonial celebration or fiesta.

Downstairs in the dining room, there were many tables set up against wood panelled walls and two large living cacti dominated the floor space in the middle. Above the cacti was a skylight and wrought iron candelabra lights hung across the rest of the room.

Mrs Cumber and Marion were still at their table with Hannah, drinking the remains of their coffee while Hannah toyed with some pineapple. Patrick, Stephen and I sat at a nearby table and Marion summoned the waiter to take our breakfast order.

'Where's Antonio? Has he had breakfast already?' I asked.

'Antonio's just had a coffee this morning and now I suspect he is outside smoking another cigarillo. He said he'll meet us in the foyer at half ten to take us to Palenque.'

Once we'd finished breakfast, we all walked back along the corridor. I noticed the prints on the walls of the corridor were the same ones Mr Anderson had in his office space at home.

Hannah stopped to look at them with me.

In the prints Mayan buildings emerged from the wildness of the jungle, the staring stone faces of statues grotesque amidst the crumbling walls. Mayan Indians lay across the front of the buildings or were busy clearing forest.

In one picture of Bolonchen Cenote the Mayan Indians were deep down underground, gathering water from a pool at the foot of an enormous wooden ladder that stretched up into the hole in the ceiling.

'These pictures were drawn by a British artist called Frederick Catherwood,' said Marion, catching sight of them, 'He was travelling with the American explorer John Lloyd Stephens when they discovered the Mayan ruins, hidden deep in the Mexican jungle. I think his drawings are beautiful and show all the drama of discovering ancient ruins for the first time.'

'They're amazing pictures,' I agreed. 'Are these the buildings we're seeing today?'

'No, these pictures are from Yucatán. Though some are of Chichen Itza. We'll see Chichen Itza once we get to Mérida.'

Antonio was in the foyer by the time we assembled again and the minibus was parked outside.

A number of American tourists were also waiting for their tour guides to appear before heading to Palenque. Antonio looked disgustedly at the tourists and said to me in a loud whisper: '¡Gringos!' I found this very amusing because it wasn't so long ago I was the one called 'gringo' at school.

I wasn't inspired with the idea of being squashed among hoards of these loud American tourists in Palenque, and once we arrived at the entrance to Palenque the sight of all the hawkers selling their wares only confirmed how busy this site was with tourists.

Food, drink, brightly-coloured jewellery, intricate hand-painted canvases depicting Mayan art and colourful tapestry purses, all vied for a prominent place in front of the grazing tourists.

However once we walked into Palenque the site was so big it didn't feel in the least bit overcrowded. At the start of the walk to the Mayan buildings, there were beautiful landscaped gardens with tropical flowers and plants.

Once we reached the archaeological site we wandered around the various temples and the Palace of Palenque, as well as the place where the tomb of King Pacal was found, the first ruler of Palenque.

After a while, having gone up and down the many steps of the Temple of the Sun, I found a flat piece of grass and lay down, leaving the others to finish exploring the ruins.

I decided I liked the fact the Mayans had several ball courts, as this clearly made them less warlike in my eyes than the Aztecs. Pictures of the warlike Aztecs dressed for battle had given me nightmares as a child. However there was no escaping both the Mayans and Aztecs were into human sacrifice. I can only assume their harsh existence, dependent on the fickle climatic conditions, made them so brutal. Now that I know a little about British history, I'm not sure it's so very different to the brutal way King HenryVIII, or his daughter Mary, behaved during their reign.

Once we'd all reunited again at the foot of the Temple of the Sun, Mrs Cumber decided to take us to see a last group of ruins, which apparently were to be found after a short walk into the jungle.

These ruins were not fully excavated and were covered in jungle vines and grass. I actually preferred them to some of the other Palenque buildings because they hinted at a long forgotten past, more than the many tidied temples we'd walked around.

In fact, we found the Temple of Inscriptions was actually getting power washed by someone when we visited it.

The last stop, before we went to have some lunch, was the Palenque museum, but by now most of us were feeling thoroughly exhausted. I could feel the sweat pooling at the base of my spine.

Patrick and Hannah waited outside, lying immobile on the grass like two colourful caterpillars, but I went into the museum with Stephen, Mrs Cumber and Marion, feeling I should show interest given their kindness in bringing me on this trip.

All I can vaguely remember from the museum were the hundreds of carved figures and inscriptions, but I was impressed with Pacal's tomb.

It was so huge it seemed incredible that it had gone unnoticed for so many years after Palenque was discovered.

I also liked the jade masks and the detailed heads of some of the Mayan sculptures. It was easy to spot the more talented Mayan sculptors, especially when you compared their work to the simplistic sculpted features and expressions of the other statues.

Once we'd left Palenque, and had eaten some lunch, we followed a tour guide to the Misol-Ha waterfall. Marion had planned this as a refreshing end to the day for us. We all stood for a moment in front of the waterfall, in awe of the power and weight of the water cascading into the pool beneath it.

'Right everyone, you're allowed to go for a swim in this which is just the thing I thought for those of you who've been complaining of the heat,' said Marion, looking pointedly at Patrick and Hannah.

Then turning deliberately to Stephen she said, 'As you'll see by the signs near the water you're not allowed to pee in this water.'

'Why not?' asked Stephen, 'What difference can it make?'

Marion rolled her eyes.

'Stephen, if you need to pee there're toilets here too. Why don't we just try to follow the rules on this trip? However, I advise you to be careful not to swallow any of this water when you swim in it, just in case.'

I now understood why Marion had been so keen on getting us to bring our swimwear. I'd never owned any swimwear until my mother had bought me a pair of swimming trunks a week ago, expressly for this trip.

'Mrs Anderson?'

'Raoul, please call me Marion. Your mother does you know.'

'I don't think I told you that I can't swim.'

The others turned and stared at me in surprise, while I felt myself go red during the awkward silence that followed my comment.

I could clearly see that Marion, thinking about the added responsibility of having someone on the trip that couldn't swim, was now starting to feel anxious.

Much later on, after the trip, my mother told me Marion felt annoyed at herself for glibly making assumptions and being insensitive about my upbringing, which was clearly so different to that of her own children. But actually my mother felt she was to blame for not having explained I couldn't swim in the first place. I didn't hold it against either of them then and I don't now. I never sensed any malice in the Anderson family.

'Raoul, you can stay on the rocks near the edge with Mrs Cumber and me. We're not going swimming either and the others will only be swimming for a short time, as we also want to do the walk that goes behind the waterfall.' Marion pointed to the far side where there was a crocodile line of people queued up, waiting to go under the waterfall. 'The waterfall walk is perfectly safe and has a rope fence along it.'

'Don't worry, you'll be able to cool down at the swimming pool when we're back at the hotel,' she added, in an effort to make me feel better.

I said nothing and followed the others as they headed down to the green pool.

For the next hour I sat and watched as the boys jumped off the rocks into the pool, envying them the cool relief they were enjoying from their swim in this hot, humid jungle.

However, when I saw the murky green colour of the water I was glad I wasn't swimming in it. I didn't like the idea of swimming in water where you'd no idea of what lay beneath you.

I smiled as Stephen waved at me, showing off as he dived into the water and resurfaced near the rocks.

Stephen was wearing a long sleeved t-shirt, as were Hannah and Patrick. The sun was still fierce this late in the afternoon and their white Anglo-Saxon skin was very vulnerable to being burnt. My mother had made me promise her I would use sun cream. Despite the many days I'd spent outside in my early childhood I was still sensitive to strong sun.

I watched as Patrick's portly figure created a miniature tidal wave when he hit the water. Hannah, the last of the Anderson children to go in, put her feet gingerly into the water.

'Push her in,' yelled Stephen to me.

I shook my head reassuringly as Hannah looked anxiously behind her.

I was too well mannered and fond of Hannah to risk incurring her anger by chucking her into the water. At least that's what I say to myself now. Possibly it was just a case of acting on my mother's orders to behave well.

In one quick graceful movement Hannah let herself slide downwards into the water. Just like a mermaid, I thought, as I watched her long blonde hair disappearing under the water.

Mrs Cumber and Marion sat next to me, a little too close for my liking, but I couldn't blame them now they knew I couldn't swim. I bent my knees and rested my head on my folded arms, feeling miserably ashamed at the many ways in which I felt I fell behind the standards of the Anderson family.

However, long before the Anderson children had had enough of swimming in the deep pool, Marion made them climb out by threatening them with a return visit to Palenque.

Mrs Cumber then led us along the short walk to the back of the waterfall. The noise and spray of the powerful hundred-foot waterfall soon soaked me to the skin. I felt so refreshed as I breathed in the humid air and felt the water droplets hit my face. I'd never seen or experienced anything like it before.

Eating slices of pizza with melted cheese and seasoned beef by the side of the waterfall restored my good humour, and I was soon laughing at Stephen's attempts to entice birds down from the trees with bits of pizza.

26

My favourite stop on this trip was Mérida. I liked the grand colonial mansions in Mérida with their ornate architecture; so different from anything else I'd ever seen before.

Mrs Cumber told me the buildings were built in the French colonial style. 'The French came to Mexico because of the trade in the plant commonly known as sisal. Sisal was used for rope, wine, paper, cloth, footwear, bags, hats and carpets to name a few. Today, you can also apparently find it in spa products, mattresses, cat scratching posts and rugs. Brazil's the biggest exporter now but in those days Mexico was seen as the main source of sisal. Even the Mayans and Aztecs used sisal to make basic fabrics and paper.'

'I remember my parents telling me about my great grand-mother,' said Marion nostalgically. 'She was Scottish and apparently came from a family involved in the jute trade. Jute's similar to sisal, it's used for many different things and the jute business became huge in Dundee. Anyway she went with her husband to live in India because during World War I many Scots set up jute factories in India, which then supplied sandbags for the war effort as well as bags for holding cotton in the USA.'

'So was our great, great grandmother really rich then?' asked Patrick. 'Rich enough to build houses like these?'

'They were well off but not rich. They didn't own the factories. Your great, great grandfather was an engineer. They eventually ended up living in a large bleak stone house in Tayport. I'll show you pictures of it when we get back home if you like.'

I'd switched off by this point in the conversation. I wasn't really that interested in the sisal or the jute trade, or Dundee (where ever that was for that matter).

I gazed at the beautiful white ornate building in front of us, and decided a house like that would be the one I would dream of owning. I would never grow tired of admiring a house like that.

Whatever brought the French to Mexico it was surely worth it for the beautiful colonial buildings they built here. I loved how many of the buildings had now acquired a Mexican flavour, painted in bright colours of orange, blue, green, yellow and even pink.

It seemed as if Mexico had finally stamped its identity on this small cosmopolitan city, a city that in the past had been isolated from the rest of Mexico for so many years in both its character and culture.

Hannah had wanted to see the city in a horse drawn carriage, but Marion refused this as she had strong feelings about how animals in general were treated in Mexico. She told me many of the horses they'd ridden on in the mountains, on the outskirts of Mexico City, looked painfully thin with their ribs exposed through their skin. Those pitiful horses looked as though they'd lost all their natural spirit.

Once apparently, when Patrick had bent down to pick up a trailing saddle rope, the horse he was on bolted, obviously expecting to be whipped and trying to avoid it by moving faster.

Therefore, in Mérida, Antonio drove us to different places in our air-conditioned minibus and while the rest of us explored the city, he happily read the newspaper 'Diario de Yucatán' instead of his usual newspaper 'La Crónica de Hoy'.

As we stood outside Mérida Cathedral I noticed several beggars sitting by the railings outside.

An elderly woman with one leg got up onto her crutches when she saw us approaching, and headed towards us. As she smiled she showed several missing teeth and blackened stumps. This disabled woman headed straight for Hannah, as I'd noticed beggars tended to do. Maybe they could see from her face that Hannah had a compassionate heart. Hannah hurriedly dropped some coins from her pocket into the woman's outstretched hand, and quickly followed us into the Cathedral.

Inside the Cathedral at Mérida I felt a lump rise in my throat as I stood in front of the huge seven metre high wooden statue of Christ, on his twelve foot cross behind the altar.

This statue, designed and made by Spanish artist and sculptor Ramón Lapayese del Rio, reminded me of my grandmother and her simple, but strong, Catholic faith. Even now when I returned home I was expected to sit by her side at mass on Sunday.

Mrs Cumber, holding on to her guidebook, leaned towards me and whispered, 'this church they reckon is one of the oldest in Latin America. The inscription at the front of the church says the Spanish King commissioned it in 1598. The stones they built this church with were unfortunately from the Mayan ruins of T'ho. T'ho was the Mayan city which existed here in Mérida before the conquistadores arrived.'

I wonder looking back now what the large Mayan population

living in Mérida, and its outskirts, thought and felt about this Cathedral and, more importantly, the Spanish conquistador who'd built it.

We'd visited Montejo's house that morning and it seemed, until very recently, the Montejo family had still owned the house. Up on the facade of his house two Spanish warriors in armour stand above the portal, each with an Indian head under each foot. The statues on the wall at the front of Montejo's house seem to boast of the many victorious battles Montejo and his family were involved in against the local Mayan population.

More tellingly, there's another man in the entrance facade, bent over, above the doorway. He's stooped and bent over uncomfortably, as he carries the weight of the upper level on his back. This more than anything else seemed to illustrate the uphill struggle for Montejo and his family as they strove to conquer and subdue the indigenous population.

A short time later we wandered up and down Paseo de Montejo.

'It's just like Champs-Élysées in miniature,' exclaimed Marion.

However here in tropical Mérida the roads were lined with exotic Jicarilla and black calabash trees and the odd palm tree. Cars drove slowly past us, so far removed from the frantic, chaotic and choked streets of Mexico City.

Despite the leafy, shady trees the walk was hot and we were all pleased to stop at a Sorbeteria and order Champolas, the sorbets made with tropical fruit. Even Antonio was persuaded to sit with us and have one.

It didn't take long before the Mexican guitarist who was busking around the tables caught sight of us and moved quickly to position himself next to us.

The others were used to seeing guitarists in restaurants (usually wearing large Mexican sombreros) and ignored him but I found the experience unnerving and tried with difficulty to concentrate on eating my Campola.

Marion stretched out her legs and tilted her face to the sun.

'The next time, if there's a next time and we come back to Mérida, I want to arrive here on a Saturday when they do the *Noche Mexicana*. Saturday night becomes one big party in the city centre with music and dancing.' Marion smiled at me. 'They also have a big colourful party on their festival days, the *Vaquerías* days. And the book says on Sunday mornings they shut down Paseo Montejo so you can cycle around which sounds fun.'

'That's the problem with holidays, you only get a quick snap-shot of a place and quite often miss many things that are part of the daily life of the place,' said Mrs Cumber wisely.

'What else are we going to look at in Mérida?' asked Patrick, reaching for the guidebook.

Marion and Mrs Cumber looked at each other. Marion then turned back to Patrick.

'I think we'll have some lunch here and then I thought we could go to Parque de las Américas which is really pretty to look at as it has some Mayan inspired park architecture.'

'No,no,no,*please*, no more parks and buildings,' said Stephen, with his forehead leaning on the table in despair. 'It's *so* boring.'

Marion sighed and looked at Stephen, trying to weigh up how much she could persuade Stephen, through bribery and negotiation of course, to do a little more sightseeing.

Mercifully Patrick, who was browsing our little guidebook, saved her the trouble.

'There's a park here with a zoo apparently and it's free.'

Stephen lifted his head, waiting for Patrick to expand on this information.

'It doesn't look as if it's too far away actually,' said Patrick, looking at his mother.

'What do you think Stephen?' asked Marion, turning back to her youngest son.

'A zoo's going to be more fun than the rubbish we've seen so far,' said Stephen. 'Why didn't we go there in the first place? I've had enough of buildings. I would never have agreed to come if I'd known it was going to be like this.'

'Stephen, we won't be living in Mexico forever you know so it's important to see all we can.'

Stephen yawned and bent his forehead to the table again.

'And I'd really like to see the Parque de las Américas. So why don't we ask Antonio if we've time to do both?'

'Only if I can stay in the minibus with Antonio while you go and see the park,' mumbled Stephen from the table.

'Stephen, will you just stop being so *spoilt*,' hissed Hannah, 'this trip is as much for Raoul as for us. Some children never get to have a holiday away.'

'Yeah, well right now I wouldn't mind never having a holiday away,' said Stephen, unrepentant and angry.

Marion turned round to look for Antonio and found him smoking his cigarillo and chatting to the owner of a horse and carriage. She got up and went to speak to him, leaving the rest of us in a silent group around the table.

'Right,' she said as she came back from speaking to Antonio, 'Antonio's told me what he wants for lunch, so now the rest of you need to decide quickly, so we can get lunch over with and

112

get started with the afternoon's activities.'

By the time we reached Parque de las Américas that afternoon Stephen's mood had mellowed somewhat and he consented to go with us to look at the Mayan inspired architectural designs in the park.

As we approached the columns leading to the park's concert shell, with its red and white Mayan warriors painted on it, we could hear the tones of an acoustic violin and a cello being played.

Two Mexicans were playing music to the tune of a popular Mexican pop song. In front of them were several CDs of their music for sale for forty pesos.

All of us stopped for a few minutes to listen to the two buskers playing a few tunes. I saw Marion looking hopefully at Stephen who was the most musical in the family, hoping he'd be enjoying the music, but he just looked bored.

'Can we go now?' Stephen asked Marion quietly, looking thoroughly unimpressed.

It was clear to the rest of us Marion was resisting the urge to shout at her obdurate son and so we all turned and walked towards the fountain with its stone snake like heads, the music following behind us.

The sight of the clear blue water and leafy trees was refreshing in the afternoon heat.

I thought to myself how pleasant this was, especially when you compared it to what was likely to be a pretty smelly zoo in this heat. With a sigh I followed Marion as she lead us back to the minibus for the last trip of the day to the Centennial Zoo Park.

The Centennial Zoo Park was busy and looking back it must've been a stressful experience for Marion and Mrs

Cumber, as they desperately tried to keep an eye on the four of us.

By the time we'd seen the big cats, the hippo, raccoons, chimpanzees and the aquarium most of us were feeling pretty worn down and, after a brief paddle in the lake, we were happy to sit on the benches and eat a marquesita.

It was pleasurable to watch the Mayan families enjoy themselves, mothers pushing pushchairs with their beautiful babies in them, their little button black eyes watching the scenery while their siblings raced around with carefree abandon.

It was hard to believe we only had three nights and two full days left before we were headed back home to Mexico City.

27

We didn't spend very long at Chichen Itza. In the end, within the space of a couple of hours, we were heading towards Cancun.

The beautiful ancient stone city of Chichen Itza had many columns, which looked like pieces of flotsam in the midst of the jungle's vast green sea of trees.

However by the time we reached Chichen Itza most of us had had enough of sightseeing. Marion decided we would do the light tour offered at the site and allow ourselves time to reach Cancún and have some fun on the beach there.

Marion had been strongly recommended by a Dutch diplomat to visit the Ik Kil Cenote after visiting Chichen Itza, because we could then have a swim and get refreshed in the cool water after a hot day.

However given that I didn't know how to swim and we didn't have much time left in Yucatán, Marion made the spontaneous decision to head straight from Chichen Itza to the Green Jade Hotel in Cancun, so we could have some relaxation time by the pool and in the sea.

Marion told us she was looking forward to catching up with her friend Barbara, who she'd last seen over a year ago.

Marion had met Barbara at a busy evening reception in the American Embassy. From what I gathered, as Marion chatted to Mrs Cumber on the way to Cancun, many people at these diplomatic gatherings are trying to suss out who is worth talking to and once they decide you're of no interest, they excuse themselves and 'circulate'.

Sitting in the seat behind Marion on the minibus, I listened with interest as Marion explained to Mrs Cumber how she'd met Barbara.

David had disappeared off to talk to his American counterpart and Marion found herself in a corner of the reception room with a champagne glass in her hand, trying to look as though she was observing closely an oil painting of Seatle hanging on the wall.

Just at the point she was starting to wonder if her outfit (a bright orange silk dress David had disapproved of her wearing to this reception) was too garish and was frightening people off, she got a tap on the shoulder.

'Hi. How are you doing? My name's Barbara,' said a strident voice beside her.

Marion turned and she found herself looking up into the pale, expertly made up face of a tall lady with ebony, long hair and expensive looking emerald earrings.

'Hi my name's Marion.'

'Oh, cool. So you're British! Let me guess-is there a hint of Scots in your voice?'

Taken aback by this lady's directness Marion nodded.

'That's so cool. I love Scotland. We were there five years ago in May. Even then we found it too cold but a stunning place. So much history!'

'So are you part of the American embassy here in Mexico?' Marion asked politely, not recalling having seen her before.

Barbara put back her head and laughed.

'No. We're part of the business contingent. Now and again the embassy likes to invite American businessmen *and women* working in Mexico to network. They're supposed to be encouraging American business to grow in Mexico after all. However Americans aren't that well liked in Latin America as you've probably noticed. I'm half Mexican so I get the best of both worlds really.'

Marion shook her head as a waiter presented her with a plate of miniature crab cakes.

'Why don't we try and find a less cramped corner than here and have a chat,' suggested Barbara. 'I find rooms stuffed full with people like this one so claustrophobic. I know the way to the outside terrace which is much nicer than here and outside we won't get the smell of Macy's perfume counters.'

Marion smiled and nodded as Barbara turned and pushed her way through the crush.

She hoped David wouldn't mind her disappearing for a bit but it certainly had to be better than staring at a painting of Seattle for an hour or alternately smiling and nodding like a mannequin at her husband's side.

Barbara found some comfortable armchairs in the terrace and sank down into the cushions with a sigh. Marion sat next to her.

'What a relief! These heels were killing me. By the way I love your dress it's so unusual! Where did you get it?'

'I had this one made from a piece of silk I found in El Palacio de las Telas in Oaxaca. I have to confess the seamstress I use is a little adventurous and I wasn't sure the dress worked, but having spent so much on it I thought I'd better wear it.'

'Why wouldn't you wear it? I think it's great!' asked Barbara, looking genuinely perplexed.

'To be honest my husband David's quite conservative and I think he thought it was a bit too flamboyant for tonight.'

'Crazy man! I can't believe in this day and age you're still deferring to your husband on matters of dress. He clearly hasn't a clue, it's absolutely stunning.'

'Thank you. If you don't mind me asking what business are you involved in?'

'Oh, my partner and myself own a couple of hotels down in Cancun. We've made quite a name for our selves with American tourists, mainly because we're providing a slice of America in the sunshine for them with a bit of Mexican culture and sightseeing thrown in. What about you, what are you doing here?'

'I'm married to a British diplomat. He's off talking to some other diplomats.'

'So what were you doing buried in the corner, looking at paintings?'

'I find some of these evening receptions quite hard going actually. Dinner parties are easier because people have to make an effort to talk to you.'

'Don't know how you stand it. We only do this once a year and we make a trip of it usually but unfortunately Craig couldn't make it this time, he's dealing with a few staffing issues. Listen, I'm here for a few days catching up with some old friends, why don't we meet for lunch and shopping one day?'

Marion smiled.

'That would be nice. If you give me your number I'll text you with mine.'

They exchanged numbers and what then followed apparently was one of the busiest weeks Marion had ever experienced. She discovered that Barbara, besides being very energetic, tended to include as many people as possible in her daily life.

Marion wasn't just invited out to lunch, she was also invited into the homes of Barbara's friends and any other activity they were involved in. What started as a planned shopping trip with Barbara would end up stretching out into a day of other diversions, sometimes it turned out to be an art exhibition, a musical concert or a new wine bar opening.

Often Marion had to excuse herself and make her way home to organise her children or the household, feeling a bit of a killjoy in the process.

When Barbara met up with Marion to say her final goodbyes before heading to the airport to catch her flight to Cancún, she thrust a Green Jade Hotel brochure into Marion's hands and insisted with her typical generosity of spirit on Marion and her family coming to stay with them. 'Just give me a call with the dates and we'll keep the rooms free, free of charge, for you. It'll be truly awesome to have you there and Craig will absolutely love meeting you all.'

Barbara had given Marion a tight hug in which Marion could feel Barbara's skeletal frame through her jacket, got into her taxi and waved out of the window as she headed north to the International Benito Juárez Airport.

'It'll be interesting to see Barbara in the setting of Cancún', Marion said to Mrs Cumber, looking out of the front window of the minibus. 'I have to admit it's hard to imagine Barbara managing to be as energetic in the relaxed atmosphere of a holiday resort.'

Antonio drove the minibus along the toll road to Cancún, quicker apparently but less interesting than the 180 toll free road.

All we could see most of the time was swathes of green vegetation along the toll road, whereas by all accounts the toll free road took you in and out of numerous small villages with speed bumps called topes, and with a quantity of children and dogs to watch out for.

Although the slower road was likely to give us a clearer glimpse of real Mayan life, by this point on the trip all of us were ready to arrive and leave the minibus as soon as possible.

28

The Green Jade Hotel was a large hotel complex surrounding a series of central pools and bar areas. Golf buggies were parked outside in rows on the right hand side of the main entrance and on the left there was a multi storey car park. A large coach was unloading its passengers at the front entrance when we arrived.

Marion had called Barbara a few minutes before our arrival to let her know we were nearly there, and as we arrived Barbara was standing at the top of the hotel stairs looking for our small minibus, totally disregarding the swarm of tourists walking past her into the main entrance.

She was wearing a loose royal blue dress full of flounces that suited her tall, thin figure.

Barbara ran down the steps once she caught sight of us, waving her hands and smiling broadly. As soon as Marion had descended from the minibus she was hugged enthusiastically. Mrs Cumber, not keen on being hugged, stood back hiding behind us. Stephen already impressed with the size of the hotel, was for once speechless and barely even noticed Barbara's hug.

Marion introduced us to Barbara and then we all walked up into the hotel foyer. Barbara calmly bypassed the queue of recently arrived tourists and went behind the reception desk to retrieve our keys.

Antonio had unloaded our bags by the time we came out of the hotel again.

'Right, Antonio, we need to get these bags into one of the golf buggies and then you can park the minibus in the car park. Here's the key for your room in the hotel and I'll take the others down to their chalet once the buggy's loaded with the luggage.'

Antonio nodded in agreement, happy to have the rest of the day to himself before heading back to Mexico City in the morning.

Within a short space of time our three golf buggies made their way slowly down the slope, leaving the hotel behind us, with Barbara leading the way along the beachfront to a chalet with its own little pool outside. There was mounting excitement as all of us saw where we'd be staying for the next two nights.

Barbara dismounted from the buggy with experienced grace and ran up the steps to try out the key. Once she'd managed to open the door she ran in quickly to check all the rooms were as they should be, and then beckoned the rest of us into the house.

'Well, here you have it, my darlings. This is your very own little chalet and pool. In the mornings they'll leave your breakfast for you out on the terrace table so as not to disturb you.' Barbara pointed to a table outside the kitchen. 'Once you've sorted yourselves out make your way to the hotel and please give me a buzz because Craig and I will meet you for lunch. And when we've had our lunch I want to show you our gorgeous sea lagoon, you'll all absolutely love it! Right then, I'll leave you all to sort yourselves out. Bye darlings, see you soon!'

Barbara swept out of the chalet and disappeared in the golf buggy back to the hotel.

'Ruth, would you be able to remember how to find the hotel again from here?' Marion asked Mrs Cumber doubtfully.

'To be honest I was so busy following both of you here I wasn't really paying much attention to how we got here in the first place,' admitted Mrs Cumber.

'Mum, it's fine. I know the way, it's really easy,' said Patrick, reassuringly.

'I hope so or we could end up having a very late lunch,' said Marion, turning to the bags now getting deposited in the hallway by Stephen and I.

It took us a good hour to unpack our bags and get settled into the chalet. We then got into the buggies again with Patrick giving Marion directions at the front of one buggy, with me sitting at the back, and Mrs Cumber following behind with Hannah and Stephen.

Marion gave Barbara a call once we were sitting in the big oversized bamboo cane sofas in the hotel reception area and while we waited for Barbara and Craig to turn up we watched the different people coming and going through the hotel lobby.

Most of the women had sun hats and bikinis on, with just a loose kaftan to cover up while the men walked in and out in brightly patterned swimming trunks, baseball caps and t-shirts. I noticed there didn't seem to be very many families staying here; mostly it seemed to be couples of varying ages.

'One of the benefits of home schooling is you can pick and choose your holiday times. It seems children and families are tied up at the moment with school', said Marion to Mrs Cumber.

At this point Barbara turned up from the hotel interior and ambling along at her side was a man slightly taller than her but very much more rotund. I liked the look of him straight away; he had a cherubic face and warm kind eyes.

'Hello again darlings. Did you all get settled in okay? This is my partner Craig Sayle. He's heard all about you and has been looking forward to meeting you.'

Craig reached forward to shake hands with us all, with an amused smile on his face. He had curly, light brown hair and warm brown eyes. He had on a big pair of over sized jeans and a collared shirt. Marion got the impression that he was naturally quite laid back but he was probably used to Barbara's way of talking and her energetic quirks.

'It's lovely to meet you all. How's your trip been so far?' Craig asked politely.

'Great. Really interesting,' said Marion at the same time as Stephen said, 'Boring!'

I bit my lips trying to repress my nervous laughter. Barbara and Craig burst out laughing.

'That's the first time I've heard a tourist tell me Chichen Itza was boring. Never mind poor Stephen, you'll have lots of fun here I promise you. In fact you probably won't want to leave and you'll have to persuade your mother to come back and see us again,' said Barbara reassuringly.

Barbara led the way into the buffet area of the hotel restaurant.

The restaurant was a large open plan room with old-fashioned colonial style fans slowly moving in the wooden ceiling above them. There were no walls to the exterior of the building, just wooden columns in a large semi-circle.

The view from the restaurant stretched out to the sea in the distance.

Bright red and purple velvet cushioned bamboo chairs of different sizes and shapes were placed around wooden tables of varying sizes. Red and purple flower arrangements were dotted about the room, red Chocolate Cosmos flowers and huge purple Dahlias. Large fern like plants were clustered together in large golden pots next to the columns.

It looked very haphazard and not quite what I had expected to see in a hotel catering mostly for Americans.

The people who were eating in the restaurant seemed to be slightly more dressed up than those we'd seen walk past us in the hotel lobby.

Barbara, correctly reading my thoughts, said to me, 'If people want to eat in a less formal setting we have a terrace cafe and barbeque but this place is a little less busy and better for catching up. Most people come here for their evening meals, once they have showered and changed from the beach.'

The adults waited behind us as we queued up eagerly at the buffet. Fresh grilled lobster salads, prawn cocktails, platters of shrimp creole as well as cold meat; cheeses and salads were laid out amongst an artistically arranged bread buffet with platters of freshly baked baguettes, bagels, pretzels and rolls.

'What do you think about the room?' Barbara asked Marion.

'It's very unusual and distinctive. I was expecting something perhaps a little more glossy and new as you said the hotel was aimed at American tourists,' said Marion diplomatically.

'Yes, it's quite different to what most people expect. For me the style is what I would call (tongue in cheek of course) the eccentric colonial. José Ramírez, who is the hottest interior designer in Mexico at the moment, designed it all. It certainly catches the eye and people always comment on it, whether they do so negatively or positively. The main thing is people remember it and in business, just as in art, that is usually a good thing.'

After lunch Craig and Barbara took us all on a walk down to their artificial lagoon.

I was glad of the walk as I was starting to feel the effect of all the rich food we'd been consuming the last few days. We walked past many one-storey chalets of different designs but all traditional with white walls, dark green shutters and red ceramic tiled roofs. Each of the chalets had a little pool next to it.

After twenty minutes we turned a corner and caught sight of a huge rocky lagoon that opened out into the sea beyond it. Around the lagoon several people were sunbathing, others were snorkelling in the clear water.

'The lagoon is very shallow at this end but it gets deeper and deeper towards the sea. There are fish to see in all parts of the lagoon so it doesn't matter where you snorkel. There's always a lifeguard on duty too', said Craig, waving a greeting at the lifeguard.

'What's the metal grill for at the entrance of the lagoon?' asked Patrick.

'That's there to make sure no sharks can sneak in on our guests,' said Craig with a twinkle in his eye.

'Seriously?' asked Patrick, unbelieving.

'No, don't listen to him Patrick,' said Barbara, 'he's just winding you up. There are sharks around of course but they congregate for the most part in reefs quite a distance from here. In fact we run excursions by boat for those tourists who do want to see sharks. You've almost zero chance of seeing a shark in the waters near here. The metal grill at the other end of the lagoon is just to keep the hotel area enclosed really. Marion, I hope you've brought your bikini with you?'

Marion blushed.

'I'm getting a little too old for bikinis I'm afraid, Barbara.'

'Nonsense, you can't stay here and not wear a bikini. Last month my eighty-five year old mother bought a white bikini. You're never too old to wear one and you have a great figure,' said Barbara, looking at Marion appraisingly, 'you can buy one at the hotel shop or borrow one from me.'

Craig laughed and shrugged expressively at those of us who were fidgeting and embarrassed by the conversation.

In the meantime I'd been staring out at the Caribbean Sea, with my hands shielding my eyes from the ferocious sun. I couldn't stop looking at the blue expanse.

This was my first glimpse of the sea other than what I'd seen on television. Hannah watched me as I took in the blue landscape dotted with a few white motorboats, and the occasional splash and roar of a jet ski disturbing the peaceful atmosphere.

'Do you like it, Raoul?'

'Yes, of course I like it,' I said smiling, 'what's there not to like?'

'I think it's beautiful. I like being near the sea. Mum and dad have a home by the sea in Edinburgh. It's rented out just now but I always feel at home when I'm by the sea.'

'It must be very different to this,' I said.

'Yes, of course, the sea's freezing cold for a start. And the sea's very rough because it's so windy. But I always feel the air's cleaner by the sea.'

Once we'd all returned to our chalet and changed into our swimsuits we spent the rest of the afternoon by the lagoon.

Stephen and Hannah stayed with me in the shallow water of the lagoon, whereas Patrick disappeared to explore the deeper end of the lagoon.

I put my goggles on and spent some time watching an aggressive triggerfish swim its way around its patch of sand; the triggerfish had two smaller fish in tow alongside it.

I was fascinated at how such a small fish could behave so aggressively towards someone as big as me. It would swim forward at me with its dorsal fin up and then swerve away. Such bravery! I found out later triggerfish have been known to give nasty nips or butts if it's the breeding season and they feel threatened.

I walked away after a minute or two to the crustacean encrusted stairs descending into the lagoon and enjoyed watching two small hermit crabs fight it out near the steps out of the lagoon, the loser disappearing into his shell.

At this point my observations were interrupted as Stephen suddenly started to howl and cry. Looking up out of the water, to see what was happening, I saw Marion helping Stephen out of the lagoon and he appeared to be hobbling on one foot.

'Calm down, Stephen, for heaven's sake! Let me see what's happened to your foot,' said Marion, 'Oh good grief! You seem to have trodden on a sea urchin.'

'I've got some tweezers in my bag, hold on a minute,' said Mrs Cumber, rummaging in her bag.

'Here we are!' she went to Stephen and bent down to look at his foot. Stephen by now was whimpering quietly. She carefully pulled a black spine out of the sole of Stephen's foot.

'Everything will be fine if it's a dead sea urchin he trod on because there'll be no venom, just a small wound,' Mrs Cumber said to Marion. 'I suggest you call Barbara and see if she can take you and Stephen to the hotel to have it checked out by the on duty medic. They'll have dealt with this before. I'll stay here with the others, it's a shame to drag them away just now.'

Poor Stephen and Marion disappeared for the rest of the afternoon, leaving us to potter about the lagoon and order coconut drinks from the waiters whenever we felt like it.

By the time we reached our chalet again we found Stephen happily seated in front of Cablevision and eating ice cream.

'Thankfully the doctor seemed to think it was a dead sea urchin when he looked at spine, so there should be no venom. His foot hasn't swollen up or gone red so he should be a little sore but fine by tomorrow,' Marion told Mrs Cumber.

'Maybe tomorrow we should just stick to the pool area,' suggested Mrs Cumber.

'I certainly think we can go to the hotel pools in the morning. If the others want to go to the lagoon in the afternoon I think we should let them, we only have one more full day here so we should do as much as we can.'

'If the others go to the lagoon I want to go too,' said Stephen, breaking off from watching his television program.

'We'll just see how everyone is in the morning, Stephen,' said Marion firmly.

In the end, the delicious barbequed lobster by the poolside kept all of us away from the lagoon for most of the day. By late afternoon Stephen was quite happy to return to the lagoon with the others and Marion, confident we'd be careful where we put our feet this time, had no objections.

Barbara and Craig joined us later for dinner in the restaurant area.

The other hotel guests seemed unaware or oblivious to the fact that Craig and Barbara owned the hotel and I could see this would be a bonus for Craig and Barbara, as then they wouldn't find themselves unexpectedly confronted with any complaints about the hotel.

I did wonder if they were ever able to relax in this beautiful place. Did Barbara sit at the table and closely observe the service provided in the dining area while she ate her lunch? Did she walk past reception keeping an eye on how messy and chaotic the hotel lobby was? Could they ever really enjoy living in this lovely coastal setting when it was their workplace?

While I sat musing and lost in thought, Marion dug down into her bag and took out a couple of small boxes. In one box she had a tiny little gold and jade pendant she'd bought to thank Barbara for her hospitality and in the other she had a pair of small gold and jade cufflinks for Craig.

'Barbara, these are small thank you for you and Craig. We've had a fantastic end to our trip thanks to you both and you've both been absolutely wonderful.'

Barbara and Craig looking deeply touched opened the boxes.

'Marion, these gifts are beautiful! Thank you so much darling! There's really no need,' said Barbara, reaching over to give Marion a hug. 'It goes without saying you're welcome any time. You're model guests which is more than we can say about some of the people who come here!'

Craig lifted his glass in a toast, 'Here's to your next visit to the Jade Green Hotel!'

Marion lifted her glass, 'and here's to your visit to number 32 Avenida de Aconcagua!'

29

In the middle of the night at the end of December 1998 I woke up suddenly.

In a half dazed state I realised my bed was shaking gently side-to-side. I sat upright for several moments, looking fixedly down at the floor, trying to gauge how strong the movement was. After about ten minutes the shaking stopped and everything went back to normal.

I discovered, when I woke up again in the morning, there'd been a minor earthquake in Mexico City during the night.

I would always in future associate this occurrence with Manolo's death, because the day after the earthquake my mother interrupted me during class, and took me outside to tell me Manolo had suffered a stroke.

As I stood in the garden numb with disbelief and shock, my mother hugged me tightly.

'Raoul, Marion's given us permission to go to Guajimalpa to see him so you need to pack your small bag and we'll take the lunchtime bus. I'll go and quickly get some sandwiches made up for us. We can go and visit Manolo in hospital; he's still able to speak although he can't move the right side of his body. You know how determined he is, apparently he keeps trying over and over again to raise his arm but only manages to raise his left arm in a salute.'

My mother laughed tearfully.

I turned and walked up to our flat, but once I got there I didn't have the mental strength to pack my bag. I sat on my bed and stared blankly at the wall.

I'd been home in Iztupalapa throughout the summer holidays while the Andersons were away in Britain on leave.

I remembered the comfort of Manolo's calm presence across the kitchen table in my grandparent's house. I remembered Manolo's childlike sense of humour, laughing at slapstick comedies on the television, but more than anything else, I remembered the wise and reassuring words Manolo had spoken to me whenever I felt weak or vulnerable.

I heard a knock on the door of the apartment and Hannah called out, 'Raoul, are you OK? Esther told us about Manolo. Do you need anything?'

I rubbed my hair vigorously, to try and dispel the fog in my mind, before opening the door and letting Hannah in. Nothing felt very real anymore and I sensed everything around me with a strange kind of detachment.

'Raoul, do you need help to pack your bag? Your mother's coming in a minute to pick you up, she's just passing things on to Aida to do when she's away.'

'No, I should be OK,' I said, turning and walking back to my bedroom.

'OK, well at least let me keep you company until your mum gets here.'

'Yeah, sure.'

I pulled my small rucksack from the cupboard and put a couple of pyjamas, some underwear and socks into it. I had no idea how long we would be away for. I put a spare shirt and trousers into the rucksack for good measure too, although I had spare clothes at my grandparent's place.

I also put my favourite book of the moment Asunder by Chloe Aridjis into the bag thinking I could at least read to Manolo in hospital in case Manolo, who loved reading, was unable to hold or read a book.

Hannah looked anxiously at me.

'Mum's saying Antonio could give the two of you a lift home but Esther said the bus was fine.'

'Yeah, we take that bus all the time to Iztupalapa. It'll be fine. Besides I'm sure Antonio has other jobs to do for your dad and mum today.'

I grabbed my toothbrush and toothpaste from the bathroom and flung it into the bag. I then sat down next to Hannah.

'Raoul, you're taking this very calmly,' said Hannah, puzzled. 'You don't seem terribly upset.'

I felt a burst of anger.

'Of course I'm upset, you idiot. Just because I'm not crying like a girl, doesn't mean I don't have feelings.'

I got up and paced to the other side of the bedroom, trying not to look at Hannah's hurt face. I looked at the garden outside the bedroom window, turning my back on Hannah.

'I'm sorry, Raoul. I didn't mean to make you feel worse. It's just difficult to know what to say.'

'Yeah, well it's difficult to know what it feels like because you don't know Manolo like I do. I think if you don't mind I'd like to be on my own. It's just easier.'

'Of course', said Hannah quietly, getting up and leaving the apartment.

I felt guilty at hurting Hannah, the one member of the

Anderson family I loved unconditionally and felt akin to.

Then I felt anger at having to deal with my complicated feelings towards Hannah, when all I wanted was to think about was Manolo, poor old Manolo, who'd be lying on a bed in a ward somewhere, wondering what was happening to him.

As we crossed the city in the bus my mother's mobile rang. My grandmother informed her that Manolo's condition had worsened and he could no longer speak. We'd better get there as soon as possible.

By the time we reached the hospital I was feeling drained and tired. My mother, protectively putting an arm around my waist (by now I was taller than my diminutive mother), guided me to the right floor and after speaking to a nurse we were directed to the ward where Manolo lay.

My grandparents met us outside the ward and gave both my mother and I a hug.

'Dios mio, it's not good. Not good at all,' my grandmother said, tears falling unnoticed down her face, 'he can't talk but apparently he can hear. He moves his foot to say yes when you ask him to. He's struggling to breathe and he's fighting hard to speak. He knows we're all here though.'

My grandfather hugged my grandmother, his face impassive and calm, like a placid pool of water surrounded by an impending storm.

'He squeezed my hand with his left hand,' my grandfather said. 'I think they said they're going to put him on a life support machine as his condition's deteriorating. I phoned his children this morning and not one of them has made it in to see him yet. Apparently they'll both come tonight.'

I walked into the busy room and straight away saw Manolo.

A shrunken small figure lay under the blankets on a bed next to the window. I stood by Manolo and placed my hand over his hand, which felt surprisingly warm and solid.

'Hi Manolo. It's Raoul. I'm here now. They tell me you can't speak but you can still hear. I don't know what's going to happen but we're all here for you so you mustn't feel you're alone. Your children are coming to you tonight.'

Manolo started to make a strange wailing noise that seemed to come from his nose. I could sense he was desperately trying to speak. The wailing noise came and went constantly and before long my face was covered in tears. My mother stood at the foot of the bed in tears too.

The nurses, who'd been watching us sympathetically, brought us some plastic chairs and we sat down.

'Your grandparents have gone home for a break and will be back in a couple of hours,' my mother said to me, as silence descended on the ward again.

I said nothing but watched Manolo's thick white stock of hair, above a forehead lined with age. Even in this frozen state Manolo's face projected calm, the bottom half of his mouth dropping down and leaving his mouth slightly open.

I wondered how much of him was alive now. Didn't a stroke kill off many brain cells? I gently stroked Manolo's veined hand, hoping Manolo could feel my presence.

I thought to myself a stroke was as bad as a sudden death. There's no chance to say one's last goodbyes. There's no consolation in a shell of a body, still alive, when everything that makes us human slowly dies away.

After a couple of hours my grandparents returned with sandwiches and drinks for us. We all looked pale and tired.

'The nurse has told us they're preparing a bed with life support for Manolo. He'll get taken there very shortly. There's a waiting room next to the ward as well.'

'Raoul, you should try and drink something. I think we're in for a long wait and we should stay until those hijos de puta turn up to see their father.'

I took the drink and swigged it down.

It was strange but it was as if every small action I could perform was filled with new significance. Poor Manolo would never be able to drink like this now. He'd never be able to open his eyes and see the people around him, appreciate the colours and the light from the window. In fact the window itself seemed to mock Manolo's helpless condition.

By contrast, the next ward they moved Manolo to was dimly lit and had no windows.

There was an almost complete silence, except for the rhythmic thumping of the life support machines, grinding away next to the beds of the unconscious patients.

There was a strange sickly smell in the air. My grandmother recognised the smell straight away having visited friends in hospital. It was the sickly smell of death that lingered on in this ward. Even though the patients were well cared for and clean, the atmosphere was that of a funeral. Maybe this is how they prepare us for what's to come I thought.

I sat by the bed holding Manolo's hand and talking quietly to him.

The others quietly watched the two of us in mutual despair.

Many hours later, as the light outside the hospital grew dim, two adults walked in and came to Manolo's bed.

The younger man was a recognisable copy of his father, but a good thirty years younger than Manolo, and he demonstrated what a dashing man Manolo must have been in his youth. He wore an expensive tailored suit, and carried a leather briefcase in his hand. Everything from his watch to his hair proclaimed his wealth.

The lady was very different in both colouring and build to her brother. She had a rounded figure; she was dressed in a chiffon black dress, and had elegant red high-heeled shoes. Her make up was bold; her eyes thickly outlined in black pencil and her lips a bright magenta red.

Her eyes were cold and appraising, I could see none of Manolo's habitual warmth in them.

'*¡Hola!* Are you Manolo's friends? I'm María Jesús. Pleased to meet you,' said the lady, cordially shaking hands with us all.

We stood aside silently and awkwardly, as the siblings walked over to Manolo's side and looked down at him.

'Have the nurses told you anything?' my mother asked María Jesús quietly.

'Yes, they've asked how we would feel about having the life support machine switched off tomorrow morning. The doctor's had a chat with the consultant and he thinks most of the brain stem's now gone. They're just keeping the body going but there's no one there anymore.'

I started sobbing again and my grandfather hugged me protectively.

'I'm sorry, I didn't mean to distress you,' the lady said politely.

I looked up at her in disbelief.

Manolo clearly meant nothing at all to her. How strange the blood ties that bind us together I thought. My family was more of a family to Manolo then this city slick brother and sister.

Why had they never visited Manolo or been to see him? Why were they turning up now after all these years? What secret sadness had Manolo carried inside of him all these years, knowing that his daughter and son were somewhere out there in Mexico City, living a life divorced from him?

Suddenly I was ready to depart and go home again. At least there I would be near Manolo's apartment and at the moment that seemed to be the closest I would get to the Manolo I knew and loved.

As if on cue my mother said our goodbyes and we all walked out together into the gathering dusk outside. I took some deep breaths of air after the confined antiseptic atmosphere of the hospital.

Manolo's funeral was only two days later.

In the meantime, his children had been busy leaving old pieces of Manolo's furniture out on the pavement for collection (or more likely theft). They lost no time in rummaging through the apartment to clear out anything unwanted, and to find anything that might be of value.

I found it very hard to see them entering, and exiting an apartment I'd spent so much time in with Manolo. It was painful to see the disdain with which they threw out his books and papers into the skip.

Manolo was always so careful and neat with his possessions; it seemed to desecrate him to have his things thrown carelessly into the skip. My grandmother seeing how distressed I felt summoned me to the kitchen and sat me down at the kitchen table.

'Raoul, before Manolo had his stroke he often spoke to me about what would happen after he died. He'd left his flat to his children and he made sure Campanita went to Pedro. However one day he came to me with a big box and said he wanted me to give it to you when he died, so you could remember him. He said you were to keep it until you needed it and then you were welcome to sell it. I've no idea what's in the box. I've kept it in my cupboard for the last two years and had just about forgotten about it until I saw you looking at Manolo's things in the skip. Here it is.'

She lifted the box carefully from the kitchen shelf and placed it on the table.

I looked at the box.

It was a plain mahogany box that had been lovingly waxed so the mahogany shone. On the top of the box was a faded brass plate with a family crest on it.

I turned the small brass key and opened up the lid, and at the same time both my grandmother and I leaned down with curiosity and peered into the box. Nestled inside the box were several worn maroon velvet pouches and underneath them there was a large envelope.

I opened up the envelope first which was addressed to me.

Inside the envelope there were several black and white photos of Manolo when he was younger, a dapper young man with his hair slicked back and shiny with oil. In one of the photos Manolo was wearing military uniform. There were also other old photographs of people I didn't know or recognise. I read the letter that encased the photos.

Dear Raoul,

By the time you read this I'll have gone and I wanted to make sure I had a chance to say my goodbyes to you because nobody knows how or when they will die. It's only a few lucky cretinos who have a chance to say their proper goodbyes. I'm getting weak and old now and I'm sure my time's getting closer.

You've been like a grandson to me; in fact you've been my only grandson as far as I'm concerned. I barely hear from my own son and daughter who have long since led successful and glamorous lives in the city but you, Raoul, have always remained true to your family and your roots even after leaving Iztupalapa. I'm so happy to see that living in the British residence hasn't changed who you are. Never be ashamed or afraid of who you are and where you come from. My own son and daughter were ashamed of me and dismissed me as out of date and poor, insignificant and unsuited to the lives they were living.

The truth is they never knew anything about their family's ancestors or their family's past achievements. My wife and I were happy to live quiet lives in Iztupalapa and we loved our neighbours and our neighbourhood. We've both given our children a good education. Neither one of us have had any regrets about our lives.

The truth is my great-great grandparents were born into great wealth and were part of the old nobility in Mexico, something that is no longer acknowledged any more in Mexico. In the past they were the Condes of Sierra Nevada. Nothing is left of their wealth now but what's in this box and I want you to have it Raoul.

You must make good use of it and I know you'll use it wisely. The contents of this box have been passed down through generations of my family. You're the special grandchild I

*always wished for and if the contents of this box help you
achieve your dreams I couldn't be happier.*

*You mustn't say anything to María Jesús and Sebastian,
they'll not understand or appreciate the relationship we
have and they'll challenge you legally for this if they find
out about my gift to you. Please honour an old man's dying
wish and keep this gift to you in secrecy until you need to
make use of it.*

*Lastly always remember me. I look forward to hopefully
seeing you in the next life at some point. Please don't get too
upset when I'm gone. I've had a good life and I certainly
don't want to be kept incapacitated and alive at any cost.
I've no regrets.*

I'll be watching you from up there so behave yourself!

Love

Manolo

With my heart full of complicated emotions I put the letter
down and looked at my grandmother.

'What is it, Raoul?'

'I don't quite understand but I think what's in that box must
be quite valuable.'

'Can I read the letter?' asked Carmela.

I passed it to her and waited patiently while she read it.

I laid out the photos Manolo had enclosed in the envelope
on the table. My grandmother slowly read to the end of both
pages and then shook her head.

'What's that old madman up to now? He always has to do
things differently. What on earth is he talking about when he

writes about the Condes of Sierra Nevada? He must be making this up. He's never said a word about this before. Maybe his mind was going more senile than I thought.'

'Don't you believe him?' I asked.

My grandmother pursed her lips thoughtfully and shook her head.

'But look at these photos,' I said, 'there're some really old ones with some wealthy looking people in them.'

My grandmother looked doubtfully at the photos Raoul was pointing at.

'I don't know, Raoul. They could be anyone,' she said slowly, 'let's see what else the box contains.'

I lifted a velvet pouch and opened the cord at the top, emptying it onto the table. A large and heavy gold necklace landed onto the table.

My grandmother and I looked at each other startled.

I then lifted up the necklace and looked carefully at it. It had an enormous emerald cross in the centre surrounded by intricate gold metalwork and pearls. From the centre-piece other round gold and pearl pieces linked onto it in ever diminishing sizes until the circle was enclosed with a gold clasp.

'*Madre de Dios*. Raoul, just look at it. It must be worth a fortune. It looks real enough to me. Why did he never say anything to us about this? I can't believe I've had that box sitting on my cupboard shelf for the last two years and he never said anything. He's an utter lunatic!'

I put the necklace back into the pouch and pushed it to one side.

I reached into the box and took hold of another pouch. This

one was smaller and lighter. I emptied it onto the table and a long gold chain slithered out.

At the end of it was a strange pendant, it was in the shape of a salamander but it actually looked more like a tool of some sort. It had what looked like a miniature gold spoon attached to it and what looked like a long gold toothpick. The salamander had only one ruby eye; the other eye had the ruby missing from it. All the way down its back little rubies were imbedded in the gold.

I looked at my grandmother in confusion. It was a weirdly shaped pendant. She shrugged and put it back into the pouch. She then had a look into the box.

'There's five more of them in here! Goodness knows where Manolo's kept this all this time. Knowing him he probably kept it under his bed, the crazy man. This should be kept in a bank. In fact that's exactly where we're going to take this tomorrow morning.'

My grandmother gazed into the space in front of her, chewing nervously on her lower lip.

'We'll take it to your mother's bank. I don't want it in the house. We'll discuss what to do with it later. I think as well, Raoul, you'll have to have a specialist look at it at some point. But they'll be asking a lot of questions that we won't be able to answer and things could get awkward for us because it'll look very suspicious. The first thing they'll think is that we've stolen this.'

I pulled out the remaining five pouches and placed the letter and photos back into the box. By the time I had emptied them out there was an enormous gold and emerald crucifix, a heavy gold signet ring with a coat of arms on it, an intricate gold and enamel brooch with a diamond in the middle, a painted gold framed miniature of a dark lady in a feathered hat with her hair done up in extravagant curls, and a small delicate coronet of dull white metal with pearls and diamonds set in it.

Both my grandmother and I, feeling quite terrified at the contents of the box, quickly placed everything back into it. Somehow we sensed that the contents of this box had the potential to change our lives in some way but at the same time neither one of us felt these things belonged to me.

We looked at each other silently.

My grandmother got up and went to put the cafetière back on to the gas hob to warm up some coffee.

'What do you think I should do with this, abuela?' I asked.

My grandmother shrugged.

'It was left to you Raoul but I'm not sure whether it's right or legal for you to have it. According to Manolo it's for you to decide what to do with it. I think we have to leave it in the bank and think about it for a bit. I just wish Manolo had explained it all in more detail. The crazy man just let me keep it there on my cupboard shelf, thinking it was nothing more than a keepsake for you. He's made me so angry! But then he probably knew I would be angry. It would be just like him.'

'If we take the box to the bank, can I keep the photos and letter here?' I asked.

'I think you should leave the letter in the box with the photos. It's the only thing we have proving he left it to you. At some point we're going to have to see a lawyer about this but leave us to worry about that.'

I reluctantly put the letter and photos back into the box

and the following morning we went to my mother's bank and deposited the box under her name.

I wanted to walk away from the bank and forget about the box. It was too big a responsibility and I wasn't ready to deal with it. I was happy to leave the box and leave it to wiser heads than mine to decide its future.

Manolo's funeral was held on a Saturday morning at the local church and it was filled with the large local community of Manolo's friends and neighbours.

Manolo's two children, who knew him the least, stood at the front of the church by the coffin. His daughter sobbed loudly and dramatically. I felt an irrational desire to laugh at her exaggerated performance. The cold and indifferent lady I met at the hospital was now all of a sudden pretending to grieve for her father.

I was sure that somewhere Manolo would be watching and laughing too. The young priest didn't know Manolo or his children but he put in a short but credible service to the crowded church.

30

1998 was the year I lost Manolo, and it turned out 1999 was the year I thought I was also going to lose the Andersons.

David received news of a new posting to Bogotá at the end of January 1999. When I look back at this abrupt interruption to what was then the placid routine of my life at the house in Chapultepec, I do start to wonder about the impact these changes must have on a diplomat's family.

I'm sure there are a lot of screwed up diplomatic kids out there. I mean if you think about it, they grow up in so many different homes and countries; their parents are given a new posting every three to four years and off they go with all their belongings to settle in a different place.

After all of this they are then, at some point, sent to boarding school in the United Kingdom (if they are British).

It's hardly what most people would call a stable upbringing, and it must've been so much worse in the days when we didn't have instant technology. In the early 1980's, for example, phone calls abroad were prohibitively expensive. Children would have had no access to email so the best they could have hoped for would be a letter in the post, or a weekly phone call.

I guess if nothing else this nomadic life breeds independence. But it's also a lonely existence as you leave behind in each country the friends you've made there.

At times I also start to wonder how easy it is for retired diplomats to return to a normal life in their home country, after all the excitement of diplomatic life.

It was Hannah actually, who filled me in on this new posting and the inevitable prospect of change for all of us. Hannah was the one who inadvertently overheard her parents talking about the move and she eventually repeated their conversation to me, but much later of course.

In the dining room one evening, as she walked towards the kitchen for a snack, she was surprised to see her parents still sitting and talking at the dining room table long after dinner had finished. David and Marion thought the children were all upstairs watching Cable.

David had taken an appreciative mouthful of red wine as he sat at the now empty table with Marion, and Marion was absorbed and completely occupied in trying to twist her dinner napkin into a swan shape.

'Marion, I've been given a new posting for next September.'

Marion lifted her eyes from her napkin and looked enquiringly at David.

'I've been given a position in Bogotá.'

Marion cleared her throat.

'I guess I'd better get in touch with Ellerslie School then and get the children ready to sit their entrance tests.'

David nodded.

They'd both agreed they'd be sending the children to boarding school to finish their education when they left Mexico.

'What about Raoul and Esther?'

'I really don't know Marion. I wish we could sort something

out for them, I really do. I just don't know what we can do. I'll ask around and see if anything comes up. There might be an opening somewhere.'

Understandably Hannah didn't tell me about this conversation until much later.

Such was my sense of security and belonging with the Andersons I'd never thought about the day when the family would have to leave Mexico for good.

My mother by contrast, with her finely tuned feminine instinct, knew almost at once something was up. Marion's anxiety about the news was clearly visible and it wasn't long before Marion sat down with my mother to talk to her about it.

'They've told David we'll be moving to Bogotá September next year so we've less than a year to get ourselves organised and get the children placed at boarding school.'

My mother said nothing, her face showing no emotion, so Marion carried on.

'I know it's going to be an anxious and uncertain time for you and Raoul over the next few months, but I want you to know that I'm going to do my best to get both of you settled in the best possible circumstances. You and Raoul are like family to us and we're not going to abandon you', said Marion, laying a hand gently on my mother's arm. 'We have a lot of contacts and there'll be lots of opportunities for you in the future, just bear with us if you can, while we try and sort everything out and see what options we have.'

My mother nodded, not finding herself able to speak.

She was tough and knew very well, having worked for diplomats for many years, diplomats always moved on. This time though I know it felt harder for my mother than at any time before. Probably because I was so happy and settled now and this meant disruption to both our lives.

'Whatever happens in the future we'll always keep in touch, Esther. You've been by far the best member of staff we've had in residence and we're going to really miss you when we go to Bogota. I'm certain we'll find you an excellent position for you to go to.'

'And Raoul?' my mother asked quietly.

'Esther, I'm totally committed to finding a good situation for Raoul too. I didn't invite Raoul into our family on a whim. We've a big responsibility to him too. He's done so well and is turning into a lovely young man. We're not going to spoil his progress by moving away and abandoning him.'

Feeling slightly reassured my mother smiled and thanked Marion.

However she told me much later she went back into the kitchen feeling many tumultuous emotions in her breast.

With age change seemed to become harder for her to accept and she was starting to long for some security in life. Still there was nothing for it but to wait and see if Marion could deliver on her good intentions.

I wasn't very happy to discover I was the last member of the household to find out about David's new posting.

The day I found out I decided to stay up late to speak to my mother about it, so I waited impatiently until I heard my mother walk wearily into our flat later that evening. I could hear her sigh of relief as she slipped on her cushioned slippers after another long day.

Then I heard her quickly walk over to my door as though she'd suddenly noticed that I, unusually, still had my light on.

She went and knocked on my half open door and then pushed it open.

'Everything OK, Raoul?'

I was sitting fully dressed on my bed sketching in my sketchbook, using my pencil with sharp, aggressive strokes.

'No.'

¿Que pasa?

'What's going on with the Andersons? Hannah told me today all of them are going to boarding school in September, and Marion and David are going to Bogotá? Was anyone going to get round to telling me?'

I turned and looked my mother in the eye. She looked dismayed at the painful intensity in my eyes.

'How long have you known?'

She sighed.

'Well, I started noticing Mrs Anderson was worried about something a few weeks ago,' she said gently, 'she's usually so cheerful no matter what happens. She only told me what was happening a couple of weeks ago. I wasn't sure how much the children knew and I didn't want to worry you just yet. She promised me she'd take care of us and I have to take her at her word. But I'll still keep an ear open for any other opportunities of course. It's a difficult situation to find ourselves in but we've been in worse Raoul.'

Looking at my mother I noticed how tired she looked. Despite her brown skin, dark circular shadows could be seen under her eyes, making her eyes look blacker than normal.

I felt compassion for her break through the anger I'd been carefully nurturing ever since I found out the Andersons had another posting. My heart would constrict painfully every time

I thought of losing my relationship with the Anderson family, especially as I'd developed a boyish crush on Hannah, but my mother was right.

Things had been bad when she'd been left with a baby at the age of fifteen. Nothing was ever going to be as precarious for us again.

I smiled at her and her face lightened. She came over and gave me a hug.

'You need to get some sleep Raoul. Now more than ever it's important for you to keep working hard and taking care of yourself. Everything's going to work out. In the worst case scenario we can always move back in with *abuelo* and *abuela* but I really don't think it'll come to that.'

And for the next few weeks those were the only words that echoed in my head as I tried not to think about the future too much. I was doing well academically and keeping up with the others. I worked hard at my studies and I was determined not to let either Hannah or Patrick outperform me. I couldn't do much else to improve things.

At various times in the ensuing weeks we'd catch Marion sitting on the sofa gazing into space.

I now know exactly what she would be thinking at these moments, having been through it all with them.

She'd be feeling tired at the thought of all that lay ahead for them as a family. The burden of the move would rest on her shoulders while David would carry on as usual with his official duties.

I know she was also in a quandary about Stephen as she felt he was far too young to be sent away to boarding school but worried how would he ever be happy away from his brother and sister. And I know Marion worried about them separating from me too. I was like a brother to Stephen.

She had to get the applications in soon for Ellerslie School in Scotland. The Anderson children would be sitting the entrance exams in February and Marion had high expectations they'd get in, especially so since David was an old alumnae.

She'd feel the need to have a chat with Stephen to see how he felt about the move, and whether he wanted to go to boarding school too. The problem was that none of them had any experience of boarding school and Stephen, at eight years of age, would have no idea what life at boarding school entailed. None of them did.

Lastly, I know Marion felt she had to figure out how to help my mother and I. To do this she'd have to speak to a few friends and see what strings she could pull to secure a good future for us. Good old nepotism again. Time was going to be tight but she had to get her head down and sort these things out which were no doubt going to give her a few sleepless nights in the process.

Marion told my mother, days later, that she had looked out of the window at the cherry trees gently shedding their blossom in the breeze blowing outside and suddenly realised she was going to miss this house because for the first time it actually felt like home.

She'd never had any regrets about leaving their diplomatic posts before.

Then she thought about the friends she'd be leaving behind in Mexico and Barbara sprung to mind. Marion decided there and then to reach into her bag for her mobile phone and make a call to Barbara.

Barbara picked up at the second ring.

'Hi honey, how are you?'

'Not so great these days, Barbara, I'm afraid.'

'What do you mean? Has something happened?'

Barbara's voice sharpened with anxiety.

'No, no, nothing like that. It's just they've given David a posting in Bogotá for September.'

There was a brief silence on the other end of the phone.

'I'm so sorry, Marion. That's going to be hard for you. It's real tough for you diplomatic folk.'

'I know it's a nightmare. I have to get the kids into boarding school now so they can finish their education properly and have a chance to get into higher education. And none of them have any idea how different that's going to be for them.'

Marion's voice broke slightly.

'Don't worry about that, Marion, children are resilient and many people have been through the same process before you. I know lots of people who've fond memories of boarding school.'

'Yeah, I know. It's just that Patrick isn't that sporty you know and that makes a huge difference to how you fit in at boarding school. And Hannah's become such an introvert recently. She's going to hate not having her own space and sharing dormitories with other girls. Stephen's only eight and I just don't know what to do with him. I know he'll insist on following his brother and sister to boarding school even when he has no idea what it's like.'

'I get that, Marion. But I also think you shouldn't worry about things until it's time to. They might all surprise you with how well they settle in. I guess the main thing is for you to show them the school and get them to meet some of the teachers.

Goodness me, boarding schools nowadays are so cushy. I mean they've counsellors on tap and are all really into what they call 'health and wellbeing' these days.'

'Yes, you're right. It's all different nowadays.'

'Nothing like the Catholic convent my mother was sent to board at. The nuns there were *so* vicious. She's left handed and as this was not seen as 'normal' in those days she was forced under punishment to write with her right hand.'

'I suppose at the moment everything seems worse than it is. I also have to do something to help Esther and Raoul too. I've a huge moral commitment to both of them and Raoul has done so well with the education we've offered him.'

'Esther's an absolute gem. She's a darling. We definitely should do something to help her out.'

There was a silence as both of them pondered this. Marion was guiltily aware of how relieved she was when Barbara had used the word 'we' in the conversation. Barbara was hugely connected and very influential in a lot of circles. Her help would be invaluable.

'Tell you what Marion leave it with me and I'll see what I can do. I'll get back to you in a few days. Try not to worry too much, honey, in the meantime. It'll all work out.'

Marion said she hung up feeling better than she had done in days. Some people have a talent for reassurance and Barbara definitely had that skill in abundance.

Marion gave herself a shake and got up to head to the kitchen to speak to Aida about this week's dinner and reception.

Needless to say my mother was also encouraged when she was told of Marion's chat with Barbara, and tried her best to trust things would work out well for us.

I think it's easier for adults to manage the stress caused by uncertainty. I had many sleepless nights at the time, which I never told my mother about of course, worrying about our future. As a child it's hard when you have no control over events in your life. As an adult there are always choices, however limited, to make.

31

It was very early summer, 1999, and the fruit trees in the garden were heavy with unripe fruit. Birds hadn't descended yet to peck at the fruit but the huge heavy ivy wall in the Anderson's garden was full of little bird nests and several small green barbet birds had made the jacaranda tree their home.

The jacaranda tree in the garden was full of floating clusters of purple trumpet like flowers. The small clouds of soft blue-lavender colour were very peaceful to look at.

The inside of the Anderson's house, however, looked anything but peaceful.

Large pale yellow wooden crates were scattered around the downstairs hallway, newspapers and rolls of bubble wrap were piled up next to them and trails of loose fill polystyrene made their way around the furniture. Some crates were full but most were half empty.

Marion had insisted on doing some of the crates herself, as she didn't want the non-essential items mixed up with essential items. Non-essential items could wait to be unpacked once they arrived in Bogotá, but the items Marion regarded as necessary were going to be put in crates that could be opened and placed as soon as they arrived. Included in the list of essential items was the family silver and all the tableware needed for diplomatic entertaining.

The abstract paintings Marion loved were going to be boxed up carefully by the packers into long rectangular wooden crates. Most of the paintings were lying stacked by the study room door and the walls in the sitting-room and hallway looked strangely bare without them.

A running battle was happening with the contents of the children's rooms. Patrick, Hannah and Stephen had all declared war on Marion's attempts to clear out their rooms of all the antiquated and unused toys and books. The prospect of change seemed to make them cling all the more fiercely to their possessions. Marion would complain to my mother she could already imagine herself in Bogotá, chucking out all the forgotten and useless things the children had lost interest in but had insisted on bringing with them.

Among the Anderson children I noticed there was a sense of anticipation and excitement building up. All of them were positive and excited about the changes happening in their lives and were looking forward to visiting their new school in Edinburgh.

They were all going to spend the summer in Edinburgh, giving them plenty of time to visit Ellerslie School and to familiarise themselves with Edinburgh. Marion had hired another very able tutor to help us all with our studies because she'd been worried we would flunk the entrance test. In the end all of us passed it.

As for me, I was going to spend the summer with my mother and then fly out to meet them all in Edinburgh at the end of the summer.

David had put his status as a former alumnus to good use and succeeded in securing me a full bursary place at the school, on the assumption I managed to pass the entrance test of course and had good references from my current teachers.

I'd passed the test and had been offered a place which in the end I'd accepted, even though my feelings on this were very mixed.

For once my mother had put no pressure on me to make a decision either way. Marion and David could only provide for me to return home to Mexico once a year so the other school holidays I'd have to stay with hospitality families linked to the school, or with Marion's mother who lived in Edinburgh.

If the Anderson family had formerly adopted me the British government would have provided for me to join my siblings in Bogotá over the Christmas and Easter break. However none of us were keen on this option, it was deemed to be both unnecessary and inappropriate. However, even given David's role in the diplomatic service, procuring a visa for me was going to be a long and arduous process. My age, especially, was a complicating factor.

Despite all these difficulties, in the three years I'd been with the Anderson family, I felt I'd become a member of their family. David and Marion were fully aware of how close I was emotionally to Hannah and Stephen. Although looking back now, I'm pretty sure of course, the Anderson children would have coped fine in the long term with the separation from my mother and I.

I think the fact Marion and David put so much effort into getting me a place at the same school as their children shows how they both must've felt a deep sense of responsibility towards me. They also managed to help my mother to find another job with good prospects.

On the fifteenth of April of that year, Barbara had called Marion's mobile and left a message asking Marion to call her back. Her phone call to Marion was to offer my mother a good job at one of their new hotels in Acapulco.

My mother told me Marion had called Barbara back straight away.

'Hi Marion. Good, good news for you. We've just been successful in buying another hotel in Acapulco and we'd like to offer Esther the position of dining manager there. We're thinking she could be in charge of the breakfast and lunch service there. She'd be perfect for the job. It'll be a big change for her but hopefully in a good way. It would also open new doors for her in the future and be great experience, wouldn't it? I'll send you an email with all the info and you can run it by her. Please let us know by the end of April if she wants it or not.'

Marion told my mother she felt a weight lift from her shoulders.

'Barbara, that sounds fabulous. I think she'd be a fantastic dining manager. She's completely trustworthy and I've never had an employee who works as hard as Esther does. Thank you so, so, much! The only problem for her might be moving so far away from her parents as she's very attached to them. But I'll let you know as soon as possible.'

'OK darling. I've got to go now but give me a call this evening and we can have a proper chinwag. Love you! Bye!'

My mother, to my surprise, was delighted when Marion told her about this new opportunity and challenge.

I hadn't realised she was starting to weary of the late and unsocial hours she had to work in diplomatic residences. If she wasn't babysitting the children, she was always involved in helping out with diplomatic functions.

She could only really call weekend evenings, spent at Iztupalapa, truly her own free time or the long summer weeks when diplomatic families vacated the residence to visit their homeland.

In the meantime, despite the expected chaos involved in packing up a house in which a family had lived in for four years, life continued more or less as normal for everyone except Marion and David who now had to attend leaving dinners given by their various friends in the diplomatic and ex pat community.

I have to confess I did slacken a little with my studies once I knew I had a place waiting for me at Ellerslie School.

One day my mother caught me playing cricket in the garden with Patrick and Stephen when I supposed to be studying.

¡Eh, Raoul! ¿Que haces?'

I turned round guiltily and shrugged.

'They asked me to play cricket with them.'

'Raoul,' said my mother in Spanish, 'if you want to keep up with this school of theirs you know you've to study hard. You'll be learning in English and it's going to be harder for you than for them.'

I sighed.

'I know that, mum, but the school knows I'm Mexican. I'll do well enough so don't worry so much about it. Mrs Cumber said I'm doing brilliantly.'

My mother's lips tightened up at my patronizing tone.

'OK, but I want to see you studying the hour before dinner, Raoul.'

I made a face.

"*Para quien quiera el ciel azul el precio es alto* (for whoever wants the blue sky the price is high)" responded my mother, retreating to the kitchen before I had another chance to argue back.

I turned back round to face Patrick who was waiting patiently for me to finish talking to my mother, tossing the cricket ball from hand to hand.

I was holding the cricket bat with both hands tightly and nervously and Stephen was in a left field position near the jacaranda tree, occupied in fixing his shoelaces.

'Stephen, are you ready?' asked Patrick.

'Yes,' said Stephen, straightening up quickly.

Patrick brushed his long fringe from his eyes. I was used to seeing Patrick brush the hair from his eyes but always thought he could do with getting his hair cut shorter. It just wasn't cool to have long hair but I guess Patrick thought otherwise.

Patrick made a short run towards me as he bowled the cricket ball over arm to me.

I gave the ball a good hit much to Stephen's delight and my relief.

A window opened on the first floor.

'Patrick, I hope you're not playing cricket in the garden again,' yelled Marion from upstairs.

Patrick's face pleaded with his mother.

'Please, mum.'

'Ten more minutes Patrick and then your time's up. I'm not having another window broken. You can play at the club with the cricket nets Patrick.'

After a few more minutes of play Patrick gave up and went indoors leaving Stephen and me in the garden.

Stephen dragged the plastic garden table over to the jacaranda tree and then went to fetch the wooden plank, which served as a swing, and was hanging from two ropes tied to the tree's branches. Carrying the plank as he clambered up onto the table he readied himself to jump on to it and swung from the table.

As I watched Stephen pushing himself to swing higher and higher, twirling rapidly just beneath the tree's branches, I hoped Marion wouldn't catch sight of him. Stephen's propensity for trouble was legendary in the family. Out of all of us, I thought to myself, Stephen was the one most likely to rise to the challenge of boarding school.

I vividly remember overhearing Marion telling her litany of woes about Stephen to a Mexican friend, Elena, who was standing in the hallway of our house, about to get into her car and leave after having had coffee with Marion.

'So on his first flight to Mexico he managed to get himself locked into the cabin toilets and the door eventually had to be broken down to extricate him!'

Elena laughed loudly. Encouraged by this Marion carried on.

'It just never stops. Within a few days of settling into the house he'd managed to slip through the stair banisters and was found hanging from the edge by his hands. And weeks before a small wedding for a couple in the embassy was due to be performed in our garden, Stephen managed somehow to get hold of some garden clippers and cut down every single one of the Cala lilies that line the pathways. He also cut down David's beloved Morning Glory flowers...David was absolutely enraged as you can imagine.'

Elena shook her head in sympathy, her large slightly bulbous dark eyes crinkled with amusement.

'One night Stephen had sneaked downstairs from his bedroom while a noisy function was being held here in the house and I later found him fast asleep on a corner sofa. I woke him up but he was so groggy I suspect he'd been helping himself to the abandoned cocktails dotted about the room.'

Marion searched her memory for more of her son's misdoings.

'And when we drove up to California they stopped us at the border for a long time as they were very suspicious because of Stephen's dark colouring. They asked him if he belonged with us and he said 'no' and that caused no end of trouble. We then had to spend the next couple of hours trying to prove we weren't smuggling a Mexican child across the border. The number of stories he'd make up and tell anyone who would listen. He's a complete nightmare.'

Elena smiled understandingly at Marion.

'Don't worry, Marion. It's just mischief. He's young; he'll grow out of it. He's probably just exceptionally bright and very active. I had a cousin much younger than me who was just the same. He was a terror, una bestia. *¡Madre de Dios!* I still remember him having a tantrum in my parent's flat and trying to kick the bathroom door down with my aunt holding the door tightly shut on the other side. She was trying to give him time out for his shocking bad behaviour but nothing ever worked. The noise he made! What the neighbours must have thought!' Elena shuddered dramatically. 'But that crazy badly behaved boy turned into the loveliest young man. He's so good with his studies, his family and his friends. So do not despair Marion,' Elena said patting Marion's arm kindly. 'They all turn out all right in the end.'

Soon afterwards Marion found Stephen sulking and knew he'd overheard her talking about him to Elena. He was obviously hurt and upset at her criticisms and it took her a considerable amount of time to restore him to good humour. After that incident I never heard Marion speak negatively about any of her children, at least not when we were within reach of hearing.

Marion wasn't her usual sunny self in the weeks leading up to our departure from Mexico.

Subconsciously we all knew the prospect of moving to Bogota, and not seeing her children for weeks on end, filled Marion with gloom but we were all too excited about boarding school to really grasp or care about what the implications were for Marion or for my mother. A good example of how selfish children can be sometimes.

32

My mother and I moved into the apartment in Acapulco on the 6th of July 1999.

The Andersons had left Mexico City for good and were back in the UK. I was only going to stay for a couple of months in Acapulco with my mother, basically whiling away time, until Mrs Anderson came back briefly to Mexico City in late August to accompany me on the journey to Edinburgh, to start school with her children.

In the meantime my mother had been given this apartment in Acapulco at low rent and within the resort where she was going to be working as the dining manager.

The grounds of the hotel complex were beautifully groomed, but inside the actual hotel a major renovation project was underway. All the bedrooms were getting refurbished and the dining area had been completely gutted. Because time's always a consideration when the hotel is empty of paying guests, all the hotel's staff members were preparing themselves so the hotel could reopen as quickly as possible after the renovation.

My mother spent her time familiarising herself with the local supply chains and the newly appointed chefs, she was in discussions with the procurement manager regarding tableware and busy recruiting staff to work with her in the restaurant.

I was left to wander round the hotel complex, getting under the feet of all the people who were trying to get the hotel functioning again.

Bored and fed up I'd become friendly with some of the professional divers in Acapulco, men who regularly plunged 40 metres off the Quebrada cliff into a small ocean cove. I accompanied a few of the divers to the various hotel nightclubs they frequented when they weren't working, but irritatingly my mother soon put a stop to my nightclub visits because she worried, as always, I might get involved with the wrong crowd.

Drugs unfortunately still had a major impact in and around Acapulco at the time and my mother, to be fair to her, was well aware of the dangers potentially ensnaring a disaffected teenager.

Brave and courageous, those divers who risked their lives entertaining the tourists had been facing an uncertain future with the drop in tourist trade at resorts in Acapulco (this decline mostly blamed of course on high levels of local crime giving Acapulco a bad name).

However with positive government initiatives cracking down on crime, Craig and Barbara, who'd bought the hotel, were optimistic things would pick up once more and some of the old glamour would return to the holiday resorts of Acapulco.

My mother was beginning to drive me crazy with her concern about my apathy and boredom, and told me she was seriously considering sending me back to Iztupalapa to stay with my grandparents, when Fernando Diaz made a sudden appearance into our lives.

I was eating my breakfast in the apartment's kitchen when I first met Fernando. The doorbell had rung just as I was debating whether to help myself to another hot chocolate. I went to open the door still wearing my slippers and pyjama shorts, expecting it to be a delivery or the post, when to my surprise I saw a complete stranger standing outside.

I stood up a little straighter. Fernando was six feet tall and had ink black hair and thick eyebrows, as well as a pair of unusually piercing light blue eyes. His face was etched with lines making me assume automatically he was in his late forties. He carried a black folder with a strap hanging carelessly on his shoulders.

'*¿Puedo ayudarte?* (can I help you?)' I asked politely.

Fernando looked very surprised to see me answer the door, which immediately made me realise he must be looking for my mother.

'My mother's up at the hotel,' I explained.

'Oh, right. Sorry to disturb you. I'm Fernando Diaz, the interior designer working on the hotel project and I need access. I've just arrived and was told to report to her if I needed access to the hotel.'

Fernando's voice was deep and raspy like that of a man who was a heavy smoker.

I was slightly shocked. Fernando did not fit in with my idea of what an interior designer should look like. He was wearing a pair of worn and ripped jeans and a faded T-shirt. His soft brown moccasin shoes were scuffed and had paint marks on them. I was absolutely sure my mother was going to disapprove of Fernando's casual and scruffy dress code.

'If you give me a minute to get dressed I can take you to her.'

I opened the door to let Fernando into the sitting-room and disappeared to my bedroom to get changed. When I came back to the sitting-room I found Fernando looking curiously at the photos we'd hung up on the wall.

'Is this your mother?'

I nodded.

'She's very beautiful. She also looks very young,' said Fernando, looking at me appraisingly.

For some unknown reason I felt annoyed at his commenting on my mother. In a protective and churlish way I didn't feel he had any right to comment on my mother, but I said nothing.

After carefully locking up the front door I led the way to the hotel, traversing a multitude of tree lined pathways to get to there. Instead of going in through the front of the hotel I led Fernando round the side to a non-descript white door and rang the buzzer.

The door buzzed open without anyone bothering to check who was arriving and we both stepped into the dark netherworld belonging to the staff quarters of the hotel.

Fernando looked around him and smiled.

'I know many hotel owners who tend to worry less about the appearance of the staff quarters in comparison to the parts of the hotel their guests stay in, but Craig and Barbara aren't like that. They want me to work behind the stage, so to speak, as well as at the front of house.'

I shot Fernando a puzzled look, not understanding what he meant.

At the end of the passage we took a sharp turn to the right and the noise of raised voices echoed towards us.

I pushed open the double swing doors that led into the kitchen and held them open for Fernando who was following behind me. The kitchen seemed to be full of people in the middle of a big debate about something, but as soon as Fernando walked in a hush descended on everyone.

'This is Fernando, the new interior designer,' I said, breaking the awkward silence.

'Of course,' said my mother coming forward, smiling and with her hand outstretched. She greeted Fernando with a quick double kiss and turned to the group of people behind her.

'You'll have to excuse me while I show Fernando around and get him some keys. Jorje, we'll talk about this later, just carry on with the training while I'm gone.'

The bubble of silence burst as soon as we vacated the kitchen.

I'd surreptitiously followed my mother and Fernando out of the kitchen. I was intrigued to meet an interior designer for the first time and I wanted to see how he worked.

I also really hoped my mother wasn't going to make me go back into the kitchen today, to spend another day training to work as a waiter with Pico, the irritable chef, and that old and pompous headwaiter, Jorje.

My mother turned and saw me walking behind them and smiled at Fernando.

'I hope you don't mind if Raoul spends a little time watching you at work,' she said to Fernando, 'he's only here for the summer holidays and he's at a loose end unfortunately. He's very artistic so he'll be genuinely interested in your work.'

Fernando smiled back at my mother, his piercing blue eyes crinkling up with understanding. He then turned to me.

'I don't mind if you'd like to see me at work. In fact it's always useful to have someone who can help me out as an assistant, especially in the early stages of implementing design work.'

'Thank you,' my mother and I said simultaneously, relieved and genuinely grateful for Fernando's goodwill.

First we walked into the newly rebuilt dining area.

The original space had been changed from a single room into two rooms. Craig and Barbara both wanted a room separate from the dining area to be available for wedding functions. Fernando had worked on the building plans with them, trying to incorporate the improvements they desired without breaking the budget they had set for the project.

Fernando looked at the space for a little while; he then walked up to the dividing wall and placed his hand on it.

'The plaster on this is still damp. Nothing can be done until everything's fully dried out obviously.'

The floors of both rooms were stripped down to grey concrete, numerous electric wires hung down from holes in the ceiling and there were large cavities in the walls.

Fernando looked up at the coving in the ceiling and shook his head disapprovingly.

'They're going to have to redo the coving. It's not a straight finish.'

He sighed, put his black folder against the wall, pulled his phone out of his pocket and started taking pictures of certain parts of the ceiling coving.

I tried to look and see the irregularities he was talking about but I couldn't notice anything. He then went up to the windows and had a good look at the two enormous patio doors leading out into the garden.

'Right,' he said finally, turning and smiling at us as we stood patiently at the other end of the room watching him, 'let's go and see what state the bedrooms are in.'

We walked down many corridors that had been stripped of their dated wallpaper, although the old light fixtures still remained in place. Each bedroom was lying empty, stripped bare of furniture and furnishings, the walls had been finished and painted a matt brilliant white awaiting the paint order that was due to arrive at the hotel that week.

Fernando checked each and every room. Every bathroom had been retiled and refitted and Fernando checked them against the plans he had in his folder. Occasionally where the tile work was sloppy Fernando made a note in his file and took photos.

Finally we made our way to the sitting-room/library at the back of the hotel. This room was a lot darker than the other spaces in the hotel and stretched right across the back of the hotel where the hotel car park was. Fernando looked out through the windows pensively.

'They're going to build a wall right here in front of the car park and eventually it'll be covered in bougainvillea flowers. It's absolutely necessary. It's impossible to relax in a room facing a car park! They really should have put the car park round the side when they first built the hotel, but anyway it can't be helped, we just have to work with it.'

Fernando looked at his watch and then turned to my mother.

'Is there somewhere I can use as an office while I'm working here? And I'll obviously need the master key and a key to access the hotel during the day. Once the furniture and all the furnishings start arriving we're going to have to make sure the hotel is very secure. I don't want to find items of furniture or furnishings going missing.'

'The hotel's very secure,' said my mother, in a frosty voice. 'You can't access the road to it without a pass and there's a security guard at the entrance twenty-four hours. We also have CCTV in the grounds and in the hotel.'

'And who has access to the master keys?' asked Fernando, enjoying putting my mother's hackles up.

'Only the Managers and the Head Chef have master keys. David Blunt is the Hotel Manager; you must've met him before. He keeps the spare master keys in his office which is always locked when he's not there, like today.'

'Well, *we* were buzzed in that side door with no checks whatsoever,' said Fernando, provocatively.

'We can see people on the door camera screen at the front desk,' insisted my mother.

'Oh, so you saw us on the camera, did you? It looked to me as though no one was paying much attention.'

My mother flushed angrily. I remained silent. I was actually surprised to see my normally docile mother getting so wound up.

'We cannot possibly at the moment keep an eye on everyone coming and going in the hotel. You're just going to have to make sure people lock up the rooms properly after they've finished decorating. At the moment most of these rooms are empty. There's always a night watchman in place when we all leave the hotel.'

'And I assume he's been properly vetted.'

My mother didn't bother to dignify him with an answer and started to walk rapidly back to the kitchen.

Fernando and I followed behind, walking quickly to keep up with her. I turned to look briefly at Fernando and saw he was grinning to himself. He's going to be trouble, I thought to myself, a mischief-maker.

33

On a roasting Tuesday in August Fernando and I were in the hotel sitting-room, bent down in front of several large paint pots with a large sheet of white paper spread out in front of us.

Silently Fernando added a small dribble of white into a yellow paint pot and mixed it in. He then dipped his brush into the paint and painted a yellow streak onto the paper. He curled his lip at the result.

'No, still too bright. I'll have to add some more white. It's such a beautiful colour but a whole room of this will start to make people feel dizzy.'

He added a little more white from the measuring beaker and stirred it in. He then painted another streak next to the original one.

'That's more like it. Can you see the difference?' he asked me. I nodded though in actual fact I could hardly see any contrast at all between the two paint stripes.

I had been given a short lesson in colour and interior design schemes by Fernando but hadn't quite grasped the fundamentals. Triadic, tetradic, tertiary, anachromatic, complementary, split complementary, analogous, monochromatic and achromatic colour schemes, tertiary and simultaneous contrast schemes were all a foreign interior design language to me.

All I'd properly grasped was that Fernando was working on the basis of a monochromatic yellow colour scheme for the sitting-room. I liked the pastel yellow colours chosen for the sitting-room, currently too dark compared to other brighter and more welcoming areas in the hotel.

'OK, I'm happy with this one,' said Fernando, writing down in his sketchbook the quantities involved. He stood up and stretched his legs. Then he looked at me.

'Have I shown you the furniture I ordered for this room? It should arrive here by next week.'

I shook my head.

'No, I've seen the furniture in the dining room areas but nothing else.'

'Come on, let's head to the office and I'll show you the plans and the furniture on my laptop. I'll see if I can grab a coffee in the kitchen on the way.'

We headed out towards the kitchen, the sound of hammering and occasionally drilling reaching us as soon as we stepped out into the corridor.

Piles of honey coloured wood flooring planks lay stacked along the corridor with two men working on laying flooring at the far end. The walls in the corridor and the skirting were freshly painted, waiting for the flooring to be finished so they too could be fully restored to their renewed glory.

Fernando poked his head into the dining room, which had been completed last week.

According to Fernando the colour scheme in this room was loosely triadic. Fernando said he'd tried to bring the green vegetation of the outdoor space into the dining room. The patio doors and the large windows all looked out onto the lush gardens outside. The green light coming in from outside was emphasized by the bright green and royal blue hues painted in the dining room ceiling recesses.

Large black metallic chandeliers hung from the ceiling. Terracotta armchairs surrounded white circular tables and the dining walls were also painted a soft terracotta colour. Each table had yellow flowers on it, standing out brightly on each table's harsh white surface. Each wall lantern gave out a dim halo of light and brought an intimate atmosphere to the room.

Placed in each wall recess were Mexican glass vases in shades of blue and green. Fernando was a big believer in resourcing local products from Mexico. Photographs had already been taken of the dining areas for the hotel brochure and website.

The room to be used for wedding functions was also finished. A huge layered red glass and black metal chandelier hung from the centre of the room. The rest of the room was white in hue with white tables and chairs placed around a circular wooden dance floor. A massive impressionistic portrait of a newly married couple, dancing in the moonlight on their wedding day, hung at the end of the room and spaced out all along the walls smaller original paintings by the same artist were hanging.

Seeing the dining room empty Fernando wandered across to the kitchen where he found my mother sitting on a bar stool and reading her way through the food list with Gonzalo, dining manager for the evening service at the hotel.

'Can I help myself to some coffee?'

My mother raised an eyebrow.

'You have a coffee service in your office, Fernando.'

'I know but I'm craving proper coffee not the instant stuff and there's no bizcochitos.'

'Well, we're going to be running out of bizcochitos at the rate everyone here devours them. I'll bring some coffee along to you in five minutes.'

'Thank you, Esther, you're an angel,' said Fernando gratefully, reaching around her trim waist with his arm and planting a cheeky kiss on her cheek.

My mother blushed and moved away.

Fernando winked at Gonzalo who shook his head and grinned at him. I pretended not to notice.

It had taken three weeks after moving into the hotel for Fernando to finally persuade Esther to go out to dinner with him and so this Friday they were both going out together to a local restaurant.

I was unaccustomed to seeing my mother have a social life with eligible men and so had mixed feelings about her going out with Fernando. No one at the hotel who worked within the vicinity of Fernando and my mother were in any doubt about their feelings for one another, in spite of my mother's determined effort to behave professionally around all the staff at the hotel.

I liked Fernando but Fernando's cheeky, laid back attitude didn't encourage me to believe that he was in any way serious about having a proper relationship with my mother. For whatever reason I still subconsciously felt very protective of my mother, something Fernando was obviously aware of, as he never spoke about my mother to me.

Fernando and I went back out to the dining room and towards the hotel room Fernando called his office.

This room would revert back into a hotel bedroom once Fernando finished up here, but at the moment the room looked like an attic filled with discards.

Two single beds had been squashed to one side and were piled high with folders of fabric samples, paint charts and invoices. A wastepaper basket was piled high with crumpled balls of paper. Some round crumpled pieces of paper were also scattered around the wastepaper basket, obviously as a result of Fernando aiming for the wastepaper basket and missing. A solid mahogany desk was facing the window and had an impressive view out into the garden.

Fernando sat on the leather armchair at his desk and switched on his laptop.

'Here we are.' said Fernando, sifting through the various room plans he had done on Autocad, until he found the sitting-room plan.

'The idea is to have five areas where people can sit on the sofas and chill out. That's where the grand piano is going to sit,' he said pointing to it on the diagram. 'Those are the coffee tables and side tables obviously.'

He scanned down some more diagrams and clicked his mouse over one.

'Here's the electric plan for the room. That's the symbol for the plug sockets in the room, there's the symbol for the wall lights and that's the one for the drop cord lights.'

He opened another window on the laptop.

'And here's the furniture I've ordered for the room.'

I looked at the furniture ordered for the sitting-room and realised with surprise the furniture was quite modern and bold, the shapes and forms were relatively unsophisticated.

'What do you think?' asked Fernando, watching my reaction closely.

'It's not what I expected,' I said diplomatically, struggling to put my thoughts into words, 'I imagined something maybe a little more fancy?'

Fernando smiled confidently.

'No need to worry, the room will look 'fancy' once I've finished with it. The accessories will transform this room into a thing of beauty.'

'Don't you think it would be good to have a more Mexican look for the sitting-room? Wouldn't it be more suitable for tourists coming to Mexico for the first time and wanting to see things that are Mexican?'

Fernando grimaced.

'I know what you're saying, Raoul, but I think people coming to Acapulco, to a resort like this one, aren't necessarily here for the Mexican culture. If you want to see a slice of real Mexican culture Acapulco isn't the best place for that. These tourists are looking for a beach holiday, rest and relaxation. A break from their normally stressful, fast paced lives. They'll spend their time soaking up the sun on the beach or pool, using the spa, having drinks at the bar.' Fernando turned to look at me. 'I'd go insane if I had to recreate Mexican interior design in every project I work on. I'm taking the Mexican and giving it a little twist. In this case I'm going for a Polynesian feel, the atmosphere of the Pacific Islands but still using Mexican artwork and textiles.'

Fernando opened another window on his screen.

'See these are some of the objects that'll be placed in this room, these terracotta pots and lamps are Mexican, as are these cushions in different shades of yellow. Everything from the lamps to the ceiling lights is sourced from here. Here's a fantastic chandelier I've purchased for the bar area...'

Fernando panned down the files and stopped at a file labelled 'BAR'. He clicked it open and enlarged the page to show me a curious chandelier, enormous in size, made completely out of green and brown beer bottles.

A gentle kick at the door announced the arrival of the coffee and I went to open the door for my diminutive mother.

'*Gracias*, Raoul,' my mother said as she walked in carrying the coffee tray and placed it on the desk. As she stood up she looked critically around the room.

'This room looks more of a mess every day. *Eres asqueroso* (you're disgusting),' she said disapprovingly to Fernando.

To my surprise Fernando got up and started to pick up the balls of waste paper from the floor and put them in the waste paper basket. Fernando smiled at my mother once he had finished picking up the wastepaper.

'For bizcochitos I'll do anything! Thank you for the sugar fix this morning.'

My mother looked at him appraisingly.

'By the way thank you for putting up with my son today. If he bothers you just let me know, Jorje could do with a hand in the kitchen.'

'He's actually been very useful as my assistant,' Fernando said quickly to my great relief, clearly not oblivious to the anxious look I'd just given him.

'Okay, as long as you're sure. I've been told Craig and Barbara are going to be arriving in a couple of weeks to look over everything,' said my mother, obviously thinking the end of the renovation would mean the end of Fernando's stay at the hotel.

'Yes, that's right. They want to arrive once everything's in place and make sure everything's in order to open up for the snow birds in the autumn.'

'Snow birds?' I asked confused.

'Yes, that's what we call the tourists who descend on our resorts in the wintertime. They're mostly old and retired and come to escape the harsh winter climate in the north.'

'Where do you go once you finish here?' asked my mother, with a valiant attempt to look nonchalant.

'Aaahh, would you look at that Raoul? She's missing me already!'

'We certainly won't be missing the mess and the ceaseless demands for bizcochitos and coffee.'

'It's just another excuse to see you, Esther, you know that.'

My mother shook her head in disapproval and left the room quickly before Fernando made her laugh and give herself away. She could never resist responding to his cheekiness. Even now as I write this in 2015, when they've already been together for sixteen years and married for nine, Fernando still hasn't lost the ability to make my mother laugh.

34

My mother was looking at herself in the mirror.

Two days ago she'd gone into Acapulco to choose a dress and had somehow ended up buying a dress costing much more than she'd intended spending.

She blamed the sales assistant that sold it to her, she blamed herself for being so gullible and finally she blamed her unaccustomed feelings towards Fernando for making her purchase the dress. Above all, I could tell she blamed Fernando for disrupting the single-minded focus of her life and causing her to feel so unsettled.

I could see my mother was torn. She liked to be in control of the situations she found herself in and because she was unaccustomed to being in a relationship she felt extremely vulnerable.

She turned around and looked at the back of the dress.

'Mum, you look beautiful. Quit worrying so much,' I said impatiently, with the typical intolerance of a child who's never had to worry about a romantic relationship.

She was wearing a dark purple lace dress with a wide neckline and the stretchy material skimmed her curvaceous hips. It was cut just below the knee. On her neck she wore a pretty fake gold and pearl necklace and two simple pearl earrings in her ears.

On her feet she wore the heels she normally wore to work. She hadn't been able to justify the expense of a new pair of shoes for one night out, in fact I know she was afraid to think what her parents would say if they ever found out how much money had been spent on the dress.

She sighed and turned back to the mirror to touch up her lipstick.

Then she heard the doorbell ring.

As she went through to the sitting-room to open the door I followed her and sat on the sofa, still trying to adjust to the sight of my mother dolled up in her dress.

She smiled at me and opened the door.

Fernando whistled slowly when he saw her. Fernando was also dressed with unaccustomed smartness and for once had ditched his ragged jeans for a pair of smart dress trousers.

'*¡Que guapa!*'

My mother smiled at him nonchalantly, as if it was normal for her to get this dressed up.

'I just have to get my bag, I'll just be a minute.'

She disappeared back into her room for it.

Fernando waited by the front door and shot me an amused look as I crashed out on the sofa.

'I take it you're not used to seeing your mother dressed up to go out.'

'No, not really.'

'I guess it's about time she had a night out... Hopefully it'll meet with her expectations. Your mother has very high standards,' said Fernando, looking slightly nervous.

'As long as you treat her well she'll be fine,' I reassured him as my mother popped out of her room with her rather large, and bulky, leather handbag slung over her shoulder.

'Raoul, I left food for you in the fridge. You can warm it

up in the microwave. Fernando, what time will we be back?'

Fernando shrugged.

'I don't know. Around eleven maybe?'

'OK. Raoul, I have my mobile on so you can phone me at any time.'

I gave her an impatient look.

'Mum, I'll be fine. Come on, get going.'

'Right, bye my love.' She kissed me on the cheek and walked out of the door, letting me shut the door behind her.

My mother didn't get back until well after midnight.

Like an anxious parent I'd stayed up watching television, waiting until she returned home again.

By the time she'd returned she was looking considerably more dishevelled, her hair was tousled and her make up slightly smudged.

'Did you have a nice time?'

'Yes, of course, but why didn't you go to bed?'

'I just wanted to make sure you were OK.'

'I'm fine, Raoul. I'll always be fine with Fernando. He's old school, my love.'

I nodded and headed to my bedroom.

Years later my mother would reminisce about her first date with Fernando.

She remembered it in minute detail (dare I say better than Fernando, who's always been hopeless at remembering these things) and often recounted it to her friends over a raucous glass of wine.

She remembered in the evening dusk the crickets were making a racket.

Fernando reached for her hand as they walked quietly along

the path to the car park, his hands felt warm, slightly calloused and strangely comforting.

It had been such a long time since someone had last held her hand that she felt her heart sing.

Fernando stopped in front of a Chevy Malibu car and opened the door for her, an old fashioned courtesy she appreciated. She was surprised to see how clean and tidy the car was given Fernando's general sloppiness in appearance and at work.

'It's not my car,' he said, correctly anticipating her thoughts and starting up the ignition, 'but I couldn't take you out in my old Toyota Tacoma truck. I don't think you would have been impressed with the state of it inside; I always use it as my work car. I have a nice car back at home but I didn't bring it with me to Acapulco so I managed to borrow this one from a friend.'

'I wouldn't have minded using the Toyota.'

"Not minding' isn't good enough for a first date as far as I'm concerned.'

'You're fairly experienced at those I take it?'

Fernando looked amused.

'Fairly. How about yourself?'

'No, not really. My life hasn't really given me many opportunities to date.'

Fernando shook his head.

'I don't believe you. I would think you'd always have plenty of Romeos wanting to take you out.'

'I've always worked in diplomatic residences, living in, and I can tell you it doesn't do anything for your social life.'

'I see. You must've met with some very interesting people though.'

'True.'

My mother fell silent until they reached the Sirocco restaurant. Fernando had booked them a seat out in the terrace with a beautiful view of the surrounding sea.

'This is lovely, Fernando,' my mother said as she sat down at the pristine white dining table.

Fernando ordered some wine and then sat back, looking out to sea.

'I like this building a lot. It's so unusual, it reminds me of Gaudi's buildings in Barcelona. It has that crazy organic feel to it.'

'Have you been to Europe a lot?'

'Yes. I worked in Madrid for a time when I was married to my ex. We used to do a lot of travelling. Cecilia, my ex, liked to travel but I was always more of a home bird. After we split up I returned to Mexico and set up my practice.'

'Did you have kids?'

'No, thank god. That complication didn't happen. I would never have left my children if I'd ever had any. Cecilia and I both figured out pretty quickly we weren't suited. In a sense we had to get married if we were going to get serious because it was too difficult otherwise for us to be together and she wasn't keen on leaving her family in Madrid.' He fiddled with his fork. 'She would've found work here in Mexico as she was a highly qualified accountant, but I think it would've been too big a culture shock for her to leave her family and friends on a long term basis.'

'She was lucky to have the choice.'

Fernando looked at my mother with his piercing blue eyes.

'I guess you haven't had many choices.'

'Oh I'm not complaining. I've been fortunate enough to

work for employers who've appreciated me and they've appreciated the work I've done for them. So far I've managed to give Raoul a good education. As you probably know, he's going to boarding school in Britain in September.'

Fernando nodded and drank some wine.

'Who knows how it'll all work out? He's not too sure about it himself. If Raoul can't handle boarding school, I know Marion, my previous employer, will help sort something else out here so he doesn't lose his education. She knew how important it was to me.'

Fernando and Esther were quiet while the waiter refilled their glasses. Fernando thanked the waiter and they then gave their food order.

'How old's Raoul?'

'He's thirteen and a half.'

'Difficult age for him. Where's his dad?'

'His dad was an American. It was a one-night stand and I didn't even know his address. He said he came from Boston. I was out with my friends in the city when we met them, him and his group of friends. He looked like a young back packer travelling through. Who knows? Anyway the next day he clearly wasn't interested in keeping in touch and we parted.'

'Poor thing.'

'No, it was just stupidity on my part. As you can imagine having a devotedly Catholic mother didn't really prepare me for messing around with the men.' She folded the napkin, smoothing down its creases. 'Once I was old enough to go out with my friends it was just a question of time before I got into trouble. However my parents were amazing and they couldn't have shown me more support when I fell pregnant. One day

186

I'd like to be able to return the favour and support them in their old age.'

My mother reached for her wine and looked at Fernando.

'How about you? Are your parents still around?'

'Yes, I have a mother who lives with my sister in Mexico City. Not far from my house. My dad passed away a few years ago.'

'I'm sorry.'

'He led a very fulfilled life and he would always say he'd no regrets. He was one of those rare people who are always content with their lot. My mother's a more negative person and it's good my sister is living with her or she'd sink into depression pretty fast.'

'And what made you want to be an interior designer?'

'My father freaked out when he found out I wanted to study Interior Design. I'd win all the art prizes at school and he'd be disappointed I hadn't won the maths prize. He couldn't see how I could be independent and earn a living from art. It worried him greatly but he was a wonderful man and once he realised I was deadly serious he was very supportive. He paid for me to go to the IED in Madrid where I did the European Double Qualification Programme in Interior Design.'

'So you come from a wealthy family, Fernando.'

'There's different levels of wealth. We're reasonably wealthy. We were never top tier. The ones in the top tier are the ones I work for now.'

They fell into comfortable silence.

'So what made you come to Acapulco?'

'I've done work for Craig and Barbara before and they're good employers. I like them. Plus they give me a certain amount of artistic freedom and that's very satisfying. Some of the clients I work for are so difficult and fussy, Craig and Barbara meanwhile are easy and appreciative clients.'

Their food had arrived. A large paella dish was placed on the table for them to share. My mother breathed in the scent of fresh seafood and garlic.

'This smells heavenly.'

'Let's hope it lives up to expectations,' said Fernando, serving her.

Later on as they arrived back at the hotel and Fernando switched off the engine, my mother turned to thank him but Fernando bent across determinedly and kissed her lips.

She started to kiss him shyly back but before long her inhibitions were gone and she was melting into his embrace. Fernando smelt of musk and tasted of the sweet sangria they had drunk. His skin was soft and his lips were gentle.

'Come back to my office with me,' pleaded Fernando quietly after a few moments.

My mother paused.

A vision of Fernando's messy office came into her head (this still makes her laugh to this day).

'We don't have to use my office, Esther. We can use one of the other rooms.'

'And how do we explain this to the night guard?'

'Esther, I don't give a fuck what the night guard thinks. Who cares what he thinks?'

She rested her forehead against Fernando's.

'OK. But I warn you I'm out of practise.'

'Don't worry about it, Esther,' said Fernando, opening his door and getting out.

She laughed and opened her door. Fernando held it open

for her as she got up and then pressed her against the side of the car as he kissed her again.

Then he held her hand and walked to the hotel with her.

The night guard, Juan, looked surprised to see them but Fernando waved confidently at him and said, 'We're just going to the office to look for some files.'

Esther tried to hide her laughter and hurried alongside Fernando, her heels clicking loudly on the hard wood floor.

As soon as Fernando had shut the office door behind them, he looked at my mother who stood smiling at him.

'You're so beautiful. You're so wasted here, Esther.'

He went up to her and took her bag off her shoulders and placed it gently on the floor. He wrapped his arms around her and kissed her again.

His lips were more demanding this time. Before long his hands were reaching for the zip of her dress and she was pulling his shirt out from his trousers and undoing his buttons.

Much later on, once they were sated, she turned around on the bed and looked at the room.

She looked accusingly at Fernando.

'You cleared the room.'

'Why, yes of course.'

'Were you so sure of me?'

'*Bonita*, I was sure of nothing. I just hoped.'

'You're a devious predator.'

'And you're so beautiful,' replied Fernando, reaching across and pulling her to him.

'Fernando I can't stay. I have to get home.'

Fernando groaned and lay back down again.

'OK, OK.'

She took pity on him and leaned over to kiss him on the lips.

'I'll see you tomorrow,' she said sternly, jumping away from him as his arms started to reach for her.

She walked calmly across the room to collect her clothes while Fernando sat up and admired the smooth brown tones of her curvaceous figure.

She dressed quickly and popped into the bathroom to look at herself in the full-length mirror before she left the room. By the time she walked out of the bathroom Fernando had quickly put his clothes on and was waiting for her.

'I'll walk you to your flat.'

She smiled gratefully at him and they both left the office holding hands. Since then the two of them have always been the template by which I would hope to live one day.

35

At the start of September my mother and I made our way back to Mexico City from Acapulco and stayed in Iztupalapa for a few days. We were waiting for Marion who would be shortly arriving in Mexico City from Bogota.

Marion was going to accompany me to my new school in Britain.

I felt excited about the prospect of leaving Mexico. Ever since the Anderson family had left Mexico I'd felt my horizons narrow and my life had slowly begun to feel constricted and mundane.

Even the sorrowful faces of my grandparents couldn't prevent the excitement building up in me at the thought of travelling to another country and being reunited with Patrick, Hannah and Stephen.

Of course I never mentioned any of this to my grandparents. They were so cross with my mother for letting me go to Scotland they were barely talking to her. Mexicans value time spent with their families and it was hard for my grandparents to accept I would be living so far away from them for the next few years.

My mother also had her doubts about sending me at such a young and vulnerable age to a school so far away from them all, but to her credit she kept her anxieties mostly to herself.

I know she didn't see any other viable alternative to letting me go and be educated alongside the other Anderson children. She was sure I'd lose all the education I'd received with the Andersons if I returned to school in Iztupalapa.

My mother and my grandparents did their best to make sure I was organised for my trip to Scotland.

My mother had bought me a laptop, so I could keep in contact with her via Skype, and with this new laptop I'd been Skyping Patrick, Hannah and Stephen. I was feeling excited about the prospect of meeting up with them again.

'Raoul, has your mother made sure you've got enough warm clothing for the school? We've been looking at the temperatures in Edinburgh and it gets very cold for most of the year.'

I looked up from my sketchbook and smiled at my grand-mother's anxious face.

'*Tranquila*. I've everything I need. Mum and I went shopping last weekend. Mrs Anderson says we'll do the rest when we get to Edinburgh, they have good outdoor shops there.'

My grandmother nodded and shuffled back to the kitchen.

I stretched my arms out as I yawned and looked out of the window into our back yard.

A chicken was doing its best to escape from its pen, pecking away at the bottom of the wire. I remember thinking that was just how I felt, eager to escape into a new and exciting phase of my life.

My mother was very happy now too.

Her relationship with Fernando had survived his move back to Mexico City, and she was spending a few days at Fernando's house in San Angel after I departed.

I wondered if she'd be looking for work in Mexico City again in the future but at the moment my mother was being cautious in her new relationship, which pleased me. Much as I liked Fernando I didn't want my mother hurt by a failed relationship.

Ever since the realities of her precarious employment became apparent to me as a child, I've always been protective of my mother. Even now when she is happily settled and secure I still worry about her. It's a strange sort of role reversal.

The doorbell rang and I quickly looked at my watch.

That would be Pedro, an old friend from school who was stopping by to accompany me to the Tertulia Cafe where we were meeting with some other kids from my old primary school. News about my departure to Britain had spread around our small community and several kids were keen to meet up with me before I left.

I got up and walked out into our small hallway where Pedro was waiting at the front door, chatting respectfully to my grandmother.

He was dressed in impeccably ironed clothes and his jet-black hair was slicked back with gel.

For a minute I enviously wondered if Pedro's mother was still religiously ironing his clothes. My mother has always been firm as far as my household education goes, and as soon as it was safe to do so, I was expected to iron my own clothes and help with cooking the meals.

My mother has worked with too many diplomatic children who were never taught the basic household skills and she was determined I wouldn't be like them.

Pedro's face brightened when he saw me.

'Hola, Raoul. Are you ready?'

'I'm ready. Abuela, you're holding us up!' I said, gently

moving her aside so I could exit the door.

'Is that the best you could do?' she asked scornfully, looking pointedly at my worn jeans.

Living with the Anderson children I'd unfortunately adopted their casual dress code. I'd realised quite early on, when I found Patrick scuffing a pair of shiny new shoes in an effort to wear them in, it was quite normal for wealthy families to wear visibly worn clothes.

My grandmother of course profoundly disapproved of this and still wanted me to look smart.

'I don't have time to change now,' I said firmly, giving her a quick hug and disappearing quickly through the front door.

'Have you heard from Miguel?' asked Pedro, as we strolled down the dusty street.

'Not recently, but I've heard he's adjusting to life in San Paolo. His dad's still on the run apparently but he and his mum seem to be comfortable enough. He's going to a private school in San Paolo.' I searched my mind for some more snippets of information. 'He seems to have really struggled with the Portuguese language. He also told me he's making new friends but he misses Mexico. I think he'd like to come back one day.'

'Does he call you often?' asked Pedro with a jealous sideways look at me.

'No, not at all. I rarely hear from him. He only replies occasionally to my emails.'

'To be honest with you Raoul, I think you're just as bad at keeping in touch as Miguel and I'm sure when you leave Mexico you'll be even worse.'

I was quick to catch the hurt in Pedro's voice and felt bad.

It's hard when you move to a new place, with all the upheaval that's involved, to keep in touch with old friends who have no understanding of what life's now like for you.

Pedro had never moved away from Iztupalapa and had his future mapped out for him at his father's garage. Pedro would always feel the absences in his life more poignantly than me, by the very act of staying fixed in one place.

'Pedro, I'm sorry,' I said remorsefully nudging Pedro with my elbow. 'I've been pretty rubbish at keeping in touch. I promise I'll try and do better when I go to the United Kingdom.'

Pedro smiled.

'You talk about it as though it were just a trip to the beach. Rather you than me. I'd miss my family too much.'

'I'm going to miss everyone a lot but the Anderson family have become like family to me too. It's hard to explain.'

Pedro nodded amicably, even though he didn't really under-stand, and changed the subject.

He started to discuss the shocking results last year from the Cruz Azul football team, of which he was an avid supporter.

When we arrived at the Tertulia Cafe I recognised most of the faces there. Apart from the elderly regulars, who met daily for their morning coffee, there were fifteen teenagers of varying ages seated in the cafe, drinking hot chocolate and munching on chocolatin.

They greeted us affectionately and made space for us around the long table.

'So Raoul I hear you're heading off to Scotland in a few days time?' asked Ramon curiously as I sat next to him.

Ramon had left school at fourteen and was now working at a glass factory. His hands were covered in callouses from handling glassware. Ramon's factory exported Mexican glassware all over the world, glasses with confetti spotting in different colours, glasses with coloured ribbons swirling round them and glasses with brightly coloured lines running through them.

I loved the feel of heavy Mexican glass and its bright colours, colours that have always been so evocative of Mexican culture.

'Yes, I'm leaving this Thursday and start at the school next Monday.'

Ramon's dark eyes looked intensely at me.

'And you're not worried about going so far away?'

'No, why should I? It's not like I'm going to be on my own.'

'I know but the British, they're nothing like us, are they?'

I smiled to myself. It was a novel experience to see things from their point of view.

'They're not that different. They do much the same kind of things that we do. I think as a nation they show more interest in travelling and seeing the world than we do.'

'Yeah, well you know why that is,' said Ramon, rubbing his thumb and forefinger, 'they have the money. People with money can travel.'

I stirred my hot chocolate thoughtfully.

The other boys started asking me questions about my trip. None of them had been on a plane before and none of them liked the idea of being confined inside a plane for so long.

They were all friendly and encouraging in their conversation with me but it was clear none of them envied me and none of them would've chosen to go so far away from friends and family.

I felt a little alone as I talked to them.

I felt I didn't belong here in Iztupalapa anymore but I also, in a strange juxtaposition, did not feel I belonged with the Anderson family either.

I was hovering between two places and didn't feel I belonged to either one.

Before too long the conversation switched to Pedro's garage.

Pedro was a font of local gossip and was a good storyteller. A diverse cross section of the local population used his father's garage and this led to many entertaining scenarios, which he was always happy to repeat to us.

I was actually very grateful for the change in conversation because I was never comfortable being the centre of attention.

Pedro told us about a man who didn't have the money to pay for his car service and so turned up with sixteen sacks of potatoes instead as payment. Pedro had no idea if they were stolen or not.

Then there was the married woman who always gave Pedro an extortionately big tip and who brought her car to the garage on the slightest pretext.

Pedro, of course, was convinced she was attracted to him but the rest of us laughed loudly and teased him about his big ego. Once we'd started giving Pedro abuse for his taste in girls, dissecting his girlfriends past and present, I felt myself relax and enjoyed the rest of the morning at the Cafe Tertulia.

36

It's strange, but now I've been settled back here in Mexico for a number of years, my memories of my time in Scotland have become rather faded and patchy to be honest.

I remember my arrival in Edinburgh for first time very clearly. If I were to give you a summary of my time in Scotland I'd say the overall impression I had was of a country which was bitterly cold for at least six months of the year and, for my personal taste, the days were too grey during the winter.

I found I could get used to the cold but I did find the lack of sunlight during the winter difficult to live with.

However Janet Anderson, Hannah's grandmother, couldn't have been kinder or more welcoming to me.

I'll always treasure my memories of her; she's an exceptional woman.

I've mixed feelings about boarding school. A polite way of phrasing it would be to say the experience was valuable, but not particularly enjoyable. I found the kids at the boarding school were nice for the most part.

There're always exceptions in any school of course. Using David's refined vocabulary, I'd say there were quite a few pompous twits at the school but they were pretty harmless.

Now, thanks in part to my education there, I'm working

in a job I love, so I won't ever say I regretted the years I spent studying in Scotland.

By the time I was a teenager I found myself spending a lot of my spare time thinking about Hannah, but actually I saw less of Hannah at boarding school than I had expected to.

This was a big disappointment for me, although I suspect not for her (if she ever thought about me at all that is). For many years she seemed to be entirely oblivious to my presence at school and the only times we managed to interact together was at Janet's home, on the weekends all of us left boarding school to stay with her.

At twenty past nine on a bright Friday morning on the 3rd September 1999 Marion and I came through security to the arrivals area of Edinburgh airport.

Waiting for us in arrivals were David, Patrick, Hannah and Stephen. Stephen launched himself onto me in glee as soon as I appeared through the sliding door. After greeting each other we turned as one and walked towards the exit and the car park.

As soon as we were outside I felt the change in temperature hit me.

Even though it was late summer a cold wind was blowing and made me realise I was very inadequately dressed for the weather. I thought longingly of the thick parka coat I had in my big suitcase.

Stephen to my surprise was dressed in a pair of shorts and a jumper, and seemed oblivious to the chilly breeze gusting at us as we walked into the car park.

Once we were in the car, and driving into Edinburgh, I remember stealing glances out of the car window as the city raced past.

I was surprised at how much vegetation there was and how green the city was.

The trees still had their summer leaves. This city seemed to be heavily populated by trees.

Traffic here was more sedate and ordered compared to the chaotic and dangerous driving of Mexico's cities.

Eventually the large rental car stopped in front of a large and imposing grey brick house at Inverleith Place, with a tall magnolia tree outside of it. The decaying pink white blossoms of the magnolia tree stood out against the deep dark green of the waxy leaves.

'Well Raoul, here we are finally. This is my mother's house. Hopefully she'll have done some of her fabulous home baking for us. She's a sprightly little lady who has more energy than I have and she's an excellent cook. In fact I think she could've even been a chef if she'd wanted to.'

'Marion, take the kids in and I'll bring in the luggage,' David said impatiently.

Marion turned and led us through the front garden to a rose pink painted door. Marion turned and smiled at me.

'My mother's a bit of an eccentric,' she said, adding as she saw me looking puzzled, 'she's unconventional, people think she's a little strange.'

She sighed a little wistfully.

'She drives David a little nuts.'

She pointed to the rose pink door.

'No one else has a pink door in this area I guarantee you,' she whispered to me as she pressed the bell.

We could hear the wooden door unlocking and then it opened revealing a tiny birdlike lady with thin fluffy white hair curled around her head.

She was dressed smartly in a royal blue suit with a circular gold and seed pearl brooch pinned to its lapel. I thought she looked very conservative, not in the least bit odd or eccentric.

'Marion,' this little lady said, giving her daughter a hug and then turning to me.

'You must be Raoul,' she said, giving me a quick hug, 'so pleased to meet you, come in, you must be so tired after such a long trip.'

'Thank you very much,' I said politely.

'He speaks English so well,' said the little lady in surprise, looking intently into my face.

'Yes, we told you that mother,' Marion said testily, 'Raoul, this is my mother Janet. Do go in, we need to have a strong cup of tea to revive us.'

I walked into a spacious hall and followed Janet into the kitchen at the back of the house.

The house smelt musty and slightly damp but as soon as I walked into the kitchen a wonderful aroma of apple and cinnamon invaded my nostrils.

'I've just made some apple scones for afternoon tea,' said Janet, busily laying out some paper napkins onto the large pine table in the kitchen.

'Raoul, just to warn you, my mother plays table tennis on this table and she'll probably want to try you out at some point during our stay,' said Marion smiling. She went over and gave her mother a big hug. 'It's good to see you mum.'

Janet moved a chair out for her daughter.

'Come on Marion, take a seat and let me get you a cup of tea.' Marion sank into the chair and I followed her example.

Patrick, Hannah and Stephen all helped themselves to scones and sat down.

A few moments later David came in and his eyes brightened at the sight of the scones.

'This looks delicious, Janet, thank you.'

I accepted a plate with a scone from Hannah and drank some tea. Living with the Andersons I had of course drunk tea with them many times but I'd never really grown to like it, or become accustomed to it.

I caught Janet looking at me.

'Would you rather have something else to drink Raoul?' she asked.

'No, this tea is fine thank you,' I said politely, surprised at how she seemed to read my mind.

I took a bite of the scone and loved the sweet flavour of apple and cinnamon that melted into my mouth. I decided I could get used to Janet's cooking.

The others were listening as Marion told them about our trip and David kindly asked after my grandparents and my mother. When I'd finished talking Hannah offered to show me around the house and garden.

Hannah looked much the same as when I'd last seen her. Today she was wearing a warm cobalt blue jumper that complimented her pale blue eyes. She seemed more self-assured than I remembered. She was obviously enjoying staying with her grandmother and felt at home in Edinburgh.

I suddenly felt tired.

I was beginning to feel the six-hour time difference between Mexico City and Edinburgh. I hadn't slept much during the flight and although we'd arrived in the morning at Edinburgh airport, in Mexico it was still the middle of the night.

Janet's house was very spacious and the attic had been converted to create another large guest room with an en suite. It was clear Janet still kept this large cumbersome house so her family could use it to stay when they needed to.

Hannah showed me around the house and then took me to the room I'd be sharing with Patrick and Stephen on the first floor.

This room was large and rather sparse with bare cream walls and three beds laid out at intervals across the far wall. I looked out of the window of our room and saw a large garden with neat flowerbeds. Hannah stood next to me as I looked out at the garden with interest.

'I'm afraid since Stephen has been banned from playing football in granny's garden he's not shown much interest in going out into the garden. He usually rushes across to Inverleith Park to kick the football and annoy all the dog walkers that go there in the mornings. He'll probably try and persuade you to join him.'

'That would be cool. We're starting school on Monday though, aren't we?'

'Yes, we start school on Monday. Mum and Dad are going to hang on here for a few days to make sure we get settled in and then they'll head off back to Colombia. It's going to be a bit weird once they're gone but granny's great and she'll have us out at weekends, which is more than a lot of diplomatic kids get when they go to boarding school. How are you feeling about starting boarding school?'

I shrugged. I was suddenly conscious of Hannah looking at me in that intense way of hers.

'I don't know how I feel. I've never stayed in a boarding school,' I said, 'I'm sure it'll be fine.'

'I'm not sure I'm going to like it. It's hard starting all over again and most of the girls have been there already for at least a year so they'll all know each other. But I guess there's no point worrying about it.'

Hannah turned around and looked at the messy room where Stephen and Patrick had scattered their belongings around their suitcases on the floor.

'Those two are going to have to learn to be tidier; they're not going to put up with this mess at Ellerslie School.'

Marion came into the room. She was beginning to look exhausted too. She was carrying her small suitcase.

'Raoul, if you want to catch up on some sleep feel free to. David's taking the others out to the cinema so the house will be quiet. Or you're welcome to go with them to the cinema. Most people I know like to stick it out until its evening to catch up on jet lag, but I like to catch a nap when I can. Feel free to do the same if you want.'

'I think I'll stay and try and catch up on some sleep, thanks Marion,' I said politely, sitting on my bed.

Hannah and Marion disappeared out of the room and I collapsed with relief onto the soft pillows, stretching out my legs. I had a throbbing headache but shutting my eyes seemed to make it feel worse so I opened them again and looked out for a few minutes at the branches of a beech tree waving outside my window.

I swung my legs off the bed and went downstairs where I found Janet clearing up in the kitchen.

'Excuse me Janet, do you have any paracetamol? I have a headache.'

'Oh you poor thing. Of course I do. If you just follow me.'

Janet scooted out of the kitchen and up the stairs to a room at the front of the house.

It had a wonderful view across Inverleith Park to Edinburgh Castle. The furnishings in the room looked at least thirty years old, the carpet was a combination of mustard yellow and ochre green in a dated pattern. The curtains were plain ochre green and the bedspread had a yellow floral pattern. The wallpaper was a dark green stripe.

'This room could look so much nicer,' I thought as I took in the high ceiling and the views from the window.

Meanwhile Janet was rummaging in her bedside table drawer for the paracetamol. The beside table looked like it was about to collapse, it wobbled and shook as Janet pulled out bits of paper out of the drawer to find the tablets.

'No, don't have any here. Let me see. I probably have some in the bathroom, come with me Raoul.'

She trotted off to the bathroom.

The bathroom felt freezing cold to me, it was a north-facing bathroom and had an old lino on the floor.

Janet opened a bathroom cabinet and brought out the Paracetamol triumphantly.

'Here we go at last, Raoul. I think they're in date. Can you just check for me? I don't have my glasses and I can't see.'

She handed the packet to me and I read out the sell by date. They were well within date.

Janet beamed.

'Great. Let's get you a glass of water and then you can go and rest. It's such a long way from Mexico. David and Marion are used to it but long distance travel isn't for everyone. I've only been to Madeira three times in my whole life and every other holiday I've been on has been here in Britain, mostly in Cambridge where my family were from. I still have two sisters who live there.'

Janet got me a glass of water and after I had swallowed the tablets and thanked her, I crashed on my bed with a book by Isabel Allende that my mother had bought for me before I left.

Isabel Allende's book ' *Mi pais inventado*' was a nostalgic look at the author's early life in Chile. My mother had dedicated it to me with an inscription '*nunca olvides de donde vienes*' (never forget where you came from).

It was such a relief to read in Spanish. I hadn't realised what it would be like to be constantly surrounded by the English language.

Even in the Anderson's residence in Mexico, Aida the cook and my mother had always addressed me in Spanish, as had Antonio the driver. I also used to listen to Spanish on the television and the radio.

I decided once I'd got my laptop up and running I'd start listening to some Spanish radio stations. After a few minutes of reading I fell fast asleep and only woke up when they came to get me for lunch.

37

Just as my arrival in Edinburgh stands out in my mind, so does my memory of those early days at boarding school.

First impressions make things vivid and easy to remember I suppose and I remember very clearly the day we first arrived at Ellerslie School.

The school wasn't based in Edinburgh; it was located on the outskirts, in East Lothian.

Just past the village of Gullane in East Lothian, a road turns to the right and winds its way through fields of pale wheat and bright yellow flowering Rapeseed.

This farmland eventually gives way to a healthy looking grassy expanse where the occasional well-kept horse grazes peacefully. The green land round about is dotted with patches of woodland and the road eventually leads to an old sandstone gateway where a big sign indicates you're approaching Ellerslie School.

Ellerslie School resides in a large red sandstone manor house built in the 1800's for a prosperous sheep farmer. Over the years many additional extensions and buildings have been added to the original building.

David was never sure whether the local council was bribed at the time and turned a blind eye to the additions, or whether the additional building work actually received proper planning permission, because none of it was in keeping with the original building.

Some of the buildings built on the grounds were of questionable taste and looked as though they had been constructed with the extreme principles of economy in mind.

Thankfully a school inspection in the seventies had declared two of the buildings as unfit for purpose and the school had raised sufficient funds to replace the buildings with an indoor swimming pool and a library very much in keeping with the old manor house.

However, as far as I could tell, the old alumnae of the school, like David, had nostalgic and fond memories of the disparate and quirky character of the now demolished school buildings.

At a quarter to eight on Monday morning, the 6th of September, the Andersons and myself made our way up the driveway to Ellerslie School. This first morning at school the sky was grey and the rain was falling in a misty drizzle.

All of us were wearing our school uniform; a hideous combination of claret blazers and navy stripe ties.

The driveway was busy with cars entering, and exiting the school after dropping off their children, so we crawled slowly at a sloth's pace towards the busy car park.

I remember looking out of the windows at the soggy landscape and feeling a tight rigid knot form at the pit of my stomach.

I was thinking of all the other school kids I didn't know and this was making me feel apprehensive, but I could see I was not alone feeling this way.

Hannah was looking decidedly miserable next to me. Her freckled face looked pale and there were dark shadows under her eyes so she'd clearly not slept well last night.

When we eventually parked the car David got out quickly and stretched his legs. He looked around with interest.

'Here we are! My goodness it's been a long time.'

He then opened the boot and started to pull out the suitcases.

'I think we'd better get a move on,' said Marion anxiously looking at her watch. 'It's not long to go before they have to be at assembly.'

'Don't panic, Marion. There's still more people arriving and they won't start until they have everyone registered.'

Inside the entrance hallway there were maps of the school building and a room plan so pupils could see which room they had to make their way to. Several teachers with badges on were helping to organise the chaotic mass of pupils and parents.

Pupils familiar with the school registered quickly with their form teacher and dispersed swiftly to their new rooms.

Families new to the school tended to stay in the hallway to question the teachers.

David and Marion's inherent politeness meant they were among the last ones to get a chance to speak to the teachers, as there seemed to be many other more pushy parents who were quick to monopolise them.

One of the teachers eventually looked up and recognised David from when he'd been a pupil at the school, and came forward to greet him.

'Why hello David! It's such a pleasure to see you! What've you been up to these last few years?'

We left David talking to the teacher while Marion impatiently pointed out the way to the boys' dorms to us, and hurried off with Hannah to the girl's boarding house.

David caught up with us shortly afterwards.

In keeping with the building's expansion some of the rooms were newly built and modern with a fully functioning heating system, whereas most of the original rooms still had the worn old wooden floors, rattling windows and an antiquated heating system.

I, of course, would have preferred to be sleeping in one of the newer rooms, carpeted and cosy they actually looked enticing, but I ended up in a large open dorm on the top floor of the manor house.

At least I had a bed by the window so I had a view outside and Stephen was in the room with me.

Patrick wasn't far away; he was only slightly further along the hallway but in a smaller room. The school tended to put the older boys together and in smaller dorms, especially those who were close to their National exams.

Our dorm had seven beds and some of the other boys had already made themselves at home.

Already there were several magazine pages or posters blue tacked to the walls by the boys; some were of football teams or stars, others of provocative looking models or singers. Duvets were already made up and piles of clothing hung untidily from all the beds and chest of drawers. David did his best to help us unpack our stuff, mainly just emptying a bag on to the bed and then trying ineffectively to divide clothes up into separate piles, leaving us to put it away.

Marion appeared a short time later to help us make up our beds. I'd never used a duvet before, as in Mexico we'd only used sheets and blankets, so Marion did her best to explain to me how to put a duvet cover on without getting in a muddle.

By the time we were more or less organised, it was time for David and Marion to leave and the school bell rang to alert all the school children to go to the main assembly hall for the school's welcome assembly with the headmaster.

The bell sounded like a strident fire alarm and I didn't like the thought of having it go off several times a day. The school seemed to follow well-accustomed routines.

I don't know of any boarding schools in Mexico, although I suppose there must be some.

However I'm pretty sure British boarding schools are uniquely traditional. It really is like stepping back into a time warp.

Before leaving the dorm Marion went over to my bed and put a small package into my chest of drawers.

'That's your birthday present from David and me, Raoul, as we won't be here to give it to you. Janet's going to do a proper birthday celebration on your birthday weekend at her house. Unfortunately we won't be able to be there for that either, but we'll be able to speak to you on the day from Colombia.'

I was touched Marion had remembered my birthday. My mother had already given me a wrapped parcel from her before I left Mexico.

'Any problems at all Raoul please let us know, we're far away physically but it'll be very easy to contact us via email or Skype, OK?'

Marion gave me a tight quick hug that did nothing to disguise her anxious feelings. I know she was worried I wouldn't cope with the school and would find it hard to fit in with the other school children.

She looked at me smiling tremulously.

211

We were all uncomfortably dressed in school uniform and I'm sure we already looked a little institutionalised.

She turned round to look for Stephen.

She was less worried about him than me.

He was standing comfortably at ease next to another boy's bed, deep in discussion about the Manchester City players on the poster this boy had pinned to the wall.

Stephen's always had the ability to make himself at home anywhere.

We all went downstairs, joining a stream of people heading down to the main entrance again.

Once at the entrance, David and Marion said their good-byes to all of us and left quickly rather than prolonging their departure.

Hannah had come down into the hallway earlier with a couple of roommates who had clearly made an effort to befriend her. The girls went through to the assembly hall together, leaving Patrick, Stephen and me to follow behind them.

Hannah told me the next day she'd caught sight of her mother crying as she left the school. The last snapshot she had of her parents was of her mother crying and David grim faced, patting Marion's leg consolingly as he drove out of the school gates.

We were all aware that Marion at times felt incredibly angry at the sacrifices David's job demanded of them as a family, and how she resented that as a family unit the rest of them had to pay the price for David's career choices.

I do think diplomatic kids have a messy family life. Marion knew as a mother she'd be missing her children's birthdays and she'd miss seeing them grow up.

Even when her children came out to stay with them in Colombia, it still wouldn't be quality time together because David and her would still have their diplomatic work and commitments to go to.

38

One thing I've never understood about boarding school is how some children seem to manage on next to no sleep.

Stephen was a prime example of this. Despite the fact he was so much younger than me, he seemed to function perfectly well on next to no sleep.

Within a few weeks of staying at the boarding school I was struggling with my lack of sleep. It wasn't just Stephen, others in the dorm liked to talk until close on midnight every night and it was like a rite of passage to see who could stay up the longest. Stephen won on that front by a mile. And I wasn't the only one who struggled with lack of sleep.

I remember a friend called Mark falling asleep during a maths lesson, his head actually on the desk, and I know some of the older kids used to resort to buying earplugs so they could get enough sleep to see them through their exams.

'Raoul, wake up!'

I groaned as Stephen tugged at me.

Stephen, who never seemed to need much sleep, was keen to go and explore the school after the lights were out.

'No!'

'Come on, Raoul. Everyone else is asleep now.'

'I know!'

'Raoul, come on. Wake up.'

I rolled over and looked at Stephen.

'I'm not going to go exploring tonight, Stephen. The last time wasn't fun. We got caught and had to do detention in the hall for three hours. I like my sleep so you can count me out tonight.'

'Oh, OK. I'm just bored. I keep trying to get to sleep but can't.'

'Why don't you read your kindle?'

'I need some new books. I've read every book on my kindle at least twice. Hey, did you hear about Dorm 4?'

'No.'

'They had a pile of food and sweets and had a midnight feast on Thursday night, downstairs in the bathrooms. Mrs Petrie caught them and she confiscated *all* their food. Apparently she's going to let them have it all back at the end of term.'

I didn't answer as I was beginning to doze off again.

Stephen shook me again.

'Raoul, are you listening to me?'

I nodded with my eyes shut.

'Can I borrow your torch?'

I opened my eyes to look at Stephen.

Unlike some of the boys in the school I didn't have many gadgets and I was protective of the things I owned.

'Why do you want my torch?'

'So I can read my library book under the duvet.'

I sighed and heaved my legs out of the bed.

I searched in my chest of drawers as quietly as I could and felt my fingers close around the plastic handle of the torch.

'Here you go, Stephen, but I want it back in the morning before you go off to breakfast.'

'Sure.'

Stephen went back to his bed.

The following morning the dorm bell rang like a fire drill through my skull, far too early for my liking.

As I've said before I was no fan of the cold weather in Scotland.

Several of the kids would talk every spring term about their skiing trips and for once I would feel no pang of envy. I yearned for the heat of the sun but more than that I missed the light.

Winter days in Scotland meant dark mornings and dark evenings. There were many grey overcast days where it was easy to forget how powerful and strong the sun could be.

Looking at grey sky made me feel very depressed and, whenever I travelled back into Edinburgh to stay with Janet, I felt the sombre grey- black stone buildings in Edinburgh aptly reflected the Scottish weather.

That first year in Scotland I thought enviously of Patrick who was in the New Wing and had a cosy room.

I'd never felt as cold before.

'Hurray, Raoul! It's snowing again', Stephen said excitedly one day in the middle of January, 'Look outside!'

I looked out of the window and saw a curtain of white snow raining down on the school grounds.

Somehow it was strangely peaceful.

I'd seen snow before on Popocatypetal, the volcano near Mexico City, but I'd never seen it falling like this.

It was Saturday and we were all staying at school for the weekend as Janet was away visiting relatives in Cambridge.

'Come on, Raoul get your boots on. Let's get outside!'

'Stephen, aren't we going to the hub for afternoon television?'

'We can do that later. Come on, it'll be fun to be out there with the snow.'

'Oh, OK.'

I went and grabbed my boots from the shoe cupboard.

The cold always made me feel loath to move quickly which was ironic given that if I kept moving I'd soon keep warm.

Stephen waited for me impatiently and rushed off ahead of me to the side entrance of the boarding house.

I pushed the door open again as it had slammed back after the fast retreating figure of Stephen.

I gasped as the wet flakes hit my face and lifted my scarf to cover my face.

I looked around to see where Stephen had gone. I didn't have to wait long as a snowball whirled out of the snowy whiteness and hit me on the shoulder.

'Ha, got you!' yelled Stephen.

Stephen rushed off as soon as he saw the look of vengeance in my eyes.

It wasn't easy to see Stephen however, as the ground around the main school building was full of children slinging snowballs and trying to avoid hitting two of the house teachers who were keeping an eye on things.

I spotted Hannah's long blonde hair and bright pink woolly hat and after hitting Stephen in the face with a well-aimed snowball I made my way across to her.

'Hannah!'

'Hello Raoul. How are you?' Hannah asked distractedly as her eyes searched the playground.

She spotted her friend Jennifer coming towards her with a snowball and hid behind me. Within minutes Jennifer was chasing Hannah from behind me, clearly not wanting to use me as a substitute for Hannah.

The snowball hit Hannah on the back of the head.

'Aarrgh! Jen I'm going to get you back for that one. Just you wait!' laughed Hannah, breathlessly building up a snowball before racing after Jennifer.

I sighed.

I didn't get many opportunities to chat to Hannah these days. She was always with other girls. I missed chatting to her but clearly she didn't seem to feel the same way.

A hard snowball hit the side of my head before I'd too much time to think about it and become morose.

My skin burned where the snowball had hit it and as I turned quickly I saw Patrick's stocky figure and black hat disappearing around the corner of the building.

'Patrick, *cabeza de mierda*, you'd better watch out,' I yelled, and I remember I then blushed as I caught sight of Mr Allan, the maths teacher, glaring at me in disapproval.

'Raoul, I hope you weren't swearing. Watch your language or you'll end up in detention this afternoon.'

'Yes sir. Sorry sir.'

I walked away quickly, skirting the corner of the building where Patrick had been.

I knew the last thing Mr Allan would want to do is to sit out detention with me on a Saturday afternoon but I didn't want to take any chances.

I started running towards a group of children who were busy throwing a hailstorm of snowballs at each other. They were all covered in a dusting of white snow on their hats, jackets and trousers.

'Stephen, have you seen your brother anywhere?'

'Patrick? No.' said Stephen absently, busily trying to aim his snowball at one of the others.

I turned and caught Patrick grinning at me from the other side of the playground.

I ran towards him and threw my snowball. The snowball curved up in the air and hit Patrick gently on the leg. Patrick looked at me with total disdain.

'Is that seriously the best you can do Raoul? Seriously? After all the cricket practise we did in Mexico? That's pathetic. Go on have another go.'

I stared at him for a minute and then bent down to make another snowball.

This one managed to hit Patrick squarely in the face.

'That's better. Give it another few months' practise and you might get quite good at this, you Mexican moron.'

My gloves were soaked through by now and I was feeling the painful chill work its way up my fingers.

'I'm going back in, Patrick. See you later.'

'See you later, Raoul. By the way, did you get into trouble with Mr Allan?'

'No. It was a close thing though.'

'You'd better watch your language or you'll be giving us Andersons a bad name.'

'Patrick, stop being such a *cojones*.'

Patrick shook his head in mock disapproval at me as he disappeared back into the school playground.

At this point I saw Hannah standing in the hallway and walked up to her.

'Hi Hannah. What are you doing here?'

'I'm waiting for Susie. She wanted to work on her tapestry rug at the barn this afternoon and I want to finish my quilted cushion. Mrs McLeane said she'd be there this afternoon if any of us wanted to put some work in on our projects. How about you Raoul, have you given up playing in the snow?'

'Yes. It's getting too cold for me. Can I join you in the barn and see what you're working on?'

'Of course. You should join our Thursday activity class if you're interested. Mrs McLeane says she wants more boys to give it a go.'

'Sounds good. Maybe next term I'll sign up for the class.'

'You might get teased for it as you'll be the only boy in the class but it's a good club to do and Mrs McLeane's lovely.'

I shrugged.

'If the club's interesting and fun I wouldn't care what people said about me.'

Hannah looked at me with reluctant admiration.

'You don't care if they tease you, do you? I heard you got a bit of stick at the start of term.'

'If you ignore them, they get bored and go for someone else. They only want to get a reaction. That's one thing I learnt in Mexico.'

'Did they laugh at you there as well?'

'They did more than that but I had a good friend who stood up for me. It's better not to care about what people say about you otherwise you're never really free, although when it gets physical that's not so great.'

'I'd *hate* it if I got picked on. I hate it when I hear other people getting teased too. It's horrible.'

I grinned at her.

'At least it hasn't happened to you.'

'No, it hasn't but that doesn't mean it'll never happen to me.'

'If it does you can let me know and I'll sort them out.'

Hannah laughed, and then laughed some more at my affronted face.

'Don't be offended, Raoul. I wouldn't tell you. You'll get a bad reputation as the Mexican hard boy if you start 'sorting' people out. You know what most people think of Mexicans nowadays. The last thing you want is for them to see you like that.'

'See me like what?'

'You know...'

I was offended but decided not to say anything to her in case I'd later regret it.

'Raoul, I've upset you. I'm so sorry,' said Hannah, putting her hand on my arm, 'you know I love you to bits. I just don't want to give people an excuse to think badly of you, which nobody does by the way,' she added hastily, clearly feeling she was digging herself into an even bigger hole.

I shrugged.

I didn't see how Hannah could make a comment like that having lived with and known Mexicans like my mother and I.

I knew I was a bit of a novelty in this school. I was probably the first Mexican to set foot in it. Yet every unkind comment that separated me from the others made me feel less and less a part of the school community and more of an outsider.

'Sorry, Raoul. I need to think things through more before I open my mouth. Do you forgive me?' Hannah pleaded with me, grabbing my sleeve and shaking it.

Realising I had momentarily mentally detached myself from our conversation I smiled at her, letting my thoughts return back to the present.

Hannah would never understand the depth of my feelings for her and I doubted my feelings for her would ever change.

Hannah's friend Susie turned up, looking less than pleased to see me standing next to Hannah. She scowled when Hannah told her I was coming with them to the barn.

Susie was a tall, slim blonde who was, in my silent opinion, far too big headed. If the school rumours were correct she was the spoilt only child of a self made couple, apparently her parents had started up a taxi business from scratch in Glasgow.

Rumour also had it her mother was a Quaker but school gossip was never the best at producing accurate information.

In the end Susie said nothing against my joining them and so the three of us walked across to the old converted barn.

The barn's lit windows held the promise of warmth and maybe, if we were lucky, some of Mrs McLeane's hot chocolate.

39

I remember it was halfway through the summer term in 2002 when I finally had the courage to ask Hannah out on a date.

It was the 8th of June and at last I was starting to feel the warmth of the sun again. Maybe the balmy summer weather was filling me with unaccustomed optimism.

April this year had been particularly cold. I would've never have believed it could possibly snow in April, but I'd been proved wrong when the sleet came down in the middle of my athletics games session.

The weather in Scotland seemed to jump along a varying scale of ten degrees so I found myself frequently checking the weather forecast but summer had arrived at last.

The 8th of June that year was a quiet weekend at the school, with only a few kids staying on at school.

I'd just finished my physics homework up at the old timber and brick library and was walking back to my dorm when I spotted Hannah sitting on the red stone tiled patio, in the sunshine, at the east side of the girls' boarding house.

I went and sat down in the shadow of a tree opposite her.

I opened up my physics prep book, but it was really only a pretext. I was hoping she'd see me and call me over.

Hannah was wrestling with a cream coloured silk object in

her hands, occasionally picking up a needle and thread to sew pieces on to it.

She was wearing a long blue skirt that I was sure I'd seen Marion wear before, and the skirt's crochet trim finish curled around her slim ankles in an enticing way.

She also had on a white summer vest, almost as white as her skin. Remembering the many occasions in Mexico when the Anderson children would have to lather on after-sun on their sensitive skin after a day in the Mexican sun, I wondered if she'd bothered with sun-cream. If she hadn't she might regret it because even I could feel my skin burning in the sun here, so unaccustomed to the sun was my skin after the long winter.

After twenty minutes of fidgeting with my physics prep book she still hadn't noticed me so I decided to get up and speak to her.

She was so absorbed in her project she didn't notice me until I'd walked right up to her.

She then looked up and smiled at me, squinting in the bright sunshine.

'Hi Raoul! Isn't it such a gorgeous day?'

'Yes, it is. What are you working on?'

'This is part of my art project but it's driving me crazy. It's supposed to be a hat but the metal wire inside of it isn't doing what it should.'

'Let's see.'

She lifted up the hat to show me. If it was a hat it was a very misshapen one.

I sat down next to her and grinned.

'It could look better.'

Hannah punched my shoulder.

'Don't say that. I've spent hours on it. I mean *hours*. I'm not doing it again.'

'Why don't you let me shape it for you?'

'Since when do you know anything about hats, Raoul?'

'It's up to you. But I could try and shape it a little better.'

'Oh all right. It could hardly look worse than it already does.' She handed over the hat.

I took it gingerly in my hands and looked at it.

'Could you open a seam?'

'Sure.'

Hannah picked up her scissors and cut through the stitching keeping the hat together. She then handed the misshapen hat to me and I carefully extricated the metal wiring from it and picked up the pliers to mould its shape.

Hannah watched with interest as I worked the wire into a circular shape and measured it against the cream coloured cloth.

After fifteen minutes I put the wire carefully back into the cream coloured cloth and passed it over to Hannah to sew up again.

Admittedly it did look marginally better but I hoped this hat wasn't the centrepiece of her art project.

Hannah sewed up the edges with careful stitches and then put the hat aside.

Both of us leant back to take full advantage of the sun. A warm breeze had started up and I could feel its gentle caress on my face.

Turning to Hannah I decided to take the plunge and let her know how I felt about her.

'Hannah?'

'Yeah?'

I paused for a second.

'What Raoul?' demanded Hannah impatiently, turning towards me when I didn't answer.

'I wondered if you'd like to go on a date with me sometime?'

Hannah looked completely taken aback.

'You mean as boyfriend and girlfriend?'

'Yes, of course.'

To my horror Hannah's blank expression turned into one of deep distress. Tears started to trickle down her cheeks. She quickly turned away from me and wiped furiously at her eyes.

I reached out to touch her gently on the arm. Hannah didn't respond.

'Hannah? I'm sorry I didn't mean to upset you. I just wanted you to know how I felt.'

Hannah turned around to face me.

'But Raoul you're like a brother to me. Why do you have to go and spoil everything? We're family, we always have been. I've never seen you as anything else.'

'Hannah, please don't take any offense to this but we're really not family. In fact our backgrounds couldn't be any more different.'

Tears were falling down Hannah's cheeks again.

'How can you say that? My parents have always behaved towards you as they would to any of us. They've always tried hard to make sure you felt you were a part of our family. This is going to spoil everything, everything that we've done together the last five years.'

I felt myself quickly losing a grip on my temper.

'With respect Hannah you can't bury your head in the sand forever. We're all growing up into adults. Your family have treated me as one of you but I'm never going to forget or lose sight of my real family or of my country. This is all a part of you' I said, waving my arm around, 'but it's not a part of me or of my background.'

Hannah grabbed her things and stood up.

'I'm not going to stay here and listen to you tell me that everything my parents did for you means nothing to you. After all they've done for you. We've always seen you as a part of our family. Now I can see that it didn't really mean anything to you. All I can say is I'm sorry if that's the way you feel about us.'

By this point I felt my blood boiling with rage.

'So I have to feel a debt of gratitude to your family for the rest of my life? It's all stored up isn't it? Every little thing is measured. And on top of everything else I'm not allowed to be honest about my feelings for you, because I've to be a brother to you and nothing else.'

Hannah looked at me for a long moment, and then got up, turned and walked away back to the boarding house, no doubt to find somewhere to cry undisturbed.

I stood up, still feeling angry.

I bent down to pick up my prep book and walked slowly back towards my dorm.

I decided on the way I'd change my clothes and go for a run to work off my anger. I used to do the same when I was younger with the garden at our home in Chapultepec.

Whenever I felt angry and isolated, which wasn't often, the school felt like a prison to me. I'd discovered that a run around the adjoining meadow often helped work off my excess emotion.

Sometimes, if I felt very claustrophobic at the school, I'd sneak out of the boarding house in the evenings and walk to this same meadow. I'd lean against the old wooden fence posts and watch the bobbing, white tails of the rabbits flash in the dusk as they munched quietly at the grass. Watching the rabbits nibble at the grass made me feel at peace because life seemed so simple and easy for them, life for them seemed to consist of eat, sleep and procreate, and of course when necessary hide from predators.

I'm sure their courtships were more successful too.

In the following weeks Hannah and I barely spoke to each other. Weekends at Janet's house were awkward but nobody said anything, although it was clear everyone had noticed how the dynamic had changed between us.

Janet would look at Hannah pensively and sigh. She told me she'd no idea how long this would take to resolve itself but she hoped it would do so soon.

I moved on.

Men are good at compartmentalising their emotions. I shelved my feelings for Hannah and started to look around at some of the other girls I found attractive.

Susie, for example, had begun to show considerable interest in me. Still feeling bruised from Hannah's painful rejection of me I began to welcome Susie's eagerness to spend time with me.

It didn't take long before the two of us were an item and were sharing deliciously illicit kisses in the small bit of woodland behind the school library.

I would've never admitted to myself that Susie's kisses were all the sweeter because Susie was a friend of Hannah's.

But looking back to those days now, I can truthfully say I hoped my relationship with Susie would hurt Hannah. At least as much as Hannah had hurt me with her rejection of me.

My relationship with Susie had the desired effect.

Hannah was never any good at hiding her feelings, and she was obviously feeling indignant at how quickly I'd recovered from our argument and found someone else to replace her in my affections. I could see she didn't get any pleasure from watching my groomed and gelled black head bend down attentively to listen to something Susie would be telling me.

I remember with clarity the frequent moments when I caught Hannah's pale blue eyes watching me from afar, when she thought I wasn't looking. I would then give Hannah an artificial smile and pretend to forget about her again when she looked away.

In the end she clearly decided her best response was to be dignified, and to ignore the pair of us.

It makes me smile a lot now. It was all so needlessly childish.

40

By the time I was sixteen years old, on the 26th of September 2003, I was really struggling emotionally.

I don't know why but turning sixteen made me feel immeasurably sad. Looking back I think I must've been wearying of leading a double life. I was in limbo between two places and torn by both of them.

In the summer holidays, when I was due to go back to Mexico, I was reluctant to leave Scotland and yet oddly after I'd said my goodbyes to my mother and grandparents, I felt terribly unhappy getting on the plane back to Scotland again.

It would always take me a few weeks to acclimatise from life as a private school pupil in Scotland to life as a Mexican and vice versa.

During the autumn term the first wake up call regarding my depression happened to be an encounter with the head boy.

I hadn't realised until then my low mood was being picked up on by others around me. The head boy, Alec Cummings, unexpectedly came up to speak to me when I was working in a quiet corner of the library.

Alec Cummings was a sporty and academic boy who was expected to apply for a place at Cambridge and Oxford University.

Despite Ellerslie being a small school I'd barely exchanged more than a few words with him so I was surprised to see Alec come and sit next to me in the library. It was lunchtime and the library was practically empty.

'Hi Raoul. What are you up to?'

'I'm just working on a maths project that needs to be in by the end of the week.'

'It's strange to see you spend so much time in the library. The other guys in your year are all out playing football.'

I didn't have anything to say to this and shrugged apathetically.

Looking at Alec's concerned face I suddenly wondered if someone had asked Alec to come and speak to me.

Alec cleared his throat awkwardly in the silence.

'Some of the boys were wondering if you'd be joining them at some point. You're a good footballer and they miss your skills in the game.'

'Yeah. I'll probably join them again at some point. Just now I'm trying to get some work done and keep on top of things,' I said in an uncompromising tone of voice, hinting him away.

'OK sure. Just wondering if you were doing OK?'

I pretended to look puzzled.

'Yeah, fine. Why?'

'A few people are concerned about you that's all.'

'Oh right. Like who?'

'Well, Mark's getting worried about you. A few others have noticed how withdrawn you've become.'

I looked at Alec silently for a long time.

Alec squirmed uncomfortably. I smiled grimly, wondering who'd snitched on me.

'I'm fine and you can tell them all I'm fine.'

Alec got up.

231

'OK, Raoul,' he said, giving me a perfunctory pat on the shoulder, 'just let us know if there's anything worrying you or anything you need to talk about.'

'Sure.'

I watched without resentment as a relieved Alec left the library.

I was aware Alec was only trying to do his job as head boy, keeping an eye on anyone that might be struggling. I shrugged and went back to concentrating on my homework.

The second wake up call came when Susie dumped me later on in the term.

I'd been seeing less and less of her since term started but, with a typically male obtuseness, it took a while for me to realise why.

Finally I asked her to meet with me behind the library, in our old woodland haunt. Susie for once hadn't made any excuses to not see me and agreed to be there one Saturday afternoon in November.

I was sitting on a mossy bank, looking at the carpet of colourful autumn leaves, when I saw Susie's tall figure walking towards me through the gaunt brown trees.

I stood up, dusting the back of my coat with my hands and waited for her to reach me.

'Hi Raoul.'

'Hi Susie, it's good to see you. I feel I haven't seen much of you this term.'

I reached forward to pull her towards me but Susie moved away, not meeting my eyes.

'What's wrong?'

'I think, Raoul, we should take a break from each other,' said Susie firmly, twisting her hands together.

I looked at Susie dispassionately. I was surprised at how little I was feeling, I just felt empty of all emotion inside. Shouldn't I have been even the slightest bit upset by her words?

'Why?'

Susie looked up at me and the pain in her eyes shocked me.

'You've changed and I'm finding it hard to be with you. It's like you're not here anymore and you aren't connecting with anyone. I don't know what's happened to you. I think you need to get help, Raoul. I really do. You aren't functioning in a normal way.'

Susie turned slightly and looked away.

'What do you want me to do?' I asked.

It was a pretty stupid thing to ask given she had made it clear she didn't want to be with me.

'I think you should see the school counsellor. It's easy to get the matron to refer you to her. She's apparently really nice. You might be able to speak to her.'

I looked away but Susie had obviously rehearsed her speech and wasn't going to let it go to waste.

'You're certainly not speaking to any of us. You just bury yourself in the library or disappear to your dorm. Even when you do get involved in activities it's as if you're not there anymore. It's like you don't care anymore and you don't want to be here anymore. It's.....' Susie's voice broke slightly,' it's as if the old you has gone somewhere else.'

I reached for her hands and pulled her to me.

'I'm sorry Susie. I really am. If you want me to go to a counsellor I will but please don't break up with me. I miss you.'

Susie gently disentangled her hands and stood back.

'I'm sorry Raoul, but I can't take it anymore. I think you need to sort yourself out first. Sorry...'

Susie turned and walked away with determined steps.

Her bulky winter jacket and bright red woolly hat made her look curiously vulnerable. I sat back down slowly and put my head in my hands.

If Susie was going to break up with me I saw no reason why I should do what she said and make an effort to see the school counsellor.

However I'd felt the changes in me as well. I certainly was feeling very detached from life at school at the moment and I didn't think it was particularly healthy to be so dispassionate.

It didn't surprise me Susie was beginning to tire of my mood swings.

I was beginning to tire of myself.

She clearly struggled to understand my difficulties with identity and didn't have the patience to empathise. I didn't blame her. Susie was the spoilt darling of her parents and lived life cushioned from reality. Whether her butterfly existence would change after school, out there in the real world, I didn't know but I doubted it.

Both of us had for a long time enjoyed a full-blown physical relationship with each other, and in many ways this had served its purpose, dulling any pain I'd felt about Hannah's rejection of me and also healing me of any lingering feelings for her.

My relationship with Susie felt comfortably real and present, as opposed to the fairy tale relationship with Hannah that had existed solely in my head.

Hannah was now dating a boy in seventh year and I was surprised by how little it bothered me.

Things had moved on since we'd first started school.

Patrick was already away to university. Stephen was a popular boy in his year and was much respected for his talent for getting into trouble.

Life was never dull at Ellerslie School when Stephen was around.

He managed to break the rules continually and yet to our surprise, no teacher saw him as a troublemaker.

In his first year at Ellerslie School Stephen had decided to augment his pocket money by lending money with interest to the other kids who'd run out of their own pocket money. The teachers discovered what he'd been up to and in the end the school decided to complain directly to David and Marion about Stephen's illicit money lending activities.

David and Marion spoke to Stephen when they saw him next and tried to explain why he shouldn't lend money with interest to his friends, but we could all see Marion was secretly quite impressed with Stephen's entrepreneurial spirit.

All of us knew he'd turn out to be very successful one day.

Hannah was shooting ahead academically, in part due to her single minded focus on her work and in part due to the fact that she didn't mix too much with the other girls.

Although she was friendly with everyone she was seen as a bit of a loner, who seemed to be mostly uninterested in all the things the other girls enjoyed doing.

Shopping trips to Edinburgh didn't appeal to her at all. She wasn't interested in plastering herself in makeup, and was genuinely horrified at the sight of girls whose faces had suddenly turned orange in colour in their mid teens. Hannah would only use a little mascara every day.

She didn't join in any gossip and avoided any school dances like the plague.

Her boyfriend Thomas was also studying hard as he was in sevenths and leaving school soon, and this seemed to suit Hannah.

To be fair to Thomas he was reliable and dependable but privately I thought he was incredibly dull. Clearly Hannah must have found some sort of comfort in his gentle stability.

However I still wonder now, all these years later, if Thomas has actually done anything remotely interesting or exciting with his life because I couldn't see any potential for it back then.

Hannah and I had by now settled into a courteous and amicable relationship, but the close bonds of family or friendship no longer applied to us anymore.

The one member of the Anderson family I was closest to at this time would be Janet.

I loved Janet to bits.

Old though she undoubtedly was, she had the spirit of a young child inside of her.

During the time I'd been living in Scotland Janet and I had become very close. I think growing up with my grandparents as a young boy has made it easier for me to relate to older people like Janet.

Of course I was also obligated to spend a lot of my time with Janet, not just at the school weekends but also during the Christmas and Easter holidays, when the other Anderson children flew to Colombia (courtesy of the embassy) to be reunited with David and Marion.

Christmas is a painful time of year to be on one's own and away from family, but despite receiving invitations from other friends at the school, I liked to spend Christmas with Janet.

Janet had lost her husband many years ago and slowly one by

one she was losing her long-time friends to illness and old age. She was always cheery and upbeat about life, but until we all came to school in Scotland her life was becoming very limited.

Both Janet and I were mutually understanding of our isolated circumstances and loneliness, and we enjoyed each other's company.

I credit Janet with bringing me out of my temporary depression in 2002. Having been a post war baby she wasn't going to put up with me moping about the house at Christmas.

In the end it was Janet Anderson who pulled me out of the abyss of self-pity I'd immersed myself in.

That Christmas, knowing I was hoping to finish school and go to Interior Design College in Mexico, she decided to let me use her house as an interior design project.

41

'Well,' said Janet, 'here we are again Raoul.'

I nodded as I cradled a hot cup of tea in my hands.

I looked at the sheep painted on the grey stoneware. I loved the solid feel of the mug.

In the hallway the grandfather clock ticked away loudly.

'Raoul, I was thinking we both need something to keep ourselves occupied this Christmas and to stop us from falling into the doldrums.'

I looked across to Janet.

'OK,' I said cautiously.

'I want to do up the house a bit Raoul. In fact I want to change it all. I've a pile of money in the bank that'll all be taken by the taxman when I die and I'd like to spend some of it making this house a little more modern. I thought you might enjoy helping me change it now that we have the house to ourselves.'

I was surprised.

'Sure. The only thing is... do you know of painters and decorators, or even joiners or builders who can help you with this? Are you sure you want all the hassle?'

Janet nodded, looking at me with a mischievous twinkle in her eye.

'Raoul, you're getting older and I know you won't be around

forever. I'd love you to leave your mark on this house. It'll be a great project for us to work on together.'

Janet got up and picked up a pile of magazines from the floor and put them on the kitchen table.

'Don't worry about the workmen, Raoul. I can get reliable recommendations but I think we need to decide what we could do with the rooms and you can use your creativity to give me a helping hand with the renovations.'

She pointed at the magazines on the table.

I've had a look at these home styling magazines and you might like to look at them later for some inspiration. Later on we can take a trip up to John Lewis and have a look around their furnishings department for some inspiration. And any other shops you think might be good to look at.'

Janet's enthusiasm made me smile.

'OK Janet, if you're really determined to do it let's do it. I'm sure it'll keep us busy. I mean are you going to change every room in the house?' I said, looking around at the kitchen.

I loved this kitchen, it was definitely the beating heart of the house, and I felt strangely resistant to changing it.

Janet, as usual reading my thoughts accurately, laughed.

'Realistically it's probably too big a project to make a major change to every room. In this room for example we could make some small improvements only. I mean it really does need a fresh lick of paint, look at all the scuff marks on the skirting and walls.'

I nodded.

Janet was right. Nothing had been done for this old house for a long time now. I looked over at the pile of magazines.

'You know, Janet, they're building new properties just down

239

the road and they've done up a few show rooms. We could take a peek in there to start with. I can always have a look through the magazines this evening when you're watching Coronation Street.'

'Also we could visit the paint shops to get some paint colours-Farrow and Ball have a shop nearby in Stockbridge. And there's the big Homebase just up the road,' I added, getting slightly carried away.

I could see Janet was pleased to see my sudden enthusiasm for the project but the more I thought about it, the more I started to wonder if she'd have the energy to keep up with all my ideas. She'd never been one to sit around but redecorating a house this size was going to be a huge challenge given nothing had been done to it in decades.

She did tell me once the house renovation was finished, which took far longer than either of us had expected, if she'd known what was ahead of her she would have changed her mind about decorating it.

At the time she was determined to do anything that would bring back some of my old enthusiasm.

She told me she missed the Raoul who'd arrived in Scotland all those years ago.

Back then, she said, I was always so interested and intelligently curious about everything. She disliked seeing me sitting in her house with a rather bloodless disinterested attitude, completely untouched by anything going on around me.

I immersed myself in the project completely, giving free rein to my imagination.

I had to contend with Janet's old-fashioned notions of how much everything would cost nowadays in terms of budget.

Given our age gap, both of us also had more than a few

tussles over my design choices. Janet's taste unfortunately was still stuck in the 1960's but ultimately, after putting up a good fight, she was willing to defer to me on matters of taste.

She was becoming very forgetful so she depended on me to remember our decisions and because of this I ended up taking notes of everything we'd decided on. This is something I still do today in my current job, so no clients can then claim I have done things without their agreement. These days I actually go over my notes with the client at each stage of the project, and I get the client to sign them at the end of the consultation.

In the end I was the only one who was really aware of what choices we'd made for the interior of Janet's house, as soon as Janet had given her assent she was quite happy to leave the rest in my hands.

It took the full three-week Christmas holiday to finish making our choices and decisions for the house.

I'd made up design boards like the ones Fernando used in his interior design work: with our colour, fabric and furniture choices for each room in the house.

The kitchen was getting a fresh lick of paint and some new blinds, as well as new cabinets, but the old wooden floor was staying, as well as the big pine dining table and chairs.

My colour choices were perhaps brighter and bolder than Janet would normally have chosen, but I think she recognised that this was very much a part of my personality and she was undoubtedly intrigued with my colour choices.

The greens, maroons and browns of her existing decor were going to be replaced with fresher and brighter colours in different room schemes; turquoise blue, rich purple, soft yellow and bright red colours all found a place in a room or in the hallway.

Patterned wallpapers and matching furnishings were going to make their way into the bedrooms and the sitting-room. I unfortunately had to limit my use of blue because although it's a colour I love; I just found blue too cold a colour for the Scottish climate. To sit in a cold room with artic coloured blue walls would've literally made me give up the will to live.

I hated the north-facing bathroom on the second floor because it was so cold.

Janet found herself agreeing to replace the old cracked lino with under-floor heating, and to installing a large floor to ceiling heated towel rail as well as an open floor shower. However she put her foot down when I suggested including a heated toilet seat.

A new log-burning stove was to make its way into the sitting-room with some warm sheepskin rugs. I worried Janet might trip up on the sheepskin rugs, which wouldn't be good given her age, but Janet thought my concerns were ridiculous.

I did try valiantly to argue the point, looking at her dainty high-heeled shoes, but she refused to listen to me. All she would tell me is that she wasn't decrepit yet and wouldn't be treated as such either.

So the sheepskin rugs stayed.

Soft lighting made an appearance into most of the rooms and the hallway. I decided to get a hands free phone as part of the hallway upgrade as Janet's phone could definitely qualify as an antique it was so old.

Old antique chairs would be reupholstered in bright and modern fabrics and the old grandfather clock still had pride of place in the hallway. But any pieces of worthless or decrepit furniture were going to be replaced. Some of Janet's furniture was in such poor condition I doubted any charity shops would even take it. We'd have to pay for the council to collect it all and take it to the dump at Seafield.

I found in no time at all the Christmas holidays had flown past.

Janet and I, as was our custom, had our Christmas lunch at the Sheraton on Lothian Road and walked back home afterwards. Mark invited me to a New Year's celebration at the Dome on George Street with some cousins of his (Janet liked an early bed even at New Year so she quite happy for me to make other plans).

I managed to relax enough under the influence of a few beers to enjoy a couple of ceilidh dances at the Dome.

An amusing mix of people were dancing at the Dome that New Year, those who took ceilidh dancing very seriously, and then those who hadn't a clue but were drunk enough to give it a go anyway. It was impossible to avoid ceilidh dances at Ellerslie School for they even did ceilidh dancing for PE occasionally, just to make sure the pupils understood how to do it.

Before going back to school again I remember looking at the shambles in Janet's house and feeling remorseful about leaving Janet to finish implementing my ideas and plans.

We'd already received most of the furnishings, paint and wallpaper, and these were carefully laid out in each room. Janet had been recommended a decent decorator and a good builder but they wouldn't be available to start until February. The new kitchen cabinets would be put in at the end of January.

'Raoul, don't worry about the house. You've done excellent plans and any problems I'll consult you. It'll all go well. We've got some excellent workmen coming and I'm sure they'll do a great job. It'll also help to keep me occupied and stop me dying of boredom.'

'I hope you can manage, Janet. Just call me anytime if there's a problem. I'm looking forward to seeing it when it starts to take shape. Just don't overdo it, I don't want you getting worn out,' I said, giving her a hug.

Janet laughed fondly.

'There's not much chance of that happening. You know I don't like sitting still for long. That and a small whisky every day are going to keep me going in my old age.'

Before I got into the car to return to Ellerslie School for the new term I made sure all the things we'd purchased were safely placed in the house so there was no danger of someone accident prone like Stephen breaking anything.

It wasn't long before the phone calls from Janet started coming in.

I wasn't supposed to have my phone switched on during school hours but anticipating Janet would have some difficulties once the workers appeared I had it on silent. Between classes, and in my morning or lunch breaks I'd hide behind the sports centre and call her back.

'Janet? Everything OK?'

'Hi Raoul. I'm so sorry to disturb you but we're a bit confused here. Which colour is getting painted on the sitting-room wall? I've got your design plan here but it has two different paint colours on it.'

'The sitting-room is getting painted in the 'Cooking Apple Green' colour.'

'Oh. Then why does it say 'Green Ground' here next to it?'

'That's the gloss paint, Janet. You know for the doors, skirting boards and windows.'

'Right you are Raoul. I'll let them know. Bye!'

'Bye!' I'd say breathlessly, starting to run to catch the start of my next lesson.

The delivery of various items of furniture caused Janet further confusion.

'Raoul, where's the oak sideboard going? Was it supposed to be in the kitchen?'

'No. The sideboard goes into the sitting-room, on the left hand side, next to the window.'

'Oh right. I'll tell them. Thank you!' said Janet hanging up rapidly.

Every weekend I went to stay with Janet I fully expected to arrive and find the wrong colours painted in the bedrooms, the wrong carpets and curtains up.

But in the end I found the workmen had read and understood my room plans better than I'd expected, and there weren't really any major mistakes. All I had to do was move a few cushions and get one of the console tables out into the hallway.

I never found out if Janet had told Marion about our joint project or what her reaction to it was. I was sure Hannah or her brothers would have reported back to their parents the dramatic transformation of Janet's house, but I still hoped blissfully it would come as a pleasant surprise when Marion saw the newly refurbished house in the summer.

42

I looked at Hannah as she absorbed herself in her textbook, every so often jotting down notes on a sheet of paper.

It was the end of May 2005 and we were both in Janet's kitchen studying hard in preparation for our final year exams at Ellerslie School. Weekends were now full of revision and the carefree days of chilling out at Janet's house were gone.

Stephen, who was younger and so had no impending exams, had disappeared to Inverleith Park with a school friend and a couple of tennis rackets and tennis balls.

Sun was blazing in through the window, brightening an already bright kitchen.

Warm red cabinets and striped red blinds were just the right shade to contrast nicely with the pine wood floor and pine table. Ivory white walls displayed a collection of black-framed black and white photos of the Anderson family (my Christmas present to Janet a couple of years ago).

A large, metal, vintage looking chandelier hung over the kitchen table. But the old pine table looked just as it had when I had first arrived, covered in mugs of half drunk tea and the remnants of scones and jam.

'Raoul?'

'Mmm?' I responded, without bothering to lift my eyes from the page in front of me.

'Who are you inviting to the end of year ball?'

I frowned slightly as I looked up from my notes.

It was only mid way through the summer term and I hadn't thought about the end of year ball. The pressure to study had taken precedence.

I looked calmly at Hannah.

'End of year ball? I've no idea. Why?'

Hannah looked slightly uncomfortable.

'I know it's early but I was wondering if you hadn't asked anyone whether you'd mind having me as your partner?'

'No, I don't mind,' I said, shaking my head and casually looking down again at my textbook, doing a good job of hiding my pleasure at Hannah's request.

'Oh, great. Thanks Raoul,' said Hannah sounding relieved and turning back to her own studies.

I smile now when I remember the end of school ball.

Hannah hated going to any school dances but the end of school ball was pretty unavoidable. Teachers and parents were expecting everyone to attend this big event in the school calendar. Parents were invited to the meal before the ball, along with the teachers, to celebrate their children having finished school.

When Janet came into the kitchen later on and was told about our decision to go together she was delighted.

'That's wonderful, what a nice way to end your journey through school.'

'Some teachers don't see it that way apparently, gran,' grinned Hannah, who'd been filled in with all the gossip by her friends of course.

'What do you mean?'

'Apparently it's not unusual for some parents to have a few

confrontations with some teachers they had issue with at the meal. You know how it is, it just takes a few glasses of wine to set them off.'

'Oh, that's ridiculous,' said Janet shaking her head, 'I hope they don't get away with that kind of behaviour. A dance is meant to be fun, not serious, after all,' she said reminiscently.

Hannah and I smiled complicity at each other knowing what was coming. It's an undeniable fact that in old age everyone repeats themselves and all of us had heard several times over Janet's stories about her dancing days.

'My goodness', went on Janet,' I used to love the jitterbug and the lindy when I was younger! After going to the dance on Friday nights I used to walk back all the way home to Cherry Hinton, by myself too! It was so much safer then.'

Janet smiled sadly.

'I also went dancing with your grandfather, Hannah, when he and I were courting. We both so loved dancing and we used to go out with our close friends too. I really miss those good times. By the way why are you two smiling?'

'Not for any important reason, Janet,' I reassured her.

'Did you wear your high heels to those dances gran?' asked Hannah, interested and procrastinating her studies once more.

'Yes, of course. I was quite short even for those days and your grandfather was very tall. Nothing would've parted me from my high heels.'

Janet glanced down with fondness at her smart navy blue shiny high-heeled shoes and sighed.

Then she remembered she had washing to bring in from the garden before it rained and she quickly disappeared through the kitchen door to bring it in.

Both of us could see how attached Janet had been to her high heels every time we caught sight of her bunions. Both Janet's big toes were bent at quite an angle due to the pointed high-heeled shoes she'd insisted on wearing for most of her life.

Hannah told me she was pretty sure she wouldn't be wearing high heels to the ball. She was the same height as me without heels, maybe even slightly taller. So that was fine by me.

Now Hannah had resolved the problem she had with the end of year ball (and I hoped she wouldn't change her mind and want to invite someone else nearer the time) she said she felt she could fully concentrate on her exams.

That last year of school always seems to be full of pressure no matter what school or country you are in.

At Ellerslie, not only did we have the pressure of our end of school exams, like everyone else we also had to decide what university or college we wanted to apply to, and what subjects we would be studying for the next few years.

A week ago a pessimistic friend of Hannah's told her how their brother had dropped out of university because quite simply he'd chosen the wrong subject.

I'd never had any doubts as to what I wanted to do after school and made no secret of it, despite the smirks from some of the other pupils who didn't see interior design as a proper profession.

In this I was for once, clear sighted and unwavering in my determination.

I felt Hannah's eyes on me again and looked up from my textbook, pushing it away.

We were clearly not going to get any work done today.

'Raoul, where are you going to go to study interior design after school?'

'I'm going to the CEDIM in Santa Catarina.... to do the Interior Design Undergraduate Course.'

'You were always going to apply there weren't you?'

'Yeah, it's where Fernando recommended I train as an Interior Designer.'

'That's pretty cool Raoul. I'm sure you'll enjoy studying there, you've been wanting to do it for so long.'

'It wasn't easy. I had to take in my portfolio and go through an interview with four different lecturers. And we had to get my reference from the school and the art department translated into Spanish. Anyway it's all done now.'

'Is what Manolo left you enough to cover the expense of studying there? It won't just be the tuition fees, you'll have accommodation and food to pay for too won't you?'

I took a mouthful of my tea while I considered her question.

'Accommodation won't be so much because my mum and Fernando have contacts in Monterrey. Fernando says it'll be easy to find friends who'll put me up in their home at a low cost to help me out. I'm going to try to find work too. After my mother had Manolo's things valued we're pretty sure I'll be able to cover the fees and my living expenses.' I shrugged. 'Just have to wait and see. How about you? Are you organised?'

Hannah shook her head.

'No, I haven't decided yet. It depends on my grades I guess. I think as long as I get the grades I'll go to St Andrews. At least we're still getting free tuition fees up here unlike in England. Patrick's fees in Durham are costing mum and dad a fortune even with him taking out student loans.'

'You're going to have to decide soon aren't you?'

Hannah grimaced.

'Yeah, thanks for that Raoul.'

'Where's Thomas studying?'

'Raoul, you know fine well Thomas and I split up ages ago. If you must know as soon as he started university he found someone more attractive than me and let me know by text we were finished. Now how about you Raoul,' Hannah said, in a dangerously icy voice, ' what happened to you and Susie, huh? I hear she dumped you?'

Wisely, I didn't rise to the bait.

'Yeah, I was getting too heavy for her liking.'

'Heavy?'

'Yeah, you know depressed, sad or whatever.'

We glanced at each other and burst out laughing, unable to restrain ourselves.

We were still laughing when Janet came back in with the washing basket. I got up to help her with the basket but sat back down again when Janet shook her head at me.

Janet was very independent and she didn't always appreciate help. I often thought she was in deep denial about her age. And I'd certainly noticed she was becoming more forgetful recently.

'What are you two laughing at?' asked Janet with a smile as she put the basket on the table and started sorting out the items of dry washing.

'It's too hard to explain', I said quickly, seeing Hannah was unwilling to talk about it.

'Fair enough, suit yourselves,' said Janet,' I don't see much studying going on you two,' she glanced up at the kitchen clock, 'Stephen's coming back soon and you won't get a minute's peace then.'

We both bent our heads over our textbooks again, and all went quiet. Having seen Patrick go through the stress of final year tests and exams I know Janet deeply sympathised with us. She often told us it wasn't easy to have so much responsibility at such a young age.

'My generation had nothing much to worry about when they were young, as far as their careers went, because there were so many jobs after the Second World War and not enough people to do them.'

Then she would pause and ruminate on the unfairness of society.

'However that said women in those days were still expected to be secretaries or housewives after the war. This despite having been roped into many of the jobs men traditionally did during the years Britain was at war, and doing a sterling job', she'd say with a disapproving sniff.

'I would've studied to be a chef if I'd been young in today's world. I love cooking and making people happy with my food. As you know I've a kitchen full of French cookery books. But I've never had any regrets about being a housewife and mother to my children. I've always been involved in different community projects and I was a part of the women's guild at my church for many years.'

It was a shame but Janet's church no longer existed.

The congregational numbers had dwindled so much the board eventually decided to sell the church building, and Janet's church had been converted into flats.

She now went along to Wardie Parish church and was quite happy to sit at the back of the church watching the new minister, a German lady, take the services. She rarely spoke to anyone there but occasionally a young harassed looking mother would sit next to her and chat to her at the end of the service.

Everything changes she'd say to me time and time again, and nothing stays the same.

Within a few minutes, with impeccable timing, Stephen and his friend came in through the front door, returning from an energetic tennis session at the park, and made their way to the kitchen.

Stephen, conveniently forgetting to wash his hands, completely ignored everyone's greetings and grabbed a scone from the kitchen table, squeezing nearly half of it into his mouth at one go.

Watching Stephen Janet smiled with amusement.

I could tell she was thinking some things don't change at all.

43

The huge marquee was stretched across the entire sports field. The summer holidays had arrived at last and the grass no longer needed to be protected from anything destructive to its pristine wellbeing.

After the school ball the grass would be sandy white in patches, due to the recent dry spell in Scotland and the plastic flooring of the marquee sealing in the heat of the day.

This was a problem the school groundsmen would contend with, no doubt with many curses, once the end of school ball had finished and the marquee had been removed.

'Mum what are you going to wear to the end of school dinner?' Hannah had asked her mother apprehensively at breakfast one morning.

'My blue dress with the white lining. You know, the one I always wear to these things. Why? Is there a problem with it?'

'No, it's fine mum. It looks really nice on you. I just wondered.'

Not deceived Marion looked at her.

'So I don't embarrass you.'

'Mum, I was just wondering that's all. OK?'

'Fine. I hope you're still OK with your outfit Hannah?'

'Yes. I really like it.'

Marion felt her shoulders loosen with relief.

Marion told me in confidence Hannah had agonised over her end of term ball dress choice for so long, she began to wonder if Hannah was starting to have unspoken romantic feelings towards me. Too wise to question Hannah directly about this Marion kept her thoughts to herself.

I said nothing because I didn't want to stir things up.

Hannah had been very much on edge over the last term of school, no doubt in part due to her anxieties over her exam performance, and as Janet said to Marion, she'd been biting everyone's heads off especially Stephen's (who seemed to positively revel in winding his sister up).

Unlike Hannah I remember I seemed to be in my element, taking the end of school in my stride. I suppose in those days I did have quite a philosophical and relaxed view towards the future, confident that whatever happened things would work out.

Returning to Mexico was something I was looking forward to. Unfortunately this talent I had when younger for being laid back and optimistic is not a characteristic I can claim to possess now I'm older.

I know Marion felt slightly emotional at the thought of both of us finishing school and was devoutly hoping I'd still keep in touch with them when I started college in Mexico.

Having lost touch with so many good friends from around the world as they moved from posting to posting, Marion was realistic about the constraints distance presented.

However she could see how close I'd become to Janet, and now here I was accompanying Hannah to the ball. She was hoping I'd still keep my connection to them alive in the years ahead.

On the day of the ball Marion and David, drinks in one hand, were mingling with other parents outside the marquee.

A few brave mothers had decided to wear hats to the pre-dinner drinks, just as they would have done to a wedding. The majority of mothers tended to go with smart summer dresses. Despite the heat of the day many of the men at the ball wore kilts and the back of their necks were soon dripping with sweat.

Patrick and Stephen always proudly wore their own kilts to formal occasions. The Anderson tartan was made up mostly of light blue and red blocks of colour with yellow and white lines threaded through it.

I'm afraid, even after living all these years in Scotland and seeing kilts at all manner of formal occasions, I still couldn't be persuaded to try on what I still saw as a skirt. So for the ball I borrowed a tux from a friend in the year below me.

I knew I was unlikely to ever need to wear one again and I was relieved I didn't have to look for one in the rental shop.

A few of the members of the school staff had lost their reserve and were dressed in unconventional and eccentric outfits. Surprisingly these eccentric staff members were not from the drama or art department as you might expect, but from the science and design technology departments.

Mr McNeil, the chemistry teacher, had on a bright orange Hawaiian shirt and Mrs Primrose, head of the DT department, had on a large purple and black tent like dress decorated with a multitude of silver chains.

Looking at the marquee I couldn't help thinking Janet should have been there with us today. After all she was the one who had provided a home for us all these years while Marion and

David were working abroad. Janet might have enjoyed the ball whereas Marion seemed to find these events hard going.

Marion told me that after the endless diplomatic social events she was forced to attend, she just didn't have the stomach to attend something like this during her holidays.

According to what David told us with amusement the next day, Marion was mentally absent for most of the dinner, and not inclined to make an effort given she didn't really know any of the other parents very well.

'Marion, are you all right?' David had asked her concerned.

'Yes of course. Why?'

'You've got that far away dreamy look on your face again, like you're not with us', David said.

'Oh sorry! I'm listening and paying attention, David. I know it looks like I'm not', whispered Marion into David's ear.

David raised his eyebrows sceptically but said nothing.

'Where've Hannah and Raoul gone, David?'

'I don't know. The last time I saw them they were in the marquee with a group of Hannah's friends.'

Marion looked at her watch.

'Well, it can't be long now before we're seated for the meal.'

David and her looked around trying to find some other parents they knew well enough to speak to. Once they spotted a group they recognised they moved in tandem and with practised ease to join them.

Meanwhile inside the marquee I was thoroughly bored. As Hannah's partner I found myself attached to Hannah's friendship group, and their partners, none of whom were particular friends of mine.

To make matters worse Susie was in our group and was

ignoring me entirely, flirting desperately with her partner and gossiping with her friends.

I knew I shouldn't be feeling bored. Hannah looked radiant and beautiful. She had on a backless red dress that clung to her slight curves. A beautician she'd been to earlier in the afternoon with some friends had done her makeup expertly.

However I found it disconcerting that Hannah didn't look like the Hannah I knew, and she certainly wasn't behaving like her either. She was laughing a little too loudly and her conversation was a little too forced. She looked nervous and out of place.

Maybe she just needs a few more glasses of prosecco to calm her down, I thought, quietly drinking my glass next to her.

I certainly felt I was going to need a few more glasses of alcohol to get through the night.

'Raoul, I hear you're going to college in Mexico in the autumn?' asked Gavin, whom I cordially disliked. He was so incredibly pretentious and full of himself, in my view.

'Yes, that's right. How about you?'

'Oh, I'm headed to Cambridge to study science.'

Of course he would be, I thought bitterly. Some people just seemed to have that golden path laid out for them. They were touched with the 'magical glitter dust' as Janet so aptly put it.

'Cambridge is a great place to live. We've been there several times visiting friends of my father's who are lecturers there.'

'Interesting', I said blandly.

Gavin looked at me with a crease in his forehead, puzzled by my abrupt response.

'Raoul won't be here over the summer', said Hannah quickly, recognising my dangerously uncooperative mood and trying to change the subject, 'he'll be back home in Mexico, won't you Raoul?'

'Yes, that's right. In a very hot, grossly polluted and smelly city', I said suavely.

'Great. Sounds good.'

Gavin started to look around and see if there was anyone else he could talk to. He clearly wasn't in the mood to pander to my whims. Once Gavin was engrossed in talking to someone else, Hannah grabbed my arm in a painfully tight pinch and pulled me away from the group.

'What do you think you're doing?' she hissed urgently in my ear.

I didn't pretend to misunderstand her.

'What do you expect? He's *engreido y orgulloso*. Full of himself.'

'Please, just for this one night, will you behave yourself?'

Feeling Hannah's proximity as she whispered in my ear made me want to not behave myself with her but I didn't feel safe joking about it.

'OK, OK, calm down, Hannah. I'll be nice. But seriously do we have to stick with them all night? They're a pretty boring group to hang around with.'

Hannah bristled.

'They're my friends, Raoul. Are you determined to offend everyone, myself included?'

I turned and looked at her. Hannah looked seriously distressed.

'No, of course not. I'm sorry Hannah. I really didn't intend to spoil the night for you. I'll be good. Promise,' I said contritely.

'It's only for a short time, Raoul', said Hannah, relenting

and softening her voice, 'Once the dancing starts everyone will do their own thing.'

I gave her a quick hug.

'OK, let's go for it then.'

As we moved back to our group the parents started streaming in, looking at the table plans trying to figure out where they were supposed to sit.

The pupils sat at separate tables to their parents, much to their relief. Even at the end of school most of us were still young enough to be embarrassed by our parents.

Hannah was glad to see I was finally making an effort to be friendly and I sensed her relaxing for the first time that evening.

She told me she wasn't planning on eating too much because her dress felt quite tight and she was sure it would be uncomfortable if it stretched any further.

I could tell she was already feeling slightly light headed after two proseccos and we had a long night ahead.

Once all the parents left, the dancing would start and would go on until one o'clock in the morning. After the dancing finished and we were all turfed out, all of us had been invited back to a party at the family estate of another pupil at the school, where no doubt we'd be staying up until the early hours of the morning.

Later on in the evening, once dessert had been served Marion walked across to our table.

'Right my little ones, we'll be heading home in the next half hour. Have you got enough money for taxis and everything else?'

Both Hannah and I nodded.

Janet had generously topped us up with cash before we left the house. I was certain Hannah, who was notoriously scatty, would lose her handbag at some point in the evening so I was glad I had my own supply of cash in case we needed it.

I'd been witness to too many diplomatic functions where women had left their bags scattered like discarded confetti around the room. It always seemed to me miraculous when none of them were stolen.

'How are you finding the evening?'

'It's OK so far, mum. The food's better than what we get at school meals so that has to be a plus. Have you enjoyed chatting to the parents?'

Marion smiled.

'Yes, it's nice to catch up with what's going on at the school after all this time. Things change so quickly. The Somervilles are divorced now apparently.'

Hannah and I nodded, disinterested. Old news. Everyone knew about the Somerville family and their divorce. It had been a highly acrimonious and public divorce with both the children and the school dragged into it at various points.

'Right, I'll see you back at Inverleith Place at some point in the morning. Be careful both of you. I'm glad you're with Raoul, Hannah. If there's anyone who knows how to look after her it's you, Raoul. Bring her home in one piece if you can.'

'Mum! I'm quite capable of looking after myself, thank you very much!'

'Of course you are, dear', said Marion pacifically, not in the least believing her.

She gave us both a hug and walked back to her table.

Hannah shrugged petulantly.

'Mum always makes me feel two years old, somehow. I'm not sure she'll ever accept I'm an adult.'

'That's normal parental behaviour Hannah. My mother's the same.'

'Is she though? I mean she was willing to let you come here to study. It's a completely different country and away from your family.'

'I guess she had a lot of faith in your mother and father in that respect. I don't think she found it easy but she's really happy I've managed to complete my school education here.'

'Well she would be, wouldn't she? Anyway when are you going to ask me to dance?' asked Hannah, abruptly changing the subject.

I turned and realised the ceilidh dancing was about to start.

I'd unconsciously tuned out the loud microphone voice belting out instructions throughout the evening. I stood up quickly and reached out for Hannah.

As she put her small hand into mine I felt a warm glow engulf me.

Maybe tonight was going to be fun after all.

44

I could feel my leg go numb under the dead weight of Hannah's head.

I tried to shift her head gently but she barely moved.

I sighed.

The night had been promising until the point Hannah, having drunk too much, had thrown up in the toilets in one of steadings used for the post ball party.

Shortly after that Hannah had lain down on the ground near the bonfire and passed out.

I'd lifted her onto my lap, hoping she'd come to soon and wondering if I'd be able to find some way of sobering her sufficiently to face the trip back to Janet's house.

Hannah wasn't the only one suffering.

Everyone had slowly descended into a state of chaos once they'd arrived at the estate.

Initially the night started with the sweet smell of a few joints and some beers but within a couple of hours a few of them had disappeared to take some coke in one of the barns, and others had begun to drink at an alarming rate.

I'd turned down the generous offer of some coke, not for the first time, and felt genuinely annoyed at the way they assumed I liked the stuff.

The music outside (run by an outdoor generator) was playing at such a volume I wondered why no neighbours had complained and no police had been summoned to the party.

I remember thinking at the time how isolated the estate must be.

I looked down at Hannah's tousled head, the hem of her dress muddy and torn, her mascara and eyeliner smudged and streaked across the tops of her cheeks.

Hannah's carefully applied makeup had disintegrated when, after I'd rejected her drunken caresses, she'd become emotional and cried, sobbing so loudly I was sure somebody would hear her.

Even now, lying quietly on my lap, drunk and worse for wear, Hannah still looked beautiful in my eyes.

I had also downed quite a few drinks but I was sufficiently self-aware to know when to stop, especially when I knew Marion expected me to bring Hannah back home safely.

I tried to warn Hannah she was maybe drinking too much but in response to that she'd wrapped her arms around my neck and kissed me on the mouth, which had taken me aback, and distracted me completely from my well meaning attempt to prevent her becoming too drunk.

Later on Hannah had dragged me away by the hand into a dark corner and proceeded to tease me with some delightful kisses.

Her exploring hands warned me she was looking for more than just kisses at which point, knowing she was very drunk, I'd gently pushed her away from me.

I told her I thought we should stop.

I was fully aware in my aroused state I would've liked nothing more than to sleep with Hannah, but I didn't want to lose Hannah's friendship when she woke up in the morning mortified by her memories of what we'd done.

At this point, Hannah had burst into tears and apologised tearfully, saying she didn't know when she'd see me again after school finished and she was going to miss me.

It wasn't long after this when she started to feel dizzy and nauseous and thankfully just made it in time to the toilet to throw up.

Now as I looked down at her I was wondering how I was going to get her home and what the Andersons were going to think of the state she was in. I started to nudge Hannah with my leg, shaking her by the shoulder.

'Hannah!'

'Hannah! Come on wake up please!'

Hannah half opened one eye and quickly closed it again.

I continued to shake her.

'Hannah, come on please! You have to wake up. We need to get back soon.'

Hannah opened both eyes and stared blearily at me.

'What's the matter, Raoul?'

'You need to get up, that's what the matter is. We have to get you sobered up and back home soon. And my leg's gone dead.'

Hannah groaned and lifted herself up into a sitting position much to my relief.

I rubbed my thigh to get the blood circulating again.

'What time is it?' asked Hannah.

'It's nearly five o'clock. Most people have crashed out or have gone home.'

Hannah looked around blankly at the discarded beer bottles,

wine bottles, the mass of paper plates and paper napkins and the last embers of the bonfire.

A few people were huddled together near the bonfire talking but the rest had all dissipated.

'Fine. Just give me a minute Raoul', said Hannah stretching and rubbing her eyes, leaving her eyes looking like a panda's after she had finished rubbing them.

I didn't bother pointing this out to her.

'Just wait here and I'll try and find some coffee for you.'

I got up feeling the pins and needles in my leg and walked to the steading, convinced the kitchen must house some coffee. As I walked down the hallway and into the kitchen I passed a couple snogging obliviously as I walked past.

Once in the kitchen I opened several of the kitchen cabinets until I'd located some coffee and then made an intensely strong cup of coffee for Hannah, with several teaspoons of sugar thrown in for good measure.

'Trying to sober up Raoul?' shouted someone as I walked outside with the coffee.

'Sort of,' I yelled back, grinning.

Once I was back outside the steading I sat down next to Hannah and passed her the coffee mug, making sure her hands were steady enough to hold it.

Hannah thanked me and drank it down slowly.

'Oh shit! Where's my handbag Raoul?'

I reached across and handed her the small clutch bag she'd brought with her to the party.

'Raoul', Hannah said urgently, with a note of panic in her voice, 'I can't go home like this; they'll all be awake soon at gran's house. They'll figure I've been drinking too much.'

'Hannah, it's normal to drink a bit too much at your end of school party. I don't think they'll be that surprised.'

Hannah buried her head in her hands.

'This is just so embarrassing. I don't think dad or mum will be impressed by my behaviour tonight.'

'They don't need to know.'

'Come on Raoul. Look at the state of me. I'm a mess and I stink of vomit. I can't go home like this. Can't we stay here and get ourselves in better shape?'

Get yourself in better shape you mean I thought to myself. I looked around.

'I guess so,' I said reluctantly,' I'll text your mother in case she's waiting up for you and tell them we'll be along later on in the morning.'

'Mum won't be up at five in the morning, Raoul.'

I thought there was a very good chance Marion (though probably not David who's more laidback) would be waiting up for us, half asleep in a sitting-room armchair.

Sure enough as soon as I'd sent her a text I received a message back: *Why so late Raoul? Surely the party must have finished at Archie's by now?*

I showed Hannah the text.

She took my phone and typed: *Still some people here so we'll stay a bit longer and be back in a couple of hours. Everything's fine. Just catching up with everyone.*

After a minute the phone pinged again: *OK. We'll see you later on in the morning.*

Not exactly a ringing endorsement for our lateness, I thought. I stood up and reached down for Hannah.

'Come on, you might as well get yourself cleaned up.'

Hannah let me pull her up and walked slowly with me into the steading.

I could see every footstep was giving her a pounding headache.

She held on to my arm as I patiently led her to the bathroom and shut the door. After she'd locked the door, I went into the sitting-room downstairs where Sky Sports was playing a rerun of a premier league football match. Two boys from my form class were hunkered down on beanbags watching the play.

'Hi Raoul. You still here?'

'Yeah. Not for too much longer I hope.'

'You can crash upstairs if you want. There's a pile of sleeping bags and camp beds set up.'

'No, it's OK thanks. I'd rather wait up.'

'Is Hannah still with you?'

'Yeah. She's just gone upstairs to get cleaned up.'

The boys snorted with laughter.

'She looked like she'd had a bit too much booze to drink.'

I smiled and didn't say anything.

'Wasn't she snogging you at one point too, Raoul?'

I started to feel uncomfortable.

'Yeah she was. Why?'

'Whoa, man, I meant no offense. Just didn't think Hannah was the type, that's all.'

I raised my eyebrows.

'What the hell do you mean by 'not the type'?'

'Oh, it doesn't matter, Raoul, just drop it.'

'No, seriously.'

'If you must know I never thought Hannah was the type to get randy when she got some booze in her. She's so uptight and boringly academic most of the time.'

'You obviously don't know her very well then.'

The two of them were convulsed with laughter again.

I gave it up and focused on the game. At regular intervals I checked my watch and wondered what Hannah was up to. I hoped she hadn't passed out in the bathroom. After half an hour I got up and stood outside the bathroom door. I could hear the sound of running water and knocked on the door.

'Hannah? You OK?'

'Raoul? Is that you? I'll be down soon.'

I sighed impatiently and went back to the television.

In the end it was an hour and a half before Hannah came downstairs. Her face was clean of all makeup and her wet hair streamed down her back.

If anything she looked more attractive than she had at the start of the night. I was relieved to see her looking relatively sober even if she might not be feeling it.

I quickly got up.

'Shall I call a taxi?'

Hannah nodded.

'See you later then guys. Thanks for a great party.'

The two boys raised their hands briefly to say goodbye and we went outside.

'Did you get a taxi sorted OK?'

'Yeah. It should be here in a few minutes.'

Hannah reached out and took hold of my hand.

'Raoul, I'm sorry I got so drunk on you.'

'It doesn't matter, Hannah,' I said, feeling seriously embarrassed but not pulling my hand away.

'I really am. I so don't want your last memories of me to be of this.'

I smiled nervously.

'We've still got two weeks before I fly back to Mexico, so don't stress about it.'

Hannah reached over and gave me a quick kiss on the cheek.

'You're such a star. Thank you for taking care of me.'

'Honestly Hannah, it's really not a big deal. Forget it.'

We turned as we heard the taxi's tires coming up the long drive and then suddenly the taxi was there to take us home.

I noticed we were still holding hands as we walked to the taxi and got into the back it.

Once in the taxi I laid my head back against the headrest, suddenly feeling very weary, and shut my eyes.

Hannah put her head on my shoulder and looked out of the car window at the passing landscape.

Half an hour later Marion, looking exhausted and anxious, opened the door at Inverleith Place before I had time to put my key into the lock.

She looked relieved to see us relatively intact and moved aside to let us in.

'Did you have a nice time?'

'Mum, do you mind if I just go and crash?' asked Hannah.

'No, of course not. I'll tell the others to be quiet when they get up. Up you go.'

We dutifully went upstairs without speaking, but before I went into my bedroom, Hannah reached across and gave me a quick hug.

I walked into my bedroom and saw Stephen's star shaped form stretched across one of the beds fast asleep.

I quietly kicked off my shoes and fully clothed, pulled the bedding over me and promptly fell asleep. I didn't even wake later that morning when the food shopping Marion had ordered from Tescos arrived at the front door.

During the next two weeks at Inverleith Place something indefinable had changed between Hannah and me.

Both of us were also very conscious we only had a few days left before we went our separate ways, so we had no real opportunity to take the time to explore our feelings for each other.

Finally, the day before I left Edinburgh for good, Hannah came out into the garden and walked over to where I was sitting at my favourite spot, on the bench next to the magnolia tree, reading messages on my phone.

'Raoul, are you going to keep in touch?'

'Of course, ' I said, conveniently forgetting the many friends in Mexico I'd lost touch with.

'Raoul, I don't want you to go,' Hannah said awkwardly, moving closer.

I watched her attentively but didn't respond.

I quickly looked up as a fat wood pigeon burst out of the tree above us. When I turned to look at Hannah again I saw she had tears rolling down her cheeks.

'Hey Hannah. Calm down. It'll be OK. We'll stay in touch.'

Hannah wiped her eyes.

'I know, I'm so sorry. I'm being so stupid.'

'Look, Hannah, there's a lot of new things happening for both of us soon. It's hard moving on, it makes you question everything but it doesn't mean it'll all be bad. It's an exciting new start for all of us.'

Hannah stared at me incredulously.

'You don't get it, you moron. I've feelings for you now and that's hard for me because you're about to leave here for another country, possibly forever, and we might not see you again,' Hannah said, welling up again.

I reached out for Hannah and enveloped her in a big hug.

When she put her hand on my chest I could feel my heart beating rapidly against the shirt I was wearing.

I really didn't know what I could say to make her feel better.

All the thoughts in my mind were already focused on the Aeropuerto Internacional de la Ciudad de México, greeting my family, all of whom I hadn't seen for a year.

I knew I'd miss Janet and the Andersons but for now I was yearning to be home again with my mother and grandparents.

However, right at this moment in time, Hannah felt good in my arms and hugging her felt like warm sunshine after a long winter.

I rested my chin briefly on her shoulder and thought for a moment with my eyes shut.

'Hannah why don't you come out and visit me?' I asked suddenly.

Hannah pulled back and looked at me in surprise.

'In Mexico?'

'Yes, in Mexico.'

'Raoul, I'm supposed to be working this summer to build up some money for university.'

'I know. But there's nothing stopping you taking a couple of weeks holiday before you start university.'

Hannah stood very still while she thought about this.

I waited patiently while she pondered, watching the bees crawling in and out of the lavender beds in the garden.

'Yeah. Why not?'

I looked at Hannah smiling at me.

'Hell, I don't know how I'll be able to pay for the ticket but who cares.'

'We can split that cost between us. Leave it to me, I'm good at booking cheap flights to Mexico.'

Everything in the garden seemed to quieten as the pair of us stood under the leafy magnolia realising we'd made some sort of commitment to each other.

It was a fragile connection that seemed as delicate as the spider webs buried in the camellia bush, but it had been built all the same.

45

It was the middle of September 2005 and waiting at Mexico City International Airport I'd started to chew my fingernails, a bad habit which my mother was constantly telling me off for.

Fernando placed a hand on my shoulder.

'Raoul, *hijo*, calm down. Security always takes a long time, especially in this airport.'

I smiled and stopped chewing.

Hannah's flight had arrived at Mexico City International Airport.

My mother was working and Fernando had kindly offered to bring me to the airport to pick Hannah up. I'd passed my driving test a few weeks ago (which of course is never difficult to pass here in Mexico), but drivers in Mexico City are so reckless I was only entrusted with driving short distances at this point in time.

My mother was extremely protective of her second hand Ford Ecosport, not so much of me, and understandably reluctant to let me drive her car. Most of my lessons had taken place in the driving instructor's car and occasionally in Fernando's shiny new Range Rover.

When Hannah finally managed to get through security she was thoroughly disgruntled with the airport staff.

She told us later she felt she'd been herded through a

two- hour immigration cattle line. The queuing had felt like a rugby scrum with those at the back of the queue clearing before those at the front.

To tell the truth for someone who was British and used to queuing, Mexico City International Airport was undoubtedly a shock to the system.

The staff Hannah spoke to for directions came across as rude and uninterested, quite happily shrugging their shoulders and saying '*no hablo Ingles*'. Some staff looked like they'd nothing to better to do than to sit and chat, or even at one point giggling and skidding on the shiny floor to relieve the boredom. The carpets were worn, the air-conditioning barely functioning and the toilets filthy.

One thing was certain, Hannah couldn't remember the airport being like this before, but then she'd been many years younger when she was last in Mexico. Maybe she hadn't noticed back then.

However Hannah's eyes brightened up noticeably when she saw us come forward to meet her; she greeted Fernando with a double kiss on the cheek and then turned shyly to hug me.

Fernando took the trolley from her as we turned and walked slowly to the airport exit.

'How was the trip?'

'Fine until I arrived at this airport. I really don't remember it being as bad as this. It was like a madhouse going through security and baggage collection.'

Fernando nodded.

'Yes. It's not a good experience for a lot of people. They're planning to rebuild the airport at some point but who knows when that'll happen.'

It didn't seem to take us very long to reach the house my mother and Fernando lived in. Their home was in San Angel, situated in the south west of the city.

The large automatic gate opened as soon as we arrived at their house and we drove up into a double driveway.

As soon as we opened the car door a beautiful longhaired rough collie dog jumped up to greet us.

'Pax! *¡Sientate!*'

The collie obediently sat down but whined in excitement and impatience.

Hannah had a quick look around at the ample walled garden and noticed the climbing frame and a swing.

Before she had a chance to ask Fernando, Fernando pre-empted her.

'Those are for my two nieces that arrive almost every week-end for a visit. Sometimes they stay the night to let their parents get a break.'

'Oh, that's nice.'

'For them maybe, but not so sure for Esther and I.'

Hannah, unsure how to take Fernando's dry humour, didn't say anything else.

There was a brief silence while Fernando opened the front door and we moved aside as Pax brushed rudely past us, impatient to get in first.

'He doesn't like sitting outside when it's this hot. He'd rather lie on the cool tiles in the kitchen,' I explained.

I noticed Hannah looking intently around at the stylish home, from the hallway we could see through to the kitchen and living room. Fernando has great taste and their house was beautifully decorated.

Fernando and I carefully lifted Hannah's suitcases from the car and put them down in the hallway.

'Raoul, why don't you take Hannah upstairs? I'm going to feed Pax in the kitchen.'

Fernando always puts his slippers on once he's inside the house, and so he padded briskly along to the kitchen.

Hannah quickly took her shoes off and left them neatly by the front door.

'You don't have to do that, he doesn't mind if you keep them on', I said.

'It's fine. It's such a beautiful home it wouldn't feel right to keep them on.'

I shrugged and led the way upstairs.

At the end of a corridor I opened the door to the guest bedroom where it was clear Fernando's nieces usually slept, as the room was jam packed with pink toys; pink teddies to Barbie dolls dressed in pink. The walls had a pretty pink flamingo wallpaper pattern on them and at the windows cute flounced curtains were hanging.

It was obvious Fernando had designed this room with his nieces in mind. The room was a large one and two canopied beds took up little space on either side of the room.

'It's so sweet. I like it. Fernando's nieces are lucky.'

I nodded.

'Yeah, he's very good with them. He pretends he finds them a pain but actually he loves having them stay. I guess he's never had children of his own, so at least he gets to play with his nieces.'

I walked over to the built in cupboard and opened it.

'We've made some room for your stuff,' I said, pointing to

some of the vacant shelves.

'Thanks, that's great.'

'Okay. Shall I leave you to get sorted? Afterwards you can come down and get a drink in the kitchen if you like.'

'No, please stay Raoul. I've come all this way to see you and it feels like it's taken forever. I only need to unpack a few things and then we can go down.'

I obediently sat down on one of the beds, feeling distinctly uncomfortable, and started to jiggle my leg impatiently as she unzipped her suitcase.

'How's the internship work with Fernando been going?' asked Hannah, as she lifted her clothes from the suitcase.

We'd been speaking regularly to each other over the summer holidays, so strangely enough we didn't have too much to say to each other.

'It's going well. I'm learning loads but there are times when the office is really busy so they can't spend the time training me up, and that's a bit frustrating.'

'That doesn't sound good.'

'It's not so bad. There's one staff member, Angela, who's really helpful and seems happy enough to spend the time with me when I'm stuck with something. It's pretty good. Great experience and I get paid a little bit too.'

Hannah was silent.

With juvenile satisfaction, I recognised on her face the pinprick of jealously that had pierced her when she heard about Angela's eagerness to help me with my work. I deliberately omitted to tell her Angela was actually in her fifties and so of no interest to me.

It didn't take long for Hannah to empty her suitcase and we

both then walked downstairs to get a cool drink of lemonade. Marisa, the lady who looked after the house twice a week, had made up jugs of fresh lemonade that morning and put them in the fridge.

I poured us a couple of glasses of lemonade and we both sat down at the kitchen table.

Before she took a drink of the lemonade Hannah lifted up her glass and watched the fresh bits of lemon swirling around in the water. As I was thirsty I finished my drink first and put my empty glass down before she'd even started her drink.

I cleared my throat.

'I was wondering what you'd like to do while you are here? Fernando has to go into work tomorrow and so does my mother, but she's offered me the use of her car. If we're going to be doing longer trips I can probably find a friend who can help take us there, as I've only just received my driver's license so I'm not too confident driving long distances.'

'I really don't mind what we do, Raoul. I came out here to see you so anything will be fine with me.'

'My mum and Fernando are taking us to a beach house the second week. Fernando and his sister own the house so they use it quite a lot at the weekends. It's literally in the middle of nowhere, right next to the jungle. There's no other houses on that beach so it's kind of special.'

'Sounds great. Where's Pax gone?'

'Pax the lazy dog, is over here at his favourite spot under the dining table.'

Hannah had a look under the dining table and laughed.

Sure enough at the far end, next to the wall and panting quietly in the heat, was Pax.

He was lying spread-eagled on the floor so he looked like a misshapen fur rug.

Hannah walked quickly across to the other end of the table and bent down to stroke Pax, who responded by wagging his tail and licking her hand, but not moving an inch away from the coolness of the wall.

'He drives mum mad because he sheds everywhere, especially in the summer.'

'He's adorable. I wish we had a pet but Janet's getting too old, and mum and dad don't want the hassle because they are constantly moving with work.'

I nodded sympathetically.

'Come on. I'll show you around the house and the garden.'

Hannah stood up, reluctantly leaving Pax lying under the table, and followed me out into the hallway.

Once we'd had a good look around the house I took her upstairs to a small outside terrace at the top of the house, where you could often get a splendid view of the houses around us as long as the smog wasn't too bad. Little blue pots full of lavender plants and sweet smelling herbs were scattered about the red tiled patio floor.

There were no chairs up here, only a brightly coloured hammock slung between the two walls enclosing the terrace.

'You can't see very far away into the distance because of the all the city smog. It's worse in the summer but sometimes if you're up here very early in the morning, just before sunset, you can get a nice view of the sunrise.'

Hannah had a look at the view and then walked back to try out the hammock.

'Is it strong enough to hold me?' she asked nervously,

tentatively sitting on it.

'Yes, of course it is. It would hold both of us. Look at the hooks that attach it to the wall, they're cemented into the wall.'

Hannah sunk back into the hammock and swung it gently by pushing against the wall with her left hand.

'This is so comfortable. I think I could spend the whole two weeks just lying here and dozing off.'

'If that's what you want to do, you can.'

She quickly lifted up her head out of the hammock and looked at me.

'Raoul, I was only joking. What were you thinking we could do?'

Taking my courage into my hands I reached over and brushed a strand of Hannah's hair away from her face.

'I was thinking... we could spend a little time, a very little time... kissing.' I said bending my head down to reach hers and covering her mouth with my own.

I took my time exploring the sweet centre of her mouth before pulling away from her to smile at her.

To my relief Hannah smiled back at me, before grabbing my arms and pulling me into the hammock, nearly oversetting us both onto the hard tiled floor in the process.

46

I watched as Hannah stretched out her toes, relishing the feel of the soft sand cushioned beneath them.

In the distance I could hear the sound of the waves gently folding over and crumpling into the sand.

A mild and warm breeze teased an annoying strand of hair that had come loose from Hannah's ponytail.

She was sitting upright gazing across at the endless blue sea.

Ten minutes ago I was fast asleep on my back with my baseball cap over my face, just like an old man. I had on a pair of old swimming trunks that had faded with use, so instead of a deep red colour they were now bleached a salmon pink colour from the sun's rays.

Unlike Hannah I hadn't bothered to lie on a beach towel, as I always liked to run into the sea to wash off the sand that had glued itself to me after lying on the beach.

We were both feeling pleasurably tired.

At least neither of us snored I thought.

We'd spent so much time up at night, enjoying each other's bodies, I would've never been able to cope if on top of everything else Hannah had kept me up with her snoring.

My mother had already given me the inevitable embarrassing chat about contraception. She'd suffered through her own carelessness as a young girl and didn't want mistakes to be repeated, especially with Hannah, when she felt she owed Marion and David so much.

However my mother clearly hadn't grasped how well educated children at Ellerslie School were as far as sexual education went, and how freely available access to contraception was.

It had taken a while but eventually, with the fatalistic calm she exuded towards most things in life, my mother had come round to accepting my relationship with Hannah.

My mother's always been determined to let nothing disturb the close, harmonious bond we both have with each other, and had realised by now this meant letting me make my own decisions.

In the end Hannah and I hadn't done a huge amount of sightseeing in Mexico City.

We'd taken Pax for a long walk every day, and we'd visited the art displays at Plaza San Jacinto several times. We walked up and down past the displays of artwork in the dappled sunlight, our shadows flickering between the overhanging trees.

Hannah decided to buy a small painting of a Quetzal bird as she said the green and red colours in its plumage reminded her of Mexico.

Hannah liked San Angel; she loved the cobblestone streets and the rich waterfalls of bougainvillea hanging down from every possible wall or doorway.

We'd visited Diego Rivera and Frida Kahlo's house in San Angel, as well as Frida's Blue house in Colonia del Carmen.

Hannah didn't like the box-like modern house in San Angel as she felt it was too clinical and functional.

In her opinion it didn't fit in with its surroundings, but she liked Frida Kahlo's more traditional Blue house.

This was Frida's childhood family home with its bright yellow kitchen and blue and red primary colours.

Every time I visit these museums I keep thinking what an odd couple these famous Mexican artists were: Diego, an obese communist supporter of Stalin, and Frida, disabled, wearing leather or plaster corsets to support her damaged spine but so strong in spirit.

Frida produced paintings that portrayed her loneliness and her pain but Diego's paintings by contrast were very organic in rich, sensual, earthy colours, showing his appreciation and enjoyment of nature.

I love the way he portrays Mexican peasants, sunflowers and lilies. The two artists strangely different given they were a couple; yet both gifted.

I looked at my watch.

We'd been lying on the warm sand like lazy slugs for the last two hours. Soon we'd have to head back indoors to join Fernando and mum for dinner.

The two of them had taken Pax out for a walk along a path that stretched along the edge of the beach and beside the dense forest of trees, but they had probably returned to the beach house by now.

There was no other house on this beach but Fernando's, and it was strange to feel so isolated from all civilization.

The first morning after arriving, Hannah had raced out of the back door of the house and onto the beach with glee; only to find the sand was so hot it burned the soles of her feet.

I found it very funny.

She'd hobbled back in and from then on would only lie on the beach in the early morning or evening.

Occasionally she'd put her plastic sandals on and refresh herself by running into the sea, closely chased by me. We'd throw ourselves into the water carelessly and with abandon.

Sometimes I'd stumble onto a giant pink conch shell washed up in the shallows and I'd pick the shell up and give it to Hannah. She'd kept two of them to take back with her to Scotland.

Hannah reached over and let her fingers crawl up my bare midriff, waking me up just as I was drifting off again.

I hated it when she did that.

I lifted my head with a jerk and let my baseball cap fall on the sand.

'¿*Que?*'

Hannah grinned at me, looking like a wicked sprite.

'Raoul, we should head back soon and join your mum and Fernando for dinner.'

I rubbed my eyes and yawned.

'OK. Are you coming to join me in the water?'

'Sure.'

I stood up and reached down to pull Hannah up.

Hannah took a deep breath and ran the short distance into the sea but I was faster than her this time, and staggered through the soft waves as I threw myself into the seawater.

Hannah followed behind me and collapsed into the sea, shutting her eyes as she slipped into the cool water. Noticing her bikini top had loosened, she stood up quickly holding on to it.

I watched her with a mischievous look on my face.

'Raoul, was that you?' asked Hannah, half laughing.

I nodded.

'Do you want me to fix it for you?'

285

Hannah turned around and presented her back to me which was too much for me to resist, so I pulled the remaining strings loose and reached from behind her to cup her breasts.

Hannah looked anxiously back at the house.

'Raoul', she protested, 'I don't want your mum to see us like this.'

I didn't answer. I was busy nuzzling her neck by now.

Hannah nudged me gently.

'Raoul, did you hear me?'

'Don't worry about mum, just move into deeper water and she'll see nothing,' I said, pulling her further into the sea, with Hannah still holding on to her bikini top.

Half an hour later we made our way, hand in hand, to the house. Gradually as we came closer to the beach house the rich smells of charred meat enticed us and made us quicken our pace.

It could only be a barbeque.

Fernando was making dinner tonight, which meant he would grill the meat over the barbeque while my mother would make a salad with freshly baked bread.

Hannah loved the simple food we ate at the beach house. The rich Mexican food we'd eaten in Mexico City the week before had upset her stomach. Used to blander and less spicy food, she struggled to acclimatise to the strong flavours in traditional Mexican cuisine.

As the evening became darker we drew the mosquito nets over the windows and the outside doors. Even our beds had hanging mosquito nets.

The indoor lights didn't just attract mosquitos; many other insects were drawn to the light.

We also had to be careful to allow no smell of food to linger after we'd eaten, because both ants and cockroaches would be attracted to it and then we'd have a nightmare trying to get rid of them. There'd been times in previous years when we'd woken up in the morning to find the kitchen swamped by a tidal wave of ants.

There was always a culprit, sometimes it was a half empty Coke glass or some cake crumbs scattered on the floor.

Ever since she was a little girl Hannah has been terrified of insects in any shape or form.

Every time a big spider snuck into this beach house, or a large moth bumped against the shutters, the rest of us had to remove it before Hannah was able to relax again.

My mother was used to Hannah's nervousness around insects. She could still remember how Hannah as a little girl had panicked whenever she saw insects near her.

When the Andersons first moved into their house in Mexico it had been full of insects. Because the house had been left unused for a few months, a multitude of little spiders had made their home on the white ceilings of the upstairs bedrooms.

From the first night Hannah had refused to sleep in her bedroom until it had been cleared of spiders.

Her brothers by contrast were completely unfazed by spiders and insects; they'd enjoyed accompanying their dad to the golf course where occasionally some of the caddies, who had nothing much to do, would dig the large hairy spiders out of their underground lairs and get the male spiders to fight each other.

Unfortunately for Hannah, outside this little beach house, the moths quite often flew onto the outdoor lamps and sizzled quickly to death. Hannah found this completely gruesome but

287

there was no way to stop this if we were going to sit or cook outside in the evenings. The rest of us had become so used to it we barely noticed the insects frying on our exposed lamps.

We sat at the kitchen table, where my mother had nicely laid out the pretty, brightly coloured and painted ceramic plates and the dark green chunky wine glasses.

I poured Hannah a large glass of red wine and shortly afterwards Fernando came in with a big dish filled with grilled steaks.

This was our last night at the kitchen table before packing up in the morning and leaving just after lunch to head back to Mexico City, returning to normal life once more.

No doubt, as with every other evening at the house, Fernando (once his confidence had been buoyed up with some wine) would bring out his guitar and play us some music that would steadily drown out the noisy crickets that would continue to rub their wings throughout the night until dawn broke.

'So Hannah, when are you going to start your university term?' my mother asked, as she helped herself to some salad after passing it around the table.

'I don't start until October. I'll be going back and doing some more shifts at the shop I've been working in over the holidays, before I head off to St Andrews.'

'St Andrews? Where Prince William met Kate?' asked Fernando.

'Yes.'

'Ouf, Raoul, you'd better look out! I believe they say one in five students who go to St Andrews University end up getting married to a fellow student.'

I didn't bother replying to his comment because I considered it in poor taste. I also suspected Fernando was trying to rile me, in much the same way as he so often wound up my mother.

'And for how long will you be studying there, Hannah?'

'Four years.'

My mother raised her small hands in horror.

'*Madre de Dios.* That's a long time. For Raoul it'll be the same. Four years in Santa Catarina. Personally, I think it's too long and for Raoul's sake I hope it'll be worth it. Studying for so long is such a big commitment in time and money.'

'I think the course he'll be doing in Santa Catarina will be perfect for Raoul. It's what he's always wanted to do and he's already had plenty of work experience with Fernando, so I'm sure he'll be at an advantage compared to everyone else there.'

As Hannah looked proudly at me, the covert look Fernando exchanged with my mother did not escape me. I pretended not to notice. I was quite happy for Hannah to be besotted with me.

'I'm going to study Chemistry at St Andrews but I've no idea what I'll be doing at the end with it. I just knew I couldn't do a subject that gave me only four lectures a week. I'd rather be in the lab working away. I like the structure and routine of work.'

Fernando nodded.

'Chemistry's a very useful and practical subject. I'm sure you'll know what to do with it once you finish.'

I swallowed some wine.

'Raoul, you're very quiet tonight', said Fernando, turning his curiously light blue eyes towards me.

I lifted my eyebrows.

'I'm fine. I'm completely full. It's making me dopey', I rubbed my stomach, 'too much food and not enough exercise.'

Fernando smiled to himself.

I knew straight away what he was thinking. I often used the running machine in Fernando's garage back in Mexico City, but I was sure Fernando was thinking I was getting plenty of other exercise with Hannah at the beach house.

I decided to change the subject and stood up.

'Hannah, let's get the washing up done and then we can play a few games of poker.'

Every evening at the beach house, which had no television, the four of us occupied ourselves by playing poker. Fernando preferred to play La Zanga but unfortunately the rest of us, who already understood how to play poker, outnumbered him in preferring poker.

Hannah was a poor loser and told me sternly she'd seen a ruthless and competitive streak in me when I played poker. She clearly wasn't enjoying playing poker as much as the rest of us were.

This didn't bother me in the slightest.

I was pleased with myself because I'd amassed a huge lead playing poker, and this meant I'd be the one to choose the restaurant in Mexico City we would eat in before Hannah returned to the UK.

Three short days later, back in San Angel, Fernando lifted Hannah's old battered suitcase into the boot of his car. The three of us got into the car and headed to the airport again.

My mother had given Hannah a fond farewell earlier that morning, giving her a sweet silver and turquoise bangle as a leaving present before she left the house to go to work.

I sat in the back of the car holding Hannah's hand as Fernando drove us through the chaotic roads on the way to the airport.

I know Hannah was dreading the thought of making her way through airport security again. She'd been very quiet this morning but she'd only say she wasn't looking forward to the trip home.

Was she also depressed at leaving me? I couldn't tell.

As soon as we were in the airport, at the departures entrance, Fernando said a quick goodbye to Hannah and then discreetly went to look for a newspaper, leaving us alone to say our good-byes to each other.

Both of us had avoided talking about the inevitable separation looming ahead of us after our holidays.

I think both of us were in denial really.

We both knew it was unlikely our relationship would survive, but in those precious moments we had together neither of us wanted to accept the inevitable ending.

I guess thinking about it now, all these years later, I never realised back then that I'd spend years in my twenties asking myself what things would have been like between us had we studied in the same country or city. Hannah would always be the big unanswered question in my life, the unresolved relationship.

I've no idea if Hannah ever asks herself these questions.

Probably unlikely, given she chose to marry someone else in the UK.

Back then I really didn't want to lose contact with Hannah and I was determined to keep in touch with her.

And right up until today we've kept in touch with each other. For the last ten years we've emailed, Skyped and Whatsapped each other with varying degrees of frequency.

Now it's 2018.

I've received this call from Austin Mitchell, and a rather ambiguous Christmas card from Hannah, and I'm debating with myself whether it's worth trying to connect properly with her again.

I've often in recent days asked myself if she could be thinking about me now she's single again.

It's one o'clock in the morning and I'm sitting in my armchair, holding the photo where Hannah and my mother have their arms around each other, wondering if I've the courage to make myself vulnerable and ask Hannah what's really going on in her life.

47

I get up from my armchair and stretch out my arms.

Gordo, my cat, has given up on me going to bed and has curled up in a huff on the sofa, with his back to me.

I decide to reach out for my phone and dial Hannah's number. Unsurprisingly it rings out. It's seven in the morning in the UK and still very early.

I try again. It picks up on the fourth ring.

'Raoul?'

'Hi Hannah.'

'Is everything OK?'

'Yes, I guess so.'

'Raoul, I've to got to get ready for work. Can we talk later?'

'Sure. I'll call you this evening.'

'This evening isn't great Raoul. I've a drinks thing at the University. Can we talk tomorrow?'

'Sure. Speak to you tomorrow.'

'OK. Bye Raoul. Take care.'

I hang up feeling dissatisfied.

Never mind, I'll call tomorrow.

For now it's time to crash and recover some sleep before another full on day at the studio. I leave the photo albums on the coffee table and disappear into my bedroom.

My bedroom's a very minimalist space because I find clutter

a burden to my mind after a day at the studio. I spend my workdays surrounded by Christina's messy disorder and I want my home to be my haven.

This room might look sparse and empty to some but it's actually restful for me.

The walls are white which make the rainbow colours of my patchwork quilt stand out like sparkling jewels.

Apart from my kindle and alarm clock there's nothing on my bedside tables.

A bright yellow chair in the shape of a Henry Moore sculpture sits in the corner of the room. The shutters on my window are also painted white. The floorboards and lights in my room are white.

Within fifteen minutes I've kicked off my slippers and collapsed into my bed.

It feels like seconds before I'm brutally awoken by my alarm clock.

I fling my clothes on; drink four espressos and race out of the flat omitting to shave, as I've no client visits today. No doubt Christina will scold me like a mother hen but I don't care because it's Friday today, and I have plans to go out tonight.

I'll be shaving later, before going to a friend's house for dinner. A few glasses of wine with a group of my close friends and their partners will mellow me enough to sleep in tomorrow and recover my lost sleep.

I always find it amazing how we are able to find ways to distract ourselves from our emotional difficulties.

I'm quite an expert at it.

Unfortunately there's also good reason to believe this talent in disconnecting has led to several failed relationships in my case. I've found it hard to be fully engaged emotionally and romantically with anyone on a long-term basis.

Christina calls me Mr Butterfly because she says I flit from one promising lady to another at the slightest pretext.

'Raoul, you look like shit', is Christina's only comment when she sees me this morning.

'Thanks.'

Christina, her laptop slung across her shoulders, whirls around the studio collecting her fabric and wall paper books before hurrying out for her first appointment.

After the door to the studio has clicked back into place, I get up and make my way into the kitchen to search for some food. It's the end of the week and there's not much to see in the fridge. I pour myself a glass of orange juice and wait for some bread to toast.

I hear my mobile ringing but ignore it. If it's important they can leave a message.

It's only when I reach my desk again and look at my mobile I realise my missed call is from Hannah. I quickly dial her number and she picks up at the third ring.

'Hi Raoul. Is it OK to talk? I'm on my lunch break but I know it's early in the morning over there.'

I rub my face with my hand, trying to waken myself up.

'Yeah. Don't worry. We're snowed under with projects here so I've come into work early. I'll probably be back in again on Sunday too.'

'It sounds like you're as busy as ever. I just wasn't sure you were OK and I felt bad postponing our conversation this morning.'

'Don't feel bad, I totally understand and thanks for calling back. It really wasn't anything important. I was looking over some old photos yesterday and thinking of you. Looking at those photos was making me feel very nostalgic.' I feel myself tensing up as I decide to ask her about Austin. 'Your Christmas card this year worried me too since Austin wasn't on it. I was hoping things were OK with you?'

There was a slight pause before Hannah spoke.

'No, things aren't great here, Raoul,' said Hannah, her voice cracking slightly. 'I don't really want to talk about it in detail, but Austin and I've split up. I'm currently in the middle of a nasty divorce. My parents have been brilliant though, and I'm really grateful for their support. They're the ones keeping me together. What photos were you looking at by the way? Are they ones from our time in Mexico or later?'

'There's photos of Mexico and Scotland, as well as some from our summer break in Mexico before we left to go to college and university.'

Hannah laughed.

'That was such a long time ago. I feel like I've aged a million years since then! Life seemed so much easier then. So you're doing OK, apart from working all hours? You should sort that out. Hire someone else or something.'

I recoiled at the thought.

'I think Christina and me are too set in our ways to cope with accepting anyone else into the business. I think we'll just have to keep raising our prices until it gets under control. That's Christina's solution to everything.'

'When did you last have a holiday?'

I grimaced.

'I think the last holiday I had was Christmas Day.'

'I meant when did you last have a proper two week holiday?'

'2013 I think', I said, laughing to myself.

'I think that's shocking. Is that even legal?' Hannah asked, not finding it funny.

I sighed.

'Hannah, this is Mexico. Anything goes. We're not tied to employment law like you are.'

'Would Christina let you take the time off?'

'Yes, she would. I'm not being forced into work. The business belongs to us both remember, so we're both motivated to make it a success. We enjoy it but it does get out of hand sometimes.'

'Raoul, I've got to head back into work in ten minutes. Was there anything else you wanted to talk to me about?'

I decide to make a bold suggestion on the spur of the moment. Adding a little emotional blackmail at the same time.

'Hannah, I'd take some holiday time off if you'd come and visit me here.'

'Why don't you come and visit us?'

'Because it wouldn't be a holiday.'

'What do you mean?' asks Hannah, sounding offended.

'I mean the weather over there isn't as good, and it sounds like your life's complicated and messy. As you should know there're plenty of nice places here to go to for a holiday. It would feel like a holiday for you too and from what you're saying, it sounds like you need a holiday.'

'It's a nice idea but it's not realistic at the moment, I'm afraid. And before you say anything don't offer to pay for the trip. It's not a financial problem.'

'I'm missing you, Hannah. I'd love us to catch up properly again.'

'I know. It would be nice. Maybe some time in the future. Just not a good time at the moment,' said Hannah, sounding weary. 'You're sounding desperately lonely.'

'Not desperate and not lonely', I said firmly. 'Nostalgic. You're a big part of my childhood.'

'I know. Likewise. Do you ever wonder if we could've made a relationship work if we were in the same country?'

'Often.'

'Anyway, I've got to go. Let's talk again soon.'

'Sounds good. Bye Hannah.'

I hang up and turn to my computer.

Thank God for work.

At least this part of my life's fulfilling. By the end of the day I've fully completed five projects. I've made a big inroad into our backlog of client work, and I'm happy to leave now and unwind with some friends this evening.

Tomorrow I'll be driving my car to San Angel to see my mother and Fernando.

Hopefully on the way I'll avoid any corrupt, yet avidly zealous, traffic policeman who might've developed a fondness for pulling car drivers up for a fabricated traffic misdemeanour, and then deciding to demand a bribe in order not to charge them.

Unfortunately this is happening in my city with increasing frequency.

48

I didn't hear from Hannah for another two weeks and even then the phone call was brief.

At this point I gave up hoping we'd ever meet up.

This year is clearly not the right time for a reunion, and as I write this it's now April 2018 and life's carrying on at its usual steady pace.

I've buried my head in my work and I've enjoyed occasional meals out with my friends, in dispersed with theatre and cinema visits.

Everything's returned to its usual clockwork routine.

Spring has arrived, the cacti outside the studio are starting to blossom, and the large palm tree in our courtyard is bustling with the activity and loud screams of the swallows nesting in it.

The only excitement we've had this year occurred in March when Christina, a force to be reckoned with, successfully won a court case against a client who hadn't settled his final payment to us for interior design work.

How she had the energy to fight it out in court I'll never know.

I'm too lazy, I'm afraid, to chase errant clients who don't pay in full. We're already rolling in it and we didn't need his final payment but Christina says we've to set a precedent.

Anyway once she'd decided to proceed to court I'd offered my full support, but she likes to fight these battles by herself.

Some people get out their unnecessary aggression in the boxing ring or in taekwondo classes. Christina lets out her aggression by lambasting any client who pays late or not at all. She reminds me of a fierce terrier at times.

My impression is she holds a lot of hidden anger inside of her.

As for myself, I'm slightly bored.

The clients I've worked with in recent weeks are well meaning enough but they're all near retirement age and very conservative.

That's the problem with providing an expensive service, you straight away cut out the younger generation who'll be keeping an eye on the bottom line.

I'd prefer to work with people who are willing to take risks with their interior design. That's where the creative process can really begin and the projects can excite me.

Christina thinks this is nonsense.

She tells me I'm in denial about my age and we're doing well enough without taking any risks. I resist telling her she's behaving just like my elderly clients.

Christina's been behaving slightly erratically recently.

You can't work for years in close proximity to someone without fathoming all aspects of their personality. I'm not normally overly sensitive to other people's emotional states, but I can tell something's changed in Christina's outlook recently.

These days she seems unusually cheerful, and this means the little things that go wrong amuse her rather than frustrate her.

She's also showing me a great deal of thoughtfulness and kindness, so much so I've started to become suspicious.

In the end, after much fruitless conjecture, I've decided to confront her about this positive change in her personality, and

I choose a moment when she's offered to help me out with one of my clients.

'Christina, something's going on and you are not telling me about it.'

Christina turns her large, slightly bulbous, eyes my way with an innocent expression on her face that doesn't deceive me for a second.

'What do you mean?'

'Something's changed in you and I can't figure it out. Do you have a new man in your life?'

I can tell right away my suggestion isn't correct.

Christina's face folds and crumples, and she laughs until tears come trickling down her lean cheeks.

I suddenly feel very foolish.

Christina wipes the tears from her cheeks and shakes her head at me.

'Raoul, trust me when I've a 'new man in my life' you'll be the first to know about it. I wish! There are few who would choose to be with a work obsessed old hag like me.'

'Christina. Come off it. You're still attractive.'

'Thank you,' said Christina laughing. 'I'm quite happy without that complication in my life thank you very much. I'm sure there'll be plenty who are interested in my bank balance but I don't have the desire to invest emotionally in anyone at the moment. I'm too selfish.'

'Christina, there's been a change in you recently. I'm not stupid. What are you hiding from me?'

'I admit I'm plotting something but it's nothing for you to worry about. I'll tell you about it another time.'

'OK', I said grumpily, 'but if it involves the business I'd like to know. I've the right to find out about any changes you're planning.'

'I promise you it doesn't involve the business.'

I look intently at Christina and see she still looks amused, but I can tell from her expression she's telling me the truth.

Whatever it is she's planning it doesn't involve work, and so by default it has nothing to do with me.

I turn back to my desk and grab my stress ball to relieve some of my tension.

As I squeeze the globe and look at my computer screen I reflect thankfully on the fact that Christina's never objected to my fidgeting.

My concentration levels often fluctuate so I'm usually constantly playing around with my stress globe, my ballpoint pen or large paperclips, and I can totally see how this restless habit could annoy Christina.

Ever since I spoke to Hannah about taking a holiday, I haven't been able to shake off the notion.

I know I need a holiday but at the moment there's truthfully nobody I'd like to go on holiday with. I've a few male friends who'd be enthusiastic at the idea of going away on holiday together to get drunk, chat up some girls and get laid.

That kind of holiday is losing its appeal for me.

I could go away on my own, I've always been happy in my own company, but I suspect I'd end up feeling slightly depressed.

The thought of visiting Hannah in Scotland has often crossed my mind, however if I'm going to take time off I selfishly want it to be restful, and I suspect her life at the moment is anything but restful.

Then I have a quick look at my desk and shake off any wishful thinking, pulling the next client file out of the pile.

Unfortunately my placid existence is marred a few days later, when I come close to losing my temper with a client who's suddenly changed his mind about the designs we'd agreed on for his house.

My designs for his home have taken me at least five days of work to finish but regardless of this he wants me to start again, completely from scratch, with a different colour scheme and a new conceptual style. Of course, at the time I found myself meekly accepting all the changes the client requested, and then I proceeded to get annoyed at myself afterwards for having done so.

That afternoon, once I'm parked outside my office, I trudge into the building thinking a myriad of bad thoughts about my difficult to please client.

Such was my bad mood I believe if I'd come across my client at this point in time I would've been tempted to punch him.

I'm generally considered reasonably even-tempered so the violence of my feelings surprises me.

I've a strong urge to break something and already I'm wondering if I can gratify this desire in the studio, assuming Christina's not around to see me.

I genuinely hope Christina's not in the studio because I might end up taking out my foul mood on her.

I open the door and as I look ahead I freeze in disbelief.

Hannah is sitting at my desk, cup of tea in her hands, chatting to Christina.

She's reclining at ease in my desk chair, dressed in a long red cotton skirt, a white top and some cheap looking espadrilles.

She looks so much older than I remember, but it probably doesn't help the images of her in my head are from photos taken when she was a teenager, or from infrequent and blurred video calls.

She's stopped talking now and is watching me carefully, smiling slightly at my confusion.

Her hair's darkened with time to hazel with blonder highlights, and where her eyes narrow with her smile I see crow's feet have already made their mark, but the smile is the same as I remember.

I drop my briefcase and hurry across the floor to give her a big embrace. Her short hair smells enticingly of jasmine.

I turn to look accusingly at Christina.

'Christina, is this what you've been planning?'

Christina nods, looking both amused and pleased in equal measure. 'When did you get here, Hannah?'

'Two hours ago. Christina picked me up from the airport. We weren't sure how long you'd be with your client but we wanted to surprise you so we decided to wait here', Hannah says.

I notice her Spanish is still fairly fluent.

'It's wonderful. Absolutely brilliant. Are you on your own?'

Hannah laughs.

'Yes, you've been let off the hook.'

I run a hand over my hair, grinning foolishly.

'How long are you here for?'

'Ten days only, I'm afraid. I've got quite a lot of stuff to get done before I go back to work so I've had to allow myself a few days at home.'

'That's fantastic, Hannah. I don't know what to say. I'm so pleased to see you. Thank you for making the trip.'

Christina interrupts us, clearly eager for us to get on with it.

'Raoul my love, you're to take ten days off and disappear somewhere nice. Don't even think about work, you need a break. I've notified your clients you'll be on vacation, so you've nothing to do but to take yourself off to where ever you want to go.'

I feel a sense of calm take hold of me. My family bring me comfort and peace and I can honestly say Hannah, even after all these years, is like family to me too.

I decide I've had enough of the studio.

'Hannah, where are your bags?'

She walks into the kitchen and stumbles out carrying a large and heavy suitcase; you'd think she was staying for a month instead of ten days.

I quickly take the bulky suitcase from her and turn to Christina.

'Thank you, Christina. You're a star. I'll pay you back in kind one day. If you don't mind we'll head out now and make the most of the time we have.'

Christina casually waves her hand at us.

'Of course, darlings. Get out of here and have some fun. This place unfortunately will still be here when you get back.'

I hold the studio door open for Hannah and within a few minutes we're in my car and driving leisurely to my flat.

As we talk to each other in the car I find I'm constantly turning my head to stare at Hannah, I'm still finding it hard to believe she's here in person. My bad mood from earlier this morning has evaporated and I feel my mind shedding my clients with every mile that distances me from my studio.

49

As soon as we arrive at my flat I take Hannah's case through to the spare bedroom and then while she's sorting out her things, I have a good look inside my kitchen cupboards.

I have literally no food in the house as I've become accustomed to long hours at work and a bachelor existence at the weekends.

I have a few beers in the fridge and some Coca Cola. I nip back to the spare bedroom to tell Hannah I'm just popping out to get some supplies. I race out of the flat to my local supermarket and pile the trolley up with miscellaneous products.

I'm a useless cook so I suspect for the most part we'll be eating out or eating with family who'll be delighted to see her.

When I get back, having lugged the shopping bags out of the lift and into the kitchen, I find Hannah's finished tidying herself up and had a good look around the flat.

'This flat's beautiful, Raoul. I love the view you have over the gardens. Is this area very exclusive?'

I shrug.

'It's a good area. I was lucky to get this flat. Christina and I knew the developer as we've done up various show homes for them over the years. I managed to book this one before they were available to reserve.'

'You've done well for yourself', said Hannah, smiling.

'So have you, Hannah', I say defensively.

In the past Hannah's always been ever so slightly scornful of the exceptionally rich in society, which I'd always felt was hypocritical given she comes from a very middleclass family, though to be honest who knows what she really thinks now.

It's been such a long time since I last saw her.

'Anyway, what would you like to drink?' I ask, changing the subject.

We both walk into the kitchen and Hannah perches on the kitchen stool, accepting a glass of orange juice from me.

I'm quick to notice how she's a little awkward, perhaps even uncomfortable, with me.

Looking at her under the harsh kitchen lighting I can see how much she's experienced the last few years.

Her skin's very pale, almost blue in tinge, and lined. The lines on her forehead hint at the worries she's had. However her eyes are the same, clear blue and unwavering in their expression. They seem to pierce like a laser right into my mind and expose those parts of myself I'd rather ignore.

Suddenly I don't feel so pleased with myself, or with the life I'm leading anymore.

Hannah's lived a life full of meaning. She works as a pharmacist at the hospital for a start. In comparison my life seems strangely hollow and artificial.

'Raoul, are you OK? What are you thinking?' Hannah asks anxiously.

I shake off my morose thoughts.

'Nothing important, Hannah', I say. ' Shall I break open the wine? I could do with a glass.'

'Of course. I hope I haven't inconvenienced you turning up like this?'

I reach over and give her a hug, kissing her on the head.

'You haven't at all. I needed to take a break from work and I'm delighted to see you again. I'd given up hope you'd ever come. What changed your mind?'

'To be honest when Christina called me I thought it was the perfect excuse to run away for a bit. Sometimes when life gets to be too difficult you need to escape the treadmill for a short time and recharge the batteries. I couldn't think of a better place to go than to visit you here.'

'What exactly did Christina tell you?'

Hannah smiled.

'Christina phoned me at the start of March and said you were missing me and needed a break. She basically wanted to arrange a surprise visit for you. She did a great job selling the idea to me. She must be an asset to your work.'

'Yes, she's an amazing saleswoman. Not that she needs to be because her work sells itself.'

I take a sip of wine and the recognizable warm notes of plum and a hint of pepper fill my palette. I often buy this particular wine from my local supermarket.

Moving to the kitchen sofa I invite Hannah to take a seat.

'What would you like to do while you're here? Is there anywhere you'd like to go?'

'I'd love to see your mum again obviously and the street we used to live in. Other than that I really don't mind. It's your holiday too.'

'I'll give it some thought. I've a few ideas but I'll sleep on it. How are your brothers by the way?'

'Patrick's doing well. He's based in London working for Quarry Bank. I don't see him very often but he was very kind and supportive towards me as I went through the divorce. Stephen's studying in Loughborough and having a great time. I've lost count of the number of girlfriends he's had since he started there. He comes up quite a lot to visit us in Edinburgh.'

'And Janet?'

'You need to visit her soon, Raoul. I'm not saying that to put pressure on you to come and see us. She's becoming quite frail and I think you'd be shocked to see the change in her. It would be sad if you didn't get a chance to see her before she passes away, she's always had a soft spot for you.'

I feel a twinge of guilt niggle at me.

'You're right. Janet always seems so indestructible. I chat to her regularly and she sounds totally with it, but a phone call never shows you how someone's doing physically. Which makes me wonder by the way, when were you planning on telling me about your divorce?'

'It's not something I particularly want to talk about, Raoul. Don't take it personally. It's all so sad and painful. The only way I manage to cope is to focus on the positive and try to avoid thinking of the negatives.'

'Yes. I get it. By the way are you OK with a platter of cold meats and cheese?'

As Hannah nods I get up and start preparing some food.

Hannah stretches out her long legs and yawns.

'I'm sure I'm going to sleep like a lead weight tonight. There's nothing like escaping from everyday life to help you forget your troubles and sleep well.'

'Feel free to crash whenever you feel like it. There are no rules in my household.'

Hannah didn't last long.

A short time later, as we watch television, she falls fast asleep on my velvet and cushioned Chesterfield sofa. I look at her as she slumbers, noting the delicate trace of her eyelashes shadowing her cheeks, and the way her long fingered hands rest peacefully on her lap. In that moment, as she sleeps next to me on the sofa, she looks so beautiful and statuesque.

The program we are watching is a documentary exploring Mexico's Pacific coast. As the documentary drones on about the prized oysters of the Mexican Pacific coast I begin to think Hannah reminds me of the enduring myths of the oyster.

She's been through so much but she's still the same beautiful person inside.

The oyster turns the irritating grains of sand into a beautiful pearl.

It's a gift to be able to bring some good out of adversity and Hannah seems to have that capacity.

Tempted to fall asleep beside her, I decide it's kinder to wake her so she can get to her bed. I shake her gently until she's sufficiently awake to make her way to her bedroom and a comfortable bed.

50

From the start I was determined to be on best behaviour during Hannah's visit although my good intentions didn't last long.

As I began to see glimpses of the old Hannah I began to fall under her spell again.

Hannah and I share a similar awareness of the ridiculous in life, and it was so nice to be able to catch her eye when something I found irresistibly funny happened. Her every gesture and facial expression felt oddly familiar to me.

I tried to restrain my Mexican tactility but before long I was hugging and touching Hannah with no conscious thought. Hannah didn't seem to mind this and before long we fell into a natural relationship, sisterly on her behalf and anything but, on mine.

My family understandably were surprised to see Hannah but welcomed her with great joy; in fact my mother had tears in her eyes when she saw her.

My mother's aged greatly since Hannah last saw her. Her ebony hair is now mixed with numerous strands of white gleaming against her brown skin, and she's cut it short into a chic bob. My mother's warm brown eyes are surrounded by fine wrinkles but she carries herself with grace and still is a beautiful woman.

She has her own circle of friends now and they meet up regularly, when she isn't travelling to the beach house with Fernando.

Both my grandparents are enjoying their retirement, although quite frankly it's a life that wouldn't suit me, it's too tame for my taste. Maybe growing up with my elderly grandparents has made the leisurely life the elderly lead an anathema to me.

I can still see myself continuing to work well into my seventies.

In the end we only made two trips during Hannah's short stay.

Hannah wasn't keen on having a beach holiday, now she was revisiting Mexico she wanted to see some of the sites she'd never been to before, so in the end we went to see the great pyramid of Cholula, which thankfully was only a day trip away.

This pyramid is the largest pyramid to exist in the world but it also, bizarrely, has a Spanish chapel built on the top of it. Legend has it when the local Indian tribe heard of the Spanish invasion they tried to disguise the pyramid with earth, and so the Spanish actually believed they were building a chapel on the top of a hill.

There are many archaeologists who are desperate to discover more about this ancient site that stretches for 154 hectares, but there's resistance to archaeological exploration from the landowners and the local indigenous population who like to preserve the sanctity of the area.

The archaeologists have discovered murals inside the pyramid. These murals are a faded version of their original selves but you can see the multitude of colours used in their decoration, red, green, ochre, blue, brown and black. Colour is in the Mexican DNA.

Outside the pyramid the chapel perches on the top of it, looking as remote as a Tibetan monastery. Dominating the horizon and hanging over the chapel like an ominous monster is the snow-capped, active volcano Popocatepetl.

The second trip Hannah and I made was to Las Pozas, a tropical coffee plantation turned into a surreal garden in the 1940's by an eccentric British gentleman, Edward James.

This trip was a long one so we stopped on the way there and on the way back at San Luis Potosi, an old mining town where we visited the Tamul Waterfall, which is considered by many to be the most beautiful waterfall in all of Mexico, and wandered among the colonial buildings and churches.

The rest of the vacation we stayed in Mexico City.

Hannah familiarised herself with coffee shops near my flat and seemed to even enjoy visiting the local supermarket. The time we had together seemed to fly quickly by, and in that short space of time we managed to fill in the many gaps in our understanding of each other's lives.

I had the opportunity to speak to David and Marion on Skype. It's been many years since I communicated with them. I can clearly see now how the stress Hannah's undergone in her life has marked her, but Marion and David were the same as I remembered them.

I only overstepped our self imposed boundaries once during Hannah's visit.

In my defence, I did so one morning when I'd just woken up and made my way to the kitchen.

I'm never at my best in the mornings and I'd consider myself a night owl. I'd been sleeping in late in the mornings, of course, whereas Hannah seemed to have no problem waking up early.

She'd just showered and come through to the kitchen, in just a towelling robe, just as I was helping myself to my second espresso.

Without thinking consciously about it, I bent down and kissed her on the lips as she stood next to me putting some bread in the toaster.

She didn't draw back straight away but soon enough.

'Raoul, what are you doing?'

'Sorry Hannah', I said, taken aback and worried I'd be in trouble, 'I wasn't thinking. It was just instinctual.'

Hannah tenderly pushed back my hair.

'I know, I get it. I just can't get involved emotionally with anyone right now. It's too painful I'm afraid after all I've been through.'

'How about getting involved physically without the emotion?' I asked cheekily, resigning myself to the fact it wasn't going to happen.

Hannah hugged me, which was meant to be sympathetic, but I wasn't feeling like receiving commiseration at that precise moment.

'I couldn't do that to you, Raoul.'

'Try it.'

Hannah grinned at me, looking so like the teenager I knew, I had to stop myself from kissing her again.

I looked at her and reached out to give her bathrobe a sharp tug so that the belt untied. Just like with the peeling of a pear, the bathrobe split apart to reveal the marble white smooth tones of her skin all the way down to her pubic hair.

I looked at Hannah's face.

Her clear blue eyes looked steadily at me, with the same amount of arousal I'm sure was reflected in mine.

Our subsequent lovemaking was tender, yet tinged with certain sadness. This wasn't a second chance at a relationship, it was a joining of two people who'd shared many precious moments in life but who were soon going to be divided yet again by the impossible barriers of distance, time, work and family.

Later on we lay calmly in each other's arms, silently looking out of the window at the scurrying clouds.

Three days later, having dropped Hannah off at the airport the previous evening, I park outside the studio and lift my briefcase out of the passenger seat.

I bend my head back to catch the early morning rays of sun for a moment and then walk resolutely into the studio with my mind fully switched on to the work awaiting me on my desk.

As was to be expected the place is a shambolic mess. To my annoyance it looks as though Christina's also encroached on my desk space while I've been away.

Christina appears at the kitchen door, looking as usual elegant and sophisticated.

'Welcome back, Raoul. You're here not a moment too soon. I've been juggling design cases and I've reached the point where I'm finding myself dealing with the clients who are protesting the most, which is no way to run a business. Have you had a nice break?' she asks, eyeing me closely.

'Yes, Christina, thank you. It was lovely,' I say shortly, 'are you going to run me through what needs to be done?'

'Oh no, Raoul. What happened?' asks Christina, looking dismayed, 'did your time with Hannah not go well?'

I smile at her.

'Yes, it did. Don't fuss. It was lovely.'

Christina, no doubt reading more into my responses than I cared for her to know, comes and sits at my desk.

As she explains what stage the different client cases are at, I try hard to focus on what she's saying.

The brightly coloured Christmas card Hannah sent me all those months ago catches my eye and distracts me when I eventually look up.

I reach across and pull it off the shelf, tearing it in two, and putting it into the bin.

Christina looks shocked.

'That bad, hey?' she asks.

'For heaven's sake, Christina! It's just a Christmas card. Of course seeing Hannah wasn't bad. It was wonderful actually.'

I smile to myself reminiscently and then look across at Christina, who's looking expectantly at me.

'We're meant to be together, Christina, I'm sure of it. But I don't think Hannah knows it yet... I'm just going to have to be patient.'

I start to tidy up the reams of paperwork in front of me. 'She'll always be the one for me.'

Christina nods in agreement, her long silver earrings tinkling softly in the silence.

'So you're going to keep in touch with her, then?'

'Of course I am.'

I glance out into our courtyard, noting several of the cacti are starting to blossom.

I love Mexico. It's my country and it's where I belong, but I would give it all up to be with Hannah.

Christina has turned her focus back to the business. She is rapidly explaining our client workload to me but already my errant mind is drifting off, busy composing an email to Hannah. In my mind's eye I visualise Hannah sitting at her desk in Scotland, reading my email, and I smile happily to myself.

THE END

Acknowledgements

With gratitude to James and Charlotte at The Conrad Press for helping my first book come to life!